WHERE THE
WILDFLOWERS DANCE

A GOOD WIND WESTERN

WHERE THE WILDFLOWERS DANCE

PHIL MILLS, JR.

FIVE STAR
A part of Gale, a Cengage Company

GALE
A Cengage Company

Farmington Hills, Mich • San Francisco • New York • Waterville, Maine
Meriden, Conn • Mason, Ohio • Chicago

LIBRARY OF CONGRESS CATALOGING-IN-PUBLICATION DATA

Names: Mills, Phil, Jr., author.
Title: Where the wildflowers dance / Phil Mills Jr.
Description: First Edition. | Waterville, ME : Five Star, a part of Gale, a Cengage Company, June 2020. | Series: A good wind western
Identifiers: LCCN 2019041831 | ISBN 9781432871055 (hardcover)
Subjects: LCSH: Ranch life—Wyoming—Fiction.
Classification: LCC PS3613.I5697 W54 2020 | DDC 813/.6—dc23
LC record available at https://lccn.loc.gov/2019041831

First Edition. First Printing: June 2020
Find us on Facebook—https://www.facebook.com/FiveStarCengage
Visit our website—http://www.gale.cengage.com/fivestar
Contact Five Star Publishing at FiveStar@cengage.com

This book is dedicated to my family and friends,
whose ongoing support and encouragement
made this project a positive and blessed experience.

ACKNOWLEDGMENTS

Any successful effort to conceive and put on paper an author's vision, thoughts, and words must always involve someone else. Such is the case with *Where the Wildflowers Dance*.

Thank you to Melody Groves for reading this manuscript, making important suggestions, and your friendship.

Thank you to Cowboy Mike Searles for your encouragement, editing skills, and friendship.

Thank you to Denise F. McAllister for your excellent editing skills, encouragement, and important suggestions.

Thank you to Diane Piron-Gelman for your excellent editing skills. You brought clarity and continuity to this story. Your time and effort are much appreciated.

Thank you to the staff of the Chugwater Historical Museum in Chugwater, Wyoming, for taking time to meet with me and for giving me a comprehensive overview and some historical insight into area life during the period about which this story is written.

Thank you to those patrons of the Chugwater Soda Fountain, "Wyoming's Oldest Operating Soda Fountain," who took the time to visit with me about the history and life in that area of Wyoming.

Thank you to my agent, Cherry Weiner of the Cherry Weiner Literary Agency, for your patience, editing suggestions, continued encouragement, support, and friendship.

Thank you to my publicist, Krista Soukup of the Blue Cottage Agency, for your promotional and marketing support, along with your friendship.

Thank you to Sonja Kabella, whose continued positive encouragement and uplifting spirit gave me the strength and support needed to finish this project.

Thank you to various members of my family, especially my daughters, Amy Mills Haler and Rebecca Mills Scott, who are always providing encouragement and support of my writing.

Finally, for all those men and women who continue to shape the American West, I thank you for helping keep the dreams and images alive out "where the wildflowers dance."

CHAPTER 1

"There will be a wedding, and Sarah Alicia Meadows will be my wife" came a shout from across the room. Jason Kelly Neal made his boisterous proclamation standing by the refreshments table, holding a half empty whiskey glass aloft for emphasis.

The screech of an out-of-tune fiddle, like fingernails sliding across a chalkboard, marked the sudden stop of music in the Meadows home. All dancing and laughter ceased.

Everyone had come by invitation to the Meadows ranch for a Saturday night dance, celebrating Sarah's return home after four years of teaching in Nebraska, along with her father's return to his ranch after being forced off his land and left for dead on the prairie. They hadn't expected a marriage proposal and neither had Sarah Meadows.

Mortified, Sarah couldn't speak at first. She started across the room toward Neal. Everyone in her way stepped back, allowing her to pass.

"As most of you know by now, I'm a good friend of Sarah Alicia," Neal said loudly. "Now, with all her friends and family present, it's a great time to ask . . . Sarah, will you marry me?"

"Jason . . . Jason, don't do this. Not now," Sarah murmured as she reached him. She looked at her father, and he spread his arms wide in astonishment.

A short time earlier, John Meadows had been talking to Jake Summers, foreman of the Box T Ranch, about recent events.

The Box T lay south of the Wheatland Flats area, a little north of Chugwater. The two men stood together along one wall, where now and then a neighbor stopped and shook Meadows's hand and engaged him in a few moments of idle conversation before returning to the party. Both men watched Sarah mix with their guests, her smile as big as Wyoming.

Every man in the room had in some way acknowledged her presence. She wore a new dress of light-blue cotton with white lace gathered around the collar. Her hair was pulled up, and around her neck gleamed a pearl necklace once belonging to her mother, who died when Sarah was born.

Looks just like her mother, thought Meadows with a blend of affection and deep melancholy. *Hard to believe she's the same rough and tumble cowgirl I sent to my sister Ruby for some refinement four years ago. Sending her to teach school in Nebraska was a good experience for her, but it's good to have her home.*

"Things are a lot different now than just a few months ago, aren't they, Mr. Meadows?" asked Jake.

"Yes," said Meadows turning his attention to the tall, lanky young foreman. "Much different. Wasn't that long ago you saved my bacon, getting me home after finding me all shot up by Harold Wayne Winston's men out on the prairie."

Jake grinned. "Fate, I guess. Just glad I happened along when I did."

"Thanks to you, your boss William Thompson, and the other Box T hands, I'm finally well and able to be with my beautiful daughter tonight." He glanced toward Sarah again and noticed Jason Neal watching her with the red-hot eyes of a hungry animal. He felt uneasy about the man and his intentions.

Just hours earlier, Neal had shown up on the Meadows ranch unannounced. He went straight to Sarah's father and asked him for permission to marry his only daughter.

"Young man, I'm afraid you have me at a disadvantage. Sarah

never mentioned you. Let me talk to her first. I need a little time to consider everything. We're having a dance tonight here on the ranch. Why don't you join us?"

Neal had agreed to attend, pleased at the opportunity "to meet Sarah's friends." For her part, Sarah was shocked to see Neal and equally surprised to learn he'd ridden almost four hundred miles to bring her back with him. Father and daughter had taken a few minutes to discuss Neal's sudden arrival, and Sarah explained she saw no future with the man. Satisfied, Meadows gave her a long hug, told her not to worry, and then suggested they return to preparations for the dance.

Now, Meadows watched Neal approach the cloth-covered table that held several plates of food. The man from Nebraska filled his glass with whiskey, raised it, and spoke. The music abruptly stopped.

"I tell you, I'm out here to get married. Nothing's going to stop me." Neal's voice grew louder. His efforts at emphasis made the amber-colored whiskey in his glass splash onto his fingers.

"Jason, you presume too much," Sarah said. "You might have asked me first. Better yet, you might have waited for my father to answer you."

"Sarah, I thought . . ."

"You thought wrong. I told you back in Nebraska, things have changed between us. Marriage won't work."

"Listen!" Neal shouted. "I came all this way. I can't believe you'd choose this God-forsaken land and cowpunchers over me. You can't be serious."

Sarah started to speak, but her father answered first. "Young man, this afternoon you asked my permission to ask Sarah about marriage. I never gave it. I take exception that you'd proceed with something so important without my blessing."

Neal turned red. "I meant no disrespect. I just figured a

11

proposal would be perfect tonight, in front of everyone."

"You should have waited," said Meadows. "But now the cow is out of the barn. You heard my daughter. Her answer is no."

In the hush that fell, Sarah's mind drifted back to Nebraska. She recalled an evening a few weeks earlier, under a full moon, when Neal had spoken of future plans for them both. She'd been thankful for the darkness as a surge of excitement and happiness brought a warm blush to her face. *Jason is so good to me, and I'm not getting any younger. Maybe this is my chance at marriage.*

Then Neal mentioned plans for moving back to Boston or even New York. He wanted to practice law in a more "civilized" part of the country. Her heart sank when he talked of city streets and office buildings that would block the "infernal wind." She'd realized for the first time that she was born to live surrounded by mountains and open prairies, not tall buildings. Neal had no use for the West, nor its rugged spirit and individualism.

Her attempts at explaining to Neal that they wanted different things from life, that she would never be happy living in a big city, fell on deaf ears. When she resigned from her teaching position a few days later and sent Neal a message that she'd been unexpectedly called home, she'd received no response. The man she thought she knew so well had not even come to see her off.

Someone coughed, bringing Sarah back to the present moment. Nobody said anything. She looked at Neal. "We have different interests and values. I can't marry you."

"Now wait," he protested. "You let me believe you wanted a future for us."

"No, I didn't. You never listened to me."

"What about our plans?"

"Your plans," Sarah answered. "You never once asked about my dreams. You just assumed we wanted the same things."

"Your dreams—"

"Jason, you have big dreams and big plans. They don't include me. Not really."

"I don't understand. I thought you cared for me."

"I do. But we could never be happy . . . me living in your world . . . you living in mine. I'm sorry."

He moved toward her as she turned away. "We'll work this out—"

Her father stepped forward. "You've got her answer. I suggest you accept that and move on. Maybe it's time you leave. You've already made a mess of our party."

"Wait!" shouted Neal as he reached for Sarah.

Three men grabbed him roughly by the arms and escorted him out the back door. One of them shouted for someone to get Neal's horse. They watched as he mounted, barring any attempt to re-enter the house. "You aren't welcome here anymore," another man told him as he rode away. "Don't come back."

Back inside, a shaken Sarah was being consoled by Molly Collins and other friends. "Things will be okay. He's gone now," said Molly. She and Sarah had met on the stage from Cheyenne during Sarah's trip home and had since become fast friends.

"I can't believe Jason would try forcing me to marry him," Sarah whispered. "He's not the man I remember from Nebraska."

Uneasy about what had happened, Sarah honestly didn't know what Neal might do next. She only knew it was important that Jake Summers somehow understood. "Where's Jake?" she asked.

"He went outside. He's on the porch," answered Molly.

Sarah hurried toward the front door.

Jake had gone outside when that Neal fellow started his foolishness. He'd heard some of the conversation, but not everything. He tried rolling a cigarette but dropped the makings. The wind quickly blew them away. Inside, the music and laughter resumed. He heard a poorly strummed guitar, then someone calling for more dancing and something to eat.

Hasn't been a whole lot to celebrate around here lately. Now a wedding. What's next?

The front door opened, and he watched Sarah come outside. Light streamed through the open doorway and spread over part of the porch.

"What happened in there? Should I congratulate you?" Jake asked.

Sarah didn't answer.

As they stood within a few feet of each other, Jake looked closely at the woman before him. Moonlight shone on her soft, brown hair, and he could see a touch of a blush on her face.

"I could never marry Jason," Sarah finally said, softly. "I intend to be a rancher's wife, out here where the wind blows wild and free. I could never be a prim and proper lawyer's wife."

Jake didn't respond. Neither spoke for a few moments as they looked at each other.

"Care to dance?" Sarah finally asked. She stepped closer and reached for his hand.

The unpleasantness of minutes earlier was lost on the Wyoming wind. But even as Sarah stepped into Jake's embrace, she felt an uneasy chill up her back. In the distance, a coyote gave a lonely wail, and the sound of Jason Neal riding away on horseback faded into an uncertain night.

CHAPTER 2

The idea had seemed simple and straightforward. Neal would ride to the Meadows ranch, sweep Sarah off her feet, and return to his law practice in Nebraska. They would get married, have children and live happily ever after. She would soon forget any nonsense about wide-open spaces and the wind that never dies.

Now he rode away from the ranch like a beaten dog with its tail between its legs. His soul was ablaze, and its fury all but consumed him. He paid scant heed to the voices in the night, the idle chatter of nocturnal insects and other creatures sharing this dark hour. The stars, whose piercing spheres of brightness might otherwise fill the black blanket of night from horizon to horizon, seemed to dim even as they held tightly to their appointed places in the sky.

How could she possibly turn me down? Why would she even consider staying in this God-forsaken, empty land over being the wife of a bright, young attorney bound for greatness?

The distant sound of music still playing, mixed with laughter, tore through Neal's brain. The sounds taunted him as he sat on his restless horse atop a nearby ridge. The music pained him, the laughter a piercing stab of humiliation. The possibility Sarah might turn him down had never entered his mind, nor that he might be thrown out of the Meadows home. He always got what he wanted. His mother had taught him to expect nothing less.

"Sarah Meadows made a fool of me. Nobody does that.

Nobody!" he said. "She and that father of hers will regret this night. I will have my revenge!"

He fumbled for his tobacco pouch and tried rolling a cigarette in the darkness. The Wyoming wind he despised so much blew his tobacco away. Feeling the empty paper made him even angrier.

The time was well past midnight when he finally wheeled his horse toward some unknown destination. He really didn't care. When he'd stopped in Chugwater earlier to get directions to the Meadows ranch, he'd made no plans on how to get back in the dark.

In the black of night every hill looked like the next, each bluff the same. Fortunately, his horse seemed to know the best route, even if he didn't. The thoroughbred plodded with the urgency of plow horse about to face another day in the fields, weaving around rocks and through sagebrush and ponderosa pine. In Neal's mind, the darkness around both man and horse became a vivid panorama of people with whom he now must deal, and deal harshly.

On nearby ridges where coyotes normally yipped and wailed throughout the night, silence prevailed. Night birds sang in hushed, melancholy tones. Other animals of the night scurried in blind indifference. Each animal sensed Neal's rising hatred for all things born of this land and the people who lived here.

As the night drifted toward morning, Neal's angry mood gave way to thoughts of how to get even with the Meadows family. "They must owe money to someone . . . probably the bank in town. That's a good place to start. Hurt them financially, and then Miss High-and-Mighty Sarah will need to come crawling. I'll set up shop in that excuse for a town and find their weaknesses. Nobody treats me with disrespect and humiliates me."

The sky gradually became an eclectic mix of oranges, blues,

and purples as sunrise claimed the hour. By the time the sun edged above the horizon, horse and rider had arrived at the north edge of Chugwater. Neal figured he'd ridden about six hours, only stopping now and then to rest.

Chugwater sat along a creek that flowed narrow and quiet at the mercy of some unseen source. Cliffs rose steep from the valley floor east of town before extending as a grassy plateau off toward Nebraska. Toward the west, the terrain was rough and defined by rocky outcroppings and sage-covered hillsides with occasional grass-covered ravines and washouts. The only trees, mostly cottonwoods, grew along nearby streams.

It wasn't much of a town. Most buildings sat along the west side of the main street facing the creek. They all needed painting, worn down by constant wind and harsh winter weather. Dust was the common bond between them, with the excess dirt hanging thick on the breeze, ready to invade any open nostril or crevice. An earthy stench filled the air, born of manure, dog feces, trash, and poorly handled chamber pots.

Off the main street a few smaller shacks pretended to be homes but barely fit the description of houses. Near the stable, a scraggly past-his-prime red rooster sat atop a corral fence preparing to start his ragged sunrise call. Neal drew up his black gelding and watched as the rooster began to crow. The noise grated on his ears. He drew a pistol from his saddlebag. His single shot sent the chicken into permanent slumber. The shot went unnoticed by town residents. Life and death of any kind were cheap in Chugwater.

"Shut up. And stay shut up!" Neal shouted at the twisted carcass and pile of bloody feathers.

He rode on. Two horses tied in front of the stable watched with tired eyes as Neal passed by. A sway-backed sorrel gelding neighed softly.

Dismounting in front of Chugwater's only café, Neal entered

17

and found a table facing the front window. Burnt coffee and some type of cleaning compound heavily laden with lye soap stung the inside lining of his nose. Fresh sawdust littering the floor, ready to absorb a day's worth of spills and casual tobacco spit, added to the assault on his senses. He sat with his back to the wall, looked around, and saw he was alone except for a young boy of thirteen or so near the back.

"Coffee! Black!" Neal ordered, with a shout and wave of his hand toward the boy. Brooding, he stared out the window at a building across the street. A simple red-brick structure, it stood apart from the others and looked badly in need of repair and upkeep.

The boy brought his coffee and set it down. "Who owns that building over there?" Neal asked.

"That one?" The boy pointed toward the red-brick structure.

"Yes, that one! Are you blind, boy?"

"Mrs. McGee. Agnes McGee. She and her husband had a general store over there until he up and died a few years back. The old woman still owns the place, I think. But mister, she ain't right in the head."

"What's that supposed to mean?"

"She took it hard when her husband passed. She ain't been right since."

"Boy?" someone shouted from the back of the room. "Get your lazy butt to work! Visit on your own time, not mine!"

"I gotta go, mister."

"Get me a menu," Neal called after the retreating boy.

Neal found renewed energy as he consumed steak and eggs washed down by a considerable amount of black coffee. He shoved back from the table, pulled out a pocket watch, and absorbed the time without emotion. Stepping outside, he decided his first stop would be the general store, to find out what he could about Agnes McGee.

The store owner had just finished sweeping off the plank walkway in front as Neal approached. He was a short, lean, hardscrabble of a man with a taut, unfriendly face that looked as if smiles seldom came to rest there. Uncombed, thinning hair gave the impression he'd gone straight from bed to store with little thought of personal grooming. Untrimmed whiskers somewhere between a full beard and several days of unshaven growth covered much of his face. Pained brown eyes spoke of a hard life. The man leaned on his broom, watching Neal with interest.

Neal called out to him. "Old man! Who owns that brick building across from the café?"

"Who wants to know?" the store owner asked.

"I'm asking the questions. Now one more time: who owns that building?"

"Mrs. McGee, why?"

"Where can I find her?"

"Mister, I don't know who you are."

"My name's Jason Kelly Neal. I plan to own that building, and real soon!"

The store owner went inside. Irritated, Neal followed. The old man busied himself adjusting some tomato cans on a shelf along the wall near the front counter. "You can save yourself some time," he said. "The old lady ain't likely to sell. Too many memories tied up in that building."

"I asked where I could find her. Not your opinion."

"End of the street. Little white house needing paint. Cottonwood tree in front."

"That's better," Neal said. "Next time I won't be so polite."

Without further comment, he strode out the front door and started down the street. A lack of spring rain along with heavy usage by men and horses had left the street inches deep in dust and scattered horse manure. Each step meant the rise and fall of powdery, thirsty dust. Black flies and gnats buzzed every-where. The smell of filth mixed with dust filled his nostrils as a freight wagon rumbled past, barely missing him. He hurried onward with a sense of urgency, his mind racing.

This will be the first step toward running this God-forsaken town. Sarah Meadows and anybody associated with her will rue ever having met me.

Agnes McGee was old and often confused. Although only five foot and frail, she could be feisty at times. Most days she was quiet and docile, given to moments of forgetfulness. Since the death of her husband, Julius McGee, the old woman's mind bounced around like a rubber ball. She lived alone, often not seen for days.

When the knock came at her front door, she cautiously opened it and looked up at the dust-covered young man standing in front of her. "Yes, may I help you?"

"My name is Neal, and I'm here to help *you*. May I come in?"

Neal pushed past Agnes into the house. "What?" she stammered. "Young man, what did you say?"

Neal slowly looked around. He found himself in a dark room with a fireplace along one wall, but no fire was lit, and it appeared there hadn't been one for quite some time. A wooden rocking chair and a badly worn sofa took up the middle of the room. A few old photos hung on each wall, along with a calendar from three years earlier that still showed November.

"Young man—?"

Neal cut her short. "I understand you own that old brick building across the street from the café?"

"Yes . . . yes, I do. But what's that—?"

"Well, I'm here to—"

The woman cut him off. Her voice and demeanor softened.

"Pardon my manners, young man. Would you please sit down?" She gestured toward a dusty armchair. At least, Neal hoped it was dust that accounted for the stained upholstery. "Would you like some coffee? When my Julius was alive, we had wonderful coffee . . . from South America, don't you know? I don't get many visitors. Not since my Julius passed."

Only then did he notice the woman still wore nightclothes. Nondescript flowers in shades of blue, purple, and pink covered her cotton gown. Threadbare, the shift had not been washed in days and reeked of sweat and human filth. Other odors—the smell of unkempt age and a lack of cleanliness—filled these darkened walls. A cat—no, two—walked quietly near him, and he could smell their urine and feces. There was a distinct smell of mold as well, but mostly of old dirt.

I wouldn't eat or drink a damn thing handled by this old coot. She needs a bath . . . badly. And this house needs some fresh air.

"Why, of course, some coffee would be nice," Neal said, perching on the chair's edge. "You have a lovely place here."

"Why, thank you," she responded, with a weak smile.

"I understand you and your late husband had a very nice store in that old building down the street. I was sorry to hear he'd passed away."

"Why yes . . . yes, we did."

"You're so kind," Neal continued. "I hate to bring you bad news."

"What? What's wrong?"

"I don't want to ruin your day. Best you forget I said any—"

"No, please tell me."

He leaned toward her, ignoring how she smelled. "You may have heard some very unscrupulous men are trying to build a railroad through Chugwater. Rumor has it they plan to tear down your building and put a railroad depot there. You could lose your building and everything you and your Julius worked

21

so hard to build. I'd hate to see that."

She gaped at him. "Oh my, I hadn't heard."

"I thought maybe you hadn't. I just heard about it myself. You see, I'm an attorney and new in town. It's my job to protect good folks like yourself. It would be terrible for you to lose that building."

"Bless you, young man. What can I do? How can you help me?"

"I'm glad you asked. Have you ever heard of eminent domain or habeas corpus?"

"No. My Julius handled all our legal and business affairs."

Neal tried not to smile as he edged forward in his chair. *This is like taking candy from a baby.* "What that means is, you sign a document allowing me as your attorney to represent your interests in such matters. I will take care of your property rights, and you won't have anything to worry about."

"Oh my . . . would you?"

"Of course." He pulled a sheet of paper from an inside pocket. "I just happen to have such a document with me. All I need is your signature. Of course, I'll waive my normal fees in exchange for a cup of your wonderful coffee."

He folded the paper in such a way so the words *Deed Transfer* were hidden from her. Once she'd signed it, Neal folded the deed and put it back in his pocket. "Thank you, Mrs. McGee."

"No, thank *you,* young man. Let me get you some coffee."

"I'll pass, thanks. I need to be going."

"Why, you just got here."

Neal stood. "I'll be moving into that building in the next few days."

"What? Why would you move into my building?"

"Because that paper you just signed makes me the new owner." He smirked. "Really, lady, you should be more careful and a whole lot smarter."

"I never agreed to sell," said the old woman. She began to tremble.

"You didn't sell. You signed it over to me. No compensation involved."

"You tricked me. You lied to me."

"Your word against mine, lady. Your word against mine."

Neal strode to the front door, almost stepping on a third cat in the process. He looked back at the stunned woman. "Have a nice day."

The front door slammed behind him as he stepped into the bright morning air. West of Chugwater, thunder rumbled along the Laramie range. Early summer was giving birth to a storm. Small streaks of lightning flashed over the distant mountains. Neal glanced casually at the distant thunderheads, taking little notice. With his shoulders back and wearing a wide, smug smile, he walked back toward the café and his horse. *I'm going to run this town. Nothing but a bunch of rubes here.*

Agnes McGee sat quietly in her parlor, trembling, one arthritic hand holding the other. She felt unsure and confused about what had just happened. Her left arm went numb, and she clutched at her chest, feeling heavy pressure as if someone were pushing her down. She cried out, "Julius!" A promising early summer morning turned to night, deep and dark. A coffee pot boiled as three near-starved, wormy cats watched in silence.

CHAPTER 3

Moonlight bathed the Meadows ranch complex and painted everything in a soft, creamy glow. It found a portal through a bunkhouse window and into an otherwise dark room. Morning would come soon enough. As moonbeams spread like a blanket across the bunkhouse, Jake Summers watched the men in various stages of sleep around him. One puncher lay sprawled on the floor where he'd passed out. The man had never reached his bed following the Meadows party. Men snored; some actually snorted, breaking the otherwise pristine quiet.

The dance was a blur, yet clear. Jake's mind raced. Feelings he'd never known engaged him in open conflict.

All the events of the past few weeks seemed surreal. Yet, Jake knew they were very real, especially his blossoming relationship with Sarah. They'd talked on the porch for what seemed like hours, but he couldn't for the life of him remember what was said. Her kiss on his cheek as they parted for the night was still alive on his face.

Jason Neal's appearance had also been real enough. Jake smiled, remembering how Sarah's well-groomed suitor had been quickly dispatched. Yet something told Jake the young attorney wasn't the type to just ride away with his ego so badly bruised.

A cowhand two bunks over snorted, gasped for air, and once again found comfort behind his closed eyelids. The room reeked of stale air heavy with body odor and cigarette smoke.

Outside, horses stirred in the early-morning darkness. On a

faraway hillside, a coyote made his final yips and cries to the night. Cows and calves bawled in the distance.

Now was the time for sorting cattle stolen by Harold Wayne Winston and returning them to their rightful owners. There were plenty of cattle needing to be found, perhaps several hundred head. Getting the animals to their owners would take time, but Jake didn't mind. Once done, everyone from the Box T would return home. After last night, he wasn't so eager for that to happen.

Jake slid from his bunk and pulled on his boots. He located a porcelain pitcher near the front door and poured just enough water in a bowl to wash his hands and face. He ran his hand over a day's worth of whiskers but decided shaving could wait. Searching his effects, he found a clean, although badly wrinkled, blue and green cotton shirt. Once he found his hat and strapped on his well-worn, leather holster and his Colt Single Action Army .45, he was ready for the day.

A handful of beef jerky and some day-old sourdough biscuits made an adequate breakfast, washed down by stale coffee poured from a pot where heat had long been lost. Jake wanted to sort through some personal things in his mind, and this noisy, smelly Meadows bunkhouse was not the place. He had tried. All night he'd tried . . . but his mind was full, and sleep wouldn't come. He stepped into the still-dark morning, going to find something, unsure of what.

The Meadows ranch complex sat along Sybille Creek, partly hidden among the isolated grassy pockets amid rocky outcroppings and ravines just east of the Laramie mountain range. The main house faced east down a narrow valley that eventually opened out toward a grass-covered prairie stretching as far as the eye could see.

A dog growled, a low guttural sound from deep in his throat. Jake assumed a coyote or some other nocturnal predator must be prowling around close. The ranch windmill creaked and turned in the early-morning breeze. A ferruginous hawk had built a nest in the windmill, but at this early hour it was empty.

Jake climbed through the corral fence and found the sorrel gelding he'd grown so fond of riding. A low nicker from among the horses shuffling about in the confined pen told him the feeling was mutual. Jake rewarded the animal with an apple.

Once saddled, Jake rode, seeking a place of solitude. His mind swirled like dust devils across a wheat field, jumping from one complicated thought to another. He sought quiet, the type of silence where you can hear your own heartbeat or the inner whispers of a divine voice. So far, he'd found neither. *I've had women in my life before. But nothing like this.*

Jake was fourteen when he left his Texas home. His family had suffered greatly from the ravages of the War Between the States. His father died from wounds received at Gettysburg, where he fought for the South. A carpetbagger killed Jake's older brother, Jesse, over who really owned the family's Texas home.

His mother gave way to insanity rather than fight a losing battle with emotional turmoil. And while his grandmother had stood firm for saving the Summers family name, even she failed. Jake left, moving north with the last trail drive Harry Haythornwaite (later known as Haythorn) led out of Texas. He eventually found his way to the Judith Basin country of Montana, where he met Tom Scott and eventually moved with him to William Thompson's Box T Ranch in Wyoming.

Jake wasn't normally given to dwelling on life, reality, and the divine role of man. The time between sunrise and sunset was filled by man's work. Love and family were seldom topics of thought, much less discussion. But long periods in the saddle gave a man time to think and even daydream. Loneliness came with the job.

A flash of lightning broke the black wall of darkness shielding the Laramie range off to the west. A second, more subdued sputter of electricity, not nearly as dramatic, followed. Then a third, smaller bolt of lightning rose and quickly died. Jake's thoughts turned to the distant storm and his surroundings.

A sagebrush lizard scurried in front of him as a jackrabbit watched nearby. Riding away from the mixed prairie grasses and sagebrush where Meadows grazed his few cattle, Jake worked his way through a dry area filled with washouts and sparse ground cover. Around him were isolated stands of buffalo grass and side-oats grama mixed with a few yucca plants.

After riding for almost three hours, he reached Chugwater Creek. Cottonwoods, box elders, and willows grew along the stream. There were also chokeberry and serviceberry shrubs, along with rushes and sedges. The entire Chugwater valley was green with several types of grasses.

In front of him, a series of high sandstone bluffs rose like a huge wall that stretched for miles along the east side of Chugwater Creek. Sixty to eighty feet in height, in some places higher, they towered over the valley floor. Most were devoid of vegetation.

Jake shuddered in the eerie quiet, sensing a ghost-like presence of death around him. His imagination sought to define the emotion that swept over him. The wind, the ever-present Wyoming wind, tugged at his hat and ruffled his hair. Cold silence, born not of the morning air but of some type of spiritual atonement, filled this sacred place.

Jake pulled hard on the reins, and his horse stopped below an outcropping of rugged rim-rock. For a moment he sat to gather his thoughts and felt his horse shift its weight under him. At the base of the cliffs, decaying piles of sun-bleached bison bones glinted in the morning light, remnants of another time. Grass and weeds grew through skulls and eye sockets where once dark eyes had surveyed a vast prairie and freedom.

He found a trail, a narrow switchback barely wide enough for a horse, used by ancient peoples for a thousand years or more. On top of the rugged bluffs and their massive rims, he saw Chugwater Creek coursing its way toward the Laramie River. Around him was a plateau known as the Chugwater Flats, a fertile area covered with a mixture of prairie grasses. A few homesteaders from Iowa had gained a foothold on the plateau with their efforts at dry land farming. Not a tree was in sight. Jake shivered as he imagined the open range giving way to homesteaders.

Jake closed his eyes so he might listen without the distractions of sight, and in his mind's eye he could see. His ears filled with a rumbling sound like the coming of a tornado. Echoes came to him, voices from the past along with the imagined sound of hooves pounding. Loud, guttural screams and a great bellowing accompanied the stampede, as bison by the hundreds plunged over these very cliffs to their deaths. Indians had chased bison over the cliffs so they might be slaughtered. Jake shivered again, feeling a conflict of spirit and mournful agony, a torture of the soul.

He shook off the strange mood and turned away. As he reined his horse down off the plateau, he could see the new day beginning. The sunrise painted the horizon with pinks, oranges, and reds gradually giving way to more yellow tones dotted with shades of dark blue and purple. Along the mountain foothills to the west, the summer thunderstorm he'd noticed earlier was growing in strength.

Needing little encouragement, the sorrel turned and headed back toward the Meadows Ranch. In the distance, Jake could see the Richeau Hills, and further still, the Laramie mountain range stretched like a wall toward the north. He pulled up long enough on top of a ridge to roll a smoke from his makings and watched the western sky.

Thunder rumbled, and the rising sun highlighted massive dark clouds reaching thousands of feet upward. Still in its infancy, the storm was already larger than when he'd first noticed it. Streaks of lightning created an electrical display worthy of any fireworks show he'd ever seen.

His cigarette burned short, and he felt the fire hot on his fingers. He lit a second cigarette and let the smoke ease gently from between his lips into the cool morning air. With his right leg curled around the saddle horn, he rested comfortably. After a time, he swung his leg back astride, touched his spur to the horse's side, and they sauntered off. One last look into the sunrise left him content. There was work to be done.

The ride had given Jake time to think, to grasp the frailty of life and its uncertainty. He'd managed to formulate some future plans. Now he felt a strong urge to go share those plans with Sarah Meadows. His senses were alive and alert. The air smelled pure and clean with a heavy dose of sage. Life was good.

CHAPTER 4

A cool, soft breeze swept over the Meadows ranch buildings. Along the eastern horizon, bright orange clouds mixed with shades of deep yellow foretold the birth of a new day. Higher up, a canvas of deep blue was tinged with orange-shaded clouds. The ranch buildings sat in deep shadows and darkness. A rooster's woeful cry broke the stillness.

Sarah woke, stretched her arms, and slipped from her warm bed. She threw back the curtains of her bedroom window and gazed outside. Horses milled in the corrals, as if anxious to begin the day. A couple of ranch hands pitched hay to them, and chaff mixed with corral dust rose like a fog on the morning air. Up close, she knew, it was hard to breathe.

Further off, down along Sybille Creek, Sarah could see prairie grasses moving gently to and fro, stretching as far as the eye could see. Toward the west, the towering peaks of the Laramie mountain range filled the sky, jagged and majestic. Only Laramie Peak at more than ten thousand feet still held tightly to last winter's snow. Storm clouds loomed to the northwest.

The previous night came swirling back to her in a rush of excitement as she recalled the welcome home party . . . and Jake Summers! *Maybe he's still sleeping,* she thought. *Or . . . maybe he's already up and out!*

Events of recent days meshed into a whirl of emotional highs and lows, joy and sadness. Sarah sought a brief escape. She felt an overwhelming urge to ride, to feel the wind in her hair and on her face. She got dressed, then found a hunting knife her father had given her years earlier and put it in a sheath attached to her belt. While it had been years since she'd fired a rifle, she decided to take her dad's Winchester Model 1873 along for the ride. "Just in case," she whispered, checking to make sure it was loaded.

With her father and the rest of the household still asleep, she left a note on the kitchen table, then slipped out of the house unnoticed. She saddled her horse, put the rifle into a scabbard securely tied to the saddle, and nudged the animal into the vast sea of grass and rolling hills . . . a bastion of solitude on this cool Wyoming morning.

Again, her thoughts turned to Jake Summers. Only last night, as the community gathered for the party, had she finally allowed her feelings for the tall, handsome Box T foreman to show. They had danced.

She pulled up on a nearby hill. As the sun broke the horizon, she watched the ranch hands catch their day mounts. She hoped for a glimpse of the rugged cowhand she'd come to like so much but didn't see him. Neighing horses and hoofbeats along with an occasional shout of "git up there" filled the air even at this great distance.

"Maybe I should go find him," she whispered softly.

Instead she rode northeast into an area where she hadn't ridden in several years. Outcroppings of sandstone and limestone surrounded her, thick with bitterbush, snowberry, and mountain mahogany. The rocky outcroppings and steep embankments mixed with ravines and swales created by flash floods. She could smell the landscape, clean and fresh. Birds sang their morning songs. A red-tailed hawk hunting for prey drifted by on a southwesterly wind. Then Sarah spotted a golden eagle as it dove to capture some unsuspecting rodent.

She remembered searching for stray cattle in this area as a

child, but that was years ago and she hadn't been back since. She let her horse choose the way while her thoughts dwelt on other, more personal interests . . . a land of possibilities involving Jake.

After riding about two hours, Sarah realized the storm in the distance was gaining strength, so she decided to turn back. At first she followed a series of ravines more toward Chugwater than the ranch, now and then crossing unnamed creeks. She wanted to get home and have breakfast.

Suddenly a jackrabbit burst from some underbrush. Her horse lunged sideways, eyes wide and nostrils flaring. She fell from her saddle and hit the ground hard, striking her head and shoulder. Pain shot through her right ankle, and she lay dazed among a pile of small rocks and soapweed yuccas. Hooves drummed in the dirt as the horse ran off.

Unseen except by meadowlarks, chickadees, and nosy ground squirrels, she gathered her wits and attempted to stand, but the pain was too great, and her ankle gave way. Her head and shoulder throbbed. She reached up and felt her forehead, wincing as her fingers brushed what must be a bad bruise. The injury to her shoulder prevented her from raising the other arm above her head.

Sarah tried pulling herself up on the rocks so she could see the landscape around her. The effort took considerable time, as her every motion met with painful resistance. Still, she managed to reach a small boulder and sat down. Nearby, a solitary ponderosa pine held tightly to a nearby slope. A high bluff behind her and the hills all around limited her view.

Her right ankle was limp. The blow to her head and the strenuous effort to reach the boulder left her dizzy and faint. Sweat covered her face, and exhaustion made breathing an effort. She called out for help but was met with silence.

"Nobody has a clue what direction I went," she whispered.

"Why do I always do these things?"

She touched her head again and realized she might pass out at any moment. *Maybe if I lie back and rest a minute . . .* "No!" she said outloud. "Pass out and I'm in deep trouble! Got to stay awake and alert."

After a few minutes, some clarity of thought returned, and she decided to try wrapping her ankle for support. She tore a piece of her riding skirt, then used her knife to cut strips of cloth, with which she tightly bound her ankle. Then she tried standing, but again the pain was too much, and she sank back down. Tears of pain and anguish welled up in the corners of her eyes. "I can't let this beat me," she murmured as she sat slumped against a larger boulder. "There's got to be a way out of this. I won't give up."

Another attempt at standing yielded the same results.

Not even a rifle to signal for help! My Winchester was in the saddle scabbard. What am I going to do?

A fox squirrel sat on a nearby rock and watched her while a horned lizard scurried away. Overhead a couple of turkey buzzards lazily circled, looking for some type of meaty carnage upon which to feast. She shuddered at the idea of their beaks tearing at her flesh.

"Can't think of such things," she told herself, as if hearing the words might make it easier. "Someone will find me. They must!"

Molly Collins slept late, still tired from the previous night, but once up she hurriedly fixed a breakfast of sourdough biscuits and honey, along with some strong black coffee and a platter of eggs and bacon. She figured everyone at the ranch house would be hungry. She'd found Sarah's note and assumed her friend would return soon for breakfast.

Molly had been lured West with a promise of marriage to a

man named Marcus Dunn, a local rancher, but Harold Wayne Winston had hanged him before she arrived, during Winston's reign of fear and death over the territory.

Sadness and disappointment were not new to seventeen-year-old Molly. She'd grown up in the back streets of St. Louis and never knew her father. He could have been any one of the numerous men her mother entertained for money. Times had been rough, her upbringing a mixture of hard realities and forced maturity.

Dunn's death left her with no means of support in Wyoming, although she worked for a short time in the local saloon. With limited options, she'd accepted Sarah's invitation to come stay at the ranch.

Molly paused, remembering the first time she'd met Sarah only a few weeks ago outside the Cheyenne stagecoach station. She was trying to ignore the eclectic mix of travelers around her when Sarah approached. All she wanted was to catch the stage to Chugwater. A young woman traveling alone was sure to attract enough attention without encouragement.

"Waiting for the stage?" Sarah had asked, before Molly realized someone was nearby.

"Yes . . . yes, I am," Molly answered, surprised to hear a woman's voice.

"Me too," Sarah said. "Mind if I sit down?"

Molly slid over on the wooden bench to make room. The bench was slick from years of being shined by the backsides of various travelers.

"What direction you headed?" Sarah asked, with a wave of her hand. "It's a big country in every direction."

"I'm going to a place called Chugwater, somewhere north of here."

"Really? Me too! My father has a ranch near Chugwater. That's where I grew up."

"That's nice." Molly paused briefly. "Is it pretty country?"

"Oh my, it's beautiful. I've been gone four years, teaching in Nebraska. And I've missed it so much. I'm finally heading home." Sarah smiled. "I'm Sarah Meadows."

Molly returned the smile, relaxing for the first time. "It's nice to meet you. I'm Molly Collins."

They'd spent the stagecoach ride talking, interspersed with long periods of companionable silence. Neither of them had any notion of what awaited them . . . Sarah a missing father, Molly herself a dead husband-to-be. But all that was over now, and Molly had found a place of sorts at the Meadows ranch. She'd kept Marcus Dunn's letters and felt wistful sometimes about what might have been. Sarah had been so kind, reassuring her when she voiced doubts about whether Dunn would like her or whether she'd be lonely. "You'll be fine," she'd said, with another warm smile. "If your Mr. Dunn is mean or bad, you'll come stay with Dad and me. In fact, if you have any doubts when you meet him, you can stay with me until you decide what to do."

They'd both laughed and then lapsed back into their own thoughts and concerns.

"When I find the right man or he finds me," Sarah said, breaking the silence, "I want us to be equals . . . like-thinking partners, if you will. My husband will be a man . . . someone I want . . . not just need. I want a man who wants an equal partner long term. I want a man who loves this land like I do."

"You think I'm settling? You think I'm going to Marcus out of need?" Molly asked.

"No," Sarah hesitated. "I think everyone has a different situation. We must each enter a marriage or relationship for our own reasons."

Molly shrugged. "Most days, I'm just concerned about having a place to sleep and finding my next meal. Let Marcus Dunn need me, want me, whatever . . . from his letters, he seems to be a good man. I will make him a good wife, and in return I'll have a permanent roof over my head, a warm fire in winter, decent food, and a man with a good heart. No more hungry days, saloons, drunks, one-night stands, and morning bruises. That will be heaven."

The sound of John Meadows and William Thompson, owner of the Box T, talking as they entered the kitchen brought Molly back to the moment at hand. "Have either of you seen Sarah this morning?" she asked.

Both men looked at each other. "No," Meadows said. "Isn't she up and around?"

"I haven't seen her. I found a note saying she was going for a ride and for us not to worry. I just wondered if she was back yet. Tom hasn't seen Jake either . . . not since daybreak! You don't suppose they went riding together?"

Meadows picked up a biscuit, split it open, inserted a fried egg, and then headed for the door. "Miss Molly, would you please fix me a cup of that good smelling coffee?" he asked. "I'll go ask the hands if anyone has seen them. Be right back."

A quick survey turned up nothing except Jake's horse was missing along with Sarah's buckskin mare. Tom Scott, another Box T hand, followed Meadows back into the kitchen.

"Good sign they took off early, maybe together," Tom said. "I know Jake likes a morning ride."

Meadows glanced at the rugged slope that rose behind the house. "You don't suppose . . . ?" he asked, rubbing his chin. "As a child, she'd go up on the ridge yonder to be alone. She called it her secret hiding place, but we all knew about it. I don't suppose they'd be up there this morning?"

Tom eyed the slope. "Jake and I hid the women up there while we were chasing down Winston. Maybe—?"

"If she's not back in the next hour or so, let's ride up that way and check it out."

After breakfast, Meadows and Thompson took their coffee out on the ranch house porch, where they sat in well-worn, light-blue rocking chairs, both in need of new paint. Thompson nodded toward Tom, who was walking from the corrals toward the house.

"You know, John, you're going to need a good foreman to help run this place. I'd suggest you consider that young man coming this way. Tom Scott knows the cattle business, and he works hard."

Meadows nodded. "I was thinking much the same thing."

Thompson chuckled. "Besides, as long as Molly Collins is staying here, that boy will be hanging around anyway. Might as well put him to work. Those two have become thicker than molasses in January."

"I agree," Meadows said with a smile. "I'll talk to him."

"He's a good man. He'll make you a solid foreman."

"I think so, too. I really do."

The sound of hoofbeats reached them. Meadows stood and glanced toward the sound and spotted Sarah's horse trotting toward the barn without a rider.

Stupid . . . just stupid. When am I going to learn? Sarah thought.

A meadowlark called out in the distance, and she could see a couple of sage grouse moving through some nearby grass. Nearer by, a fox squirrel watched her with bright-eyed interest.

Suddenly, a ground squirrel raced past her, either unaware of her presence or in such fear not to care. Abruptly, the fox squirrel disappeared into the underbrush. She looked in the direction the ground squirrel had come running from, and her eyes widened in fear. Not fifty yards away she could see three—no, four—wolves, moving toward her. They acted as if they hadn't seen her yet.

Shaking, she braced her hands on the closest rock and tried pulling herself up. Despite the wrap on her ankle, pain drove up her leg, and fresh agony shot through her shoulder and right arm. The wolves were closer now, moving silently in unison . . . stalking. They had seen her.

She tried moving again, but her body failed her. She wanted to scream, but no words came. Vertigo made her mind swim, and a black-billed magpie sitting nearby taunted her for being so stupid. Thunder reached her ears, followed by a strange falling sensation as darkness came calling.

CHAPTER 5

Ominous clouds, black and ugly, clung to the craggy mountain-tops, hiding their peaks down to the treeline and rising several thousand feet above them in puffy folds of white and grey. More frequent distant thunder announced the storm's rising intensity. Jake felt a tension in the air, an electric energy as the storm gained strength along the ragged range.

Rain clouds swept down forest-covered slopes and started out over the prairie. The storm would arrive soon, bringing with it heavy rain and wind. Birds and other animals sensed the storm's approach and moved by instinct and common sense for cover.

Grey clouds covered the mountaintops, hiding their peaks down to the tree line.

Cold raindrops fell intermittently and scattered, leaving small craters in the dusty soil. At higher elevations, the moisture would be falling as wet snow along tops of the Laramie range. Not wanting to get any wetter than necessary, Jake pulled on his rain slicker and continued riding toward the Meadows ranch. The chilly rain touched his face, and he shivered at the iciness.

He touched his spurs to the horse's flanks, striving for a swifter gait. "Git along," he said, using his entire body to urge the horse onward. The foothills of the Laramie range rose before him. His horse loped toward home, eating up the distance. The cliffs looming over Chugwater Creek were soon out of sight and out of mind. He rode among steep clay stone bluffs, still two hours or more from the ranch and shelter.

A clap of thunder in the distance and a quick flash of lightning were followed by another roll of thunder. "Boy, we may have ridden into a passel of trouble," Jake muttered, as if his horse understood. He scanned the landscape for someplace to safely ride out the storm. Off to his right, a large open basin stretched for miles toward the north. Sage and other native short grasses grew everywhere. On his left, a series of low rocky outcroppings rose to rugged bluffs. In the distance, Sybille Creek flowed toward the ranch.

The rain fell with increased intensity as Jake rode into an area filled with swales, ravines, and large boulders. He slowed his horse, not wanting to risk harm to the animal or to himself. A flash of movement ahead caught his attention, and he pulled up.

Approximately forty yards away, he spotted a wolf moving slowly as if stalking something. *Could be some cattle wandered to the top of the ridge. Maybe one is injured.*

Then he saw three more wolves, also moving slowly as if approaching their prey.

"We probably should see what's up, boy," he said softly to his horse.

A loud clap of thunder followed by lightning nearby added to his sense of urgency. The air felt colder, and the wind was rising. Maybe approaching the wolves was a bad idea. He decided to turn his horse toward home.

Then one of the wolves, a dark grey with several battle scars, suddenly stopped. The animal's tail was up, signaling his leadership of the small pack. Jake reined up again and watched.

The sight of them made him shudder, and a story from his Montana days came to mind. An old rancher by the name of Griffin had set some of his dogs loose to chase a pack of wolves. The dogs trailed the wolves along several ridges and into some deep brush before the wolves turned back against their pursuers. Griffin and his men hadn't been able to keep up. The dogs were killed, and the wolves remained. They weren't to be taken lightly.

"We'd better see what's stirring," he whispered to his horse.

At the ranch, the return of Sarah's horse caused major concern. The rain had changed from an easy drizzle to a heavy downpour. Sheets of rain swept across the open area between house and barn, making it hard to see. A dog dashed toward the barn for shelter, splashing through muddy puddles along the way.

Raindrops pounded on the metal roof of the ranch house, spilling off the edge and creating a waterfall as gravity pulled the water toward earth. Water flowed in wide rivulets away from the buildings, gradually joining together in a rush toward Sybille Creek.

Molly stared out at the downpour. "We can't just sit here," she said.

Meadows shook his head. "But we don't have a clue where she might have gone, or Jake either, for that matter."

"I'd bet money she's hurt or something," said Tom. "I've got horses saddled."

Meadows turned to him. "Young man, I hate to ask—"

Tom hurried out the door before the old rancher could finish. As he mounted his horse, several ranch hands joined him to help search. Their rain slickers shone brightly with wetness as they rode out in different directions, their horses' hooves splashing up water and mud.

Miles away from the ranch, Jake spotted a flash of yellow. All he could make out through the rain was an indistinct figure lying on the ground, unmoving among the rocks. The yellow must be the shirt the person wore.

41

"Can't be good," he said. He was certain now this was the prey the wolves were stalking. Whoever it was lay against a boulder, totally exposed, maybe already dead. Or maybe not. He urged his horse forward. "Gotta move quickly."

Sarah regained consciousness, wet and cold. Each movement was painful. She shivered, not only from the weather, but from fear. She could see two wolves, a young grey female and an older black male, twenty yards away. The rest of the pack must be nearby. She squeezed the hunting knife in her right hand but realized she was virtually defenseless.

A bolt of lightning shattered the sky. The cold wind picked up anything loose and hurled it against everything in its path. The rain was loud, falling hard. Undeterred, the hungry wolves moved forward. Their yellow eyes gleamed in anticipation.

Jake aimed his rifle carefully. The rain kept getting in his eyes, and twice he had to wipe excess moisture from his face. The rifle exploded as he brought down a young black wolf that had circled in from above. A quick second shot fatally wounded another, much older animal. The two remaining wolves refused to leave. Perhaps driven by hunger, they stood their ground.

Jake urged his horse off the ridge, allowing the animal to pick its own path. The boulder-covered terrain made reaching the injured person difficult. Rainwater ran down the hillside, creating a fast-moving stream at the base of the ravine. Jake realized the person below him was not only in danger from the wolves, but also from the swiftly rising water.

The only path available to him led directly into the flood, and he momentarily lost sight of the wolves and their human prey as he urged his reluctant horse into the belly-deep water and rode toward where he figured he'd last seen the body.

"Hurry, boy. Those wolves have the advantage. We may be too late."

As they waded through the water, Jake felt it pulling at his stirrups. He and the horse cleared a large pile of rocks just as one of the two remaining wolves moved to within a few yards of the injured and helpless person. Jake pulled up in shock as he realized who it was. "Oh my God, that's Sarah!"

The wolf moved closer, ready to spring. Jake yanked his rifle from the saddle scabbard, shoved a shell into the chamber, and aimed. His horse stumbled, and Jake lowered his rifle. The animal regained its footing, and he quickly brought the wolf into his sights once more. Rain streamed into his eyes, making any kind of clear shot impossible.

"It's now or never," he whispered as he squeezed the trigger.

Sarah heard the earlier gunshots and saw two wolves die, one falling off a nearby boulder into the rising water in the ravine. The older black male was closer now. She looked directly into his yellow eyes. His tongue dripped with saliva in anticipation of a fresh kill.

With her back against the boulder, she swept the knife wildly from side to side, praying it might slow or deter the wolf's steady advance. Still, the animal moved closer. The smell of his dirty hide filled her nostrils, a putrid, musky odor. Wet from the rain, his black coat shone. Any moment, he would leap on her, fangs and teeth seeking her throat for the kill. Terrified though she was, the will to live forced Sarah to her feet. She lunged forward, pointing the knife directly at the wolf.

A gunshot caught the animal just as his front feet came off the ground. His warm blood washed down the rocks into the rising waters nearby.

Sarah turned her head, wincing at fresh pain, and saw a man on horseback riding toward her, wearing a black slicker and hat dripping with water. Smoke rose from the barrel of the man's rifle.

"Help me! Please help me!" Sarah shouted. Then she recognized him. Relief and gratitude swept over her. Tears welled up and spilled over, mixed with the raindrops on her face. "Jake . . . oh my God . . . Jake!"

He swung down from his horse. "What're you doing out here? What happened?"

"I'm hurt bad. Can't walk. My horse threw me and bolted. I think my ankle's broken. Maybe my shoulder."

He knelt in front of her. "We gotta find shelter from this storm. It's getting worse, and the water is rising fast. I saw a place back over the ridge that might work."

Movement hurt, but, with Jake's help, Sarah managed to stand, holding tight to his arm and leaning heavily against his shoulder. With considerable effort, Jake managed to get her on his horse, and he climbed on behind. They rode toward the spot Jake remembered, a cave-like opening in the side of a rocky wall. While not large enough to include his horse, it did provide enough cover for Jake and Sarah to get out of the rain.

Still groggy and light-headed, Sarah was barely aware of her surroundings. She held out her hand and touched Jake, to reassure herself it wasn't a dream. "I can't believe you found me," she whispered.

From a dark and secluded corner, a small deer mouse watched intently with bright eyes. A flash of lightning reflected the animal's gaze, but he made no sound. These human guests were not welcome in his quiet home.

CHAPTER 6

Neal sat behind a stack of old newspapers and stared out his office window. With a freshly lit cigar in one hand, he sighed and stroked the beginnings of a beard. A puff on the cigar sent smoke swirling around his head.

"Fortunes are being made every day in this country," he said to himself. "The papers are full of success stories, and I intend to get my share. Men are getting rich in cattle, land, and railroads. Smart men, and I'm as smart as any of them."

Neal tried to remember a time when money wasn't an issue in his life.

Nobody understands me. I'm a good person. Nobody gives me a chance. All I want is respect, to be treated like I deserve. I deserve to have money like everyone else.

Thoughts of Sarah came then and brought anger . . . at her, at her father and the ranch hands who'd thrown him out the other night. At his domineering mother, too, and everyone who'd wronged him.

Even as a kid, my classmates made fun of me. Called me a momma's boy. The girls laughed at me. And in Chicago, Momma said people tried cheating us, and we had to leave town. It's always her way. She always tells me what to do, never lets me prove myself. I'll show her. I'll show Sarah, and everyone. One day I'll be rich and famous.

Neal failed to notice the fire at the end of his cigar had died. The fire within him burned hot and bright. He returned to the business section of a Denver newspaper and began to read about railroad expansion into Wyoming and Montana. He needed to make some money. The news about such ventures and his lack of involvement only frustrated him more.

I'm going to show everyone. This is my big opportunity, and nobody—nobody!—is going to stop me. Just let them try.

The wealth inherited by his mother would only last so long. His grandfather had built a New Hampshire haberdashery supply company and made a fortune, but Neal and his mother had already spent thousands of dollars from the sale of the family business. *I'll show them, Momma. I'm going to make thousands of dollars out here, in land and cattle. We'll have everything we've always wanted, and more.*

One thing he should take care of right away. What he intended here in the Wyoming Territory would make him plenty of enemies. Not that he cared, except for concerns about his personal safety. He got up and strode out of his office, to pay the local gunsmith a visit.

The gunsmith was an old man with unkempt white hair and beard. Even indoors, he wore a well-worn brown derby hat and sported a wad of chewing tobacco in his mouth. A dribble of tobacco stain oozed onto his hairy chin.

Neal entered the man's shop and looked around. Several rifles hung on the wall. Other disassembled weapons in various stages of repair lay on a table in the back. New and used pistols lay on shelves under a counter where the old man was cleaning. More used than new, like everything else in this place.

"Morning, Mr. Neal," the gunsmith said.

"You know me?"

"Everyone in town knows you. Word travels fast about strangers in Chugwater. How can I help you?"

"I'm needing a handgun. I already have one . . . could use another."

"You have something special in mind?"

"I'll know it when I see and hold it. Show me what you've got."

After showing Neal several pistols, the gunsmith suggested a Colt .45. "This one will give you more flexibility, and you can use different cartridges."

"What about this one? I like this one." Neal held up a Smith and Wesson Schofield .45-caliber revolver.

"Sir, that's a great weapon, but it only uses Schofield .45 cartridges. Whereas the Colt—"

"What did I just say?" Neal snapped.

The gunsmith shrugged. "It's your choice and your money. I'm just saying, the Colt .45 cartridges will be too long to fit that gun you want."

"I'm buying what I want. Now write me up, and give me plenty of cartridges."

Neal paid for the Schofield and stepped from the store with the idea of getting something to eat. The town's only public café was a small, rundown establishment somewhere between unhealthy and outright certain illness (if you dared to eat there). Still, he'd survived steak and eggs and bad coffee. Dinner couldn't be worse.

The sun burned hot on the midday street. Neal watched women in plain, long dresses and colorful bonnets walking in the dust. They hurried along past him and tried not to make eye contact. Temperatures hovered near 100 degrees, with unusually high humidity. Within sight of the main street, children of nearly every size, age, and shape played games near a small, one-room schoolhouse. The kids, like everything and everyone in Chugwater, were dirty and dust-covered.

On one side of the café was the town's feed store and on the other side a Chinese laundry. Neal started toward the café and its greasy excuse for nourishment and noticed two dirt-covered, sweat-stained horses tied to the hitch rail in front of the saloon. Both animals stood with their heads down and had dried sweat marks on their flanks and legs. They looked ridden hard and exhausted.

Curiosity overcame hunger. Neal decided a cold beer and a couple of hard-boiled eggs would suffice, at least temporarily. Both were readily available in the saloon.

The place was empty except for the bartender and two strangers standing at the bar. A pungent smell of stale cigars and long spent cigarettes mixed with the smell of dirt . . . the human kind. One of the strangers stood half turned toward the door, watching him. The dim light inside made it difficult to get a clear look at anything.

Neal moved further into the room. The man watching him stood more than six feet and Neal guessed was about thirty years old. He had dark-brown eyes and brown hair. His unshaven face had not seen soap or any type of cleaning for quite some time, and his lips were blistered. The man's hat was turned up on the sides and covered in a thick layer of dust. A Colt .45 hung low at his right hand, and he held a shot of whiskey in his left.

The second man, talking to the bartender, was shorter than the first. Dirty, brown hair covered his head, and he had a full beard. His exact age was hard to determine, but Neal fixed him at about twenty-five. He spoke in an annoying, high-pitched squeal. A checkered, brown and black vest covered his thin and well-worn blue shirt. Pistols hung on both hips. Both weapons were well-used Remington Model 1875 single-action Army revolvers.

Both men were missing teeth, and the taller man had tobacco stains on his lips. His left foot rested on a spittoon, but every attempt at making a deposit missed its mark. Fresh tobacco spit oozed along the floor in narrow brown rivulets.

Neal headed toward a table. "Bring me a beer," he shouted to the bartender.

Now both men were watching him, but they said nothing. Neal spoke first. "Gents, you look hot and thirsty. How 'bout I buy you each a cold beer?"

The taller man stepped away from the spittoon and turned fully to face Neal. No one said a word.

Neal allowed himself a grin. "How 'bout it? You gents thirsty?"

The men looked at each other. Then the younger man spoke. "Maybe we are!" he said, one hand resting on the butt of a pistol. "Maybe we ain't. Who are you to be concerned about it?"

"Why, gentlemen, my name is Jason Kelly Neal. Maybe you've heard of me?"

Neither man responded.

Neal stood and stepped toward them, with a hard stare. "If you haven't, you will. I aim to run this town."

"That a fact?" The taller man lowered his right hand closer to his own pistol. "Who put you in charge?"

"I put myself in charge. But, seeing as how I'm expanding my interests, I could use some help. How about I buy you boys a steak along with a beer, and we discuss a mutually beneficial business proposition?"

The two men looked at each other and then back at Neal. "What kind of proposition?" asked the taller man.

Neal took a couple more steps forward, hands held out from his sides to avoid any type of threatening gesture. He was certain either man was capable of outdrawing him. "Where you gents from?"

"We just drifted up from Texas," the younger man answered. "We heard somebody named Winston might be hiring."

"Now that's mighty interesting . . . mighty interesting," said Neal. "Winston is dead. I'm doing the hiring now, providing you have the skills and temperament I need."

"Such as?" asked the older man.

"Well, take for instance those pistols. You boys know how to use 'em?"

"We ain't dead yet!"

"We can take care of ourselves," the younger man said.

"You fellas wanted for anything? Say, down Texas way?"

The older man shrugged. "We've had a few run-ins with the law. Nothing we couldn't handle."

"Mighty fine. Mighty fine. I believe you boys just might work out. Can you take orders? You willing to shoot and kill to protect my interests?"

"We might if you pay well enough."

"That's good. That's real good. Let's just say this town is in need of some law . . . my kind of law. Get my meaning?" He turned to the older man. "You ever wear a badge? How would you like to be sheriff of Chugwater? And this young man next to you can be your chief deputy. No one's filling those jobs at present. You'll work for me, of course, and my word will be the law in this town."

The younger man laughed. "Lawmen? Now that's funny. That's real funny."

"You take care of us, we'll back you!" said the older man. "I'm Bob Swagger. This here's Ellis Lake."

"Great! Let's get you some food and a place to stay. Take your horses to the stable, and tell the old man who runs it to water and grain them. Give them some hay, and put it on my account. Welcome to Chugwater. Welcome!"

As the three men left the saloon and stepped down into the street, a wagon and team of horses nearly ran over them. The driver shouted, "Look out!" but his warning almost came too late. Swagger reached up, grabbed the man, and pulled him from the seat of the still-moving wagon. He shoved the fellow against a hitch rail with a pistol against his head.

"Don't you have nothing better to do than running down folks in the street?"

"It was an accident," the man stammered. "I tried warning you."

Lake and Neal stood back, amused at the rancher's plight.

Swagger pushed his pistol under the man's jaw. "Won't be a next time. You understand, old man? I just hired on as sheriff of this rundown excuse for a town. And I'm telling you to stay clear of me, my deputy, and Mr. Neal here."

Swagger shoved the man to the ground, laughed, and walked away. Neal looked at the humiliated rancher, rubbing his jaw and struggling to stand, and smiled as he rejoined his new sheriff and deputy.

The summer thunderstorm that had built all morning slid north, leaving the town hot and dry. Neal glanced at the distant clouds and smiled. He was having a good day, a very good day!

CHAPTER 7

The rain eased, and the storm moved northeast toward Fort Laramie and the Platte River. Jake peered from the cave-like overhang and saw a bright rainbow on the horizon, while rivulets of water sought lower ground around them. The air smelled clean and fresh. The ground was slick in places, the footing treacherous with the rough terrain.

Jake managed to get Sarah back on his horse, then climbed on behind her. The trek home took time, but he soon had her in Molly's tender care. A rider was sent to get the doctor, who would later confirm what they'd already guessed. Sarah's ankle wasn't broken, just badly sprained. She was told a "tincture of time" was her best medicine and she should stay off her feet.

"For once in your life, listen," Molly admonished her friend with a smile. Suggesting Sarah rest and stay off her badly injured ankle was like asking the sun to stop rising each day. It wasn't going to happen.

The days passed. Jake, Tom, and the other ranch hands slowly gathered the stolen cattle and sorted them by brand. William Thompson returned home to the Box T and took several of his men with him. Jake and three others, including Tom Scott and Trace Johnson, stayed behind to assist in getting the cattle to their rightful owners. Tom and Trace had both agreed to stay and work for Meadows. Switching his employment would allow Tom to see Molly more.

Most of the local ranchers agreed any cattle lacking a brand or displaying an altered brand would remain part of the Meadows herd temporarily, until a more equitable means of sorting could be arranged. A few dissenters grumbled that John Meadows stood to gain considerably more stock than he was entitled to, but no one wanted any more trouble over it.

Nobody bothered to tell Neal. The city-born attorney had let it be known that, since no one actually owned the disputed cattle, he would hold them in his own name until something was decided. The local men felt it was none of his business, and all were in agreement the animals in question didn't belong to the man from Nebraska.

Jake stopped by and checked on Sarah each day, but even he couldn't keep her boredom at bay. After two weeks of convalescing, Sarah was ready to get out and do something, anything. Staying home resting had grown tiresome.

"Let's go into town," she suggested to Molly one morning over breakfast. "We could get some supplies, and I've got to get out of here."

Molly laughed, knowing better than to argue.

"I'll send Trace Johnson along with you," Sarah's father said. "You both sit tight and enjoy the ride."

Since the night of the barn dance, Sarah had heard nothing about Neal, so she assumed he'd returned to Nebraska to stay with his mother. It surprised her somewhat that he'd gone away so quietly. During her own time in Nebraska, he'd been more than a friend. They had grown close, bordering on love, and she felt guilty at the way he'd been embarrassed in front of everyone. *Still, he brought it on himself by making that marriage proposal in front of my family and friends. It's not like him to just fade away, though it's probably for the best.*

As she slowly followed Molly out of the ranch house, hobbling on a makeshift crutch, Sarah put all thoughts of Neal to the back of her mind. She just wanted to get into town and catch up on the latest news. She also wanted to mail a letter to her Aunt Ruby and Uncle Lewis, bringing them up to date on everything. She and Molly would look at fabrics for Molly's hope chest.

Ever since they'd met during the Winston debacle, Molly and Tom's mutual attraction had grown, and now they were making wedding plans. Thoughts of Jake snuck into Sarah's mind, but she put them firmly away. *I don't even know if he wants to get married.*

Outside the barn, Trace hitched horses to the wagon. Molly helped Sarah into it, and they were soon ready to leave. "I'd tell you to keep them out of trouble," Meadows said with a laugh, "but keeping those two girls from mischief is like telling the wind not to blow out here."

Trace climbed onto the seat and slapped the reins across the horses' backs. The wagon moved forward with a jolt. The fresh morning air and bright Wyoming sunshine on Sarah's face felt like a tonic for her soul. Her healing ankle barely hurt at all. The trip took time, but she and Molly enjoyed the sights and sounds along the way.

"Smell the fresh air?" Sarah asked. "Ever wonder where the wind starts? Where it's been? How many faces has it touched before it found you? Where will it go from here? Was it born in some distant thunderstorm, or as a soft breeze in some secluded mountain forest? Ever wonder? I do."

Molly merely shook her head and glanced at Trace, who was intent on the trail ahead of them. He often snapped the reins and urged the horses onward but said nothing to his passengers. Now and then mice and rabbits scurried out of their path, eager to avoid any interaction with humans.

They rounded a high, jagged rocky point along the trail. Off in the distance spread cottonwood and willow trees growing along Chugwater Creek, with a small group of buildings beyond.

Bluffs along the eastern side of the creek towered over the valley floor. Smaller outcroppings rose from the western side of the creek, but the terrain allowed for easy traveling.

Sarah gazed at the cliffs on the opposite side of the creek. "Ever wonder just how many bison were herded off those cliffs so the Indians had food?"

"What?" Molly asked, caught up in her own thoughts.

"Those bluffs. The Indians used to run bison over those cliffs and rimrocks. They called it a bison jump. The animals would fall to their deaths, or would be so badly injured they could easily be killed. That's one of the ways the Indians hunted in ancient times, before they had horses."

"That's how the town got its name," Trace explained, speaking up for the first time. "Those old bison would make a chugging sound as they fell near the creek. So the creek and town were named Chugwater."

They sat in silence as the team pulled the wagon toward town. The only sounds were of leather and harness rubbing against wood. Now and then one of the horses snorted or let out a deep breath. Their shod hooves struck rocks underfoot with a pinging sound.

Once in town, Trace tied the team in front of the general store and helped the women climb down. Sarah stretched her arms and legs, tucked the crutch under her arm, and started toward the store's front door. She was thinking about material for a new dress, maybe some new curtains for the house. Trace excused himself and told them he would return soon. First, he had to run an errand at the telegraph office and then go by the stable. Sarah remembered she had a letter to mail and handed it to Trace as he left.

Sarah and Molly spent a pleasant hour buying supplies for the ranch and sighing over new fabrics. Neither knew the unpleasant store owner. Molly giggled when Sarah compared the man's unruly appearance to an alley cat's after a night of prowling.

Once they'd settled their purchases in the wagon, the two women started along the wooden sidewalk toward the café. They hadn't seen Trace since he left to run his errand. A wagon pulled by two bay mules rolled past, hauling corn. Two older women in calico dresses and matching bonnets walked by, hesitating just long enough to say hello. Sarah remembered them as Victoria Swanson and Emily Goodrich, neither ever married and both often grouchy. They'd never been especially friendly, even when she was a child. Apparently, nothing had changed while she was away teaching in Nebraska.

In the distance, she spotted Missy Fernsmith, wife of the town's only blacksmith, walking toward her home. Too far away to shout hello and be heard, Sarah waved instead. The gesture went unseen.

A pistol shot behind them, followed by a scream, startled both women. They turned quickly and saw two rough-looking men standing in the middle of the street, confronting an elderly couple. Sarah recognized them . . . the rancher Chris Little and his wife. The taller of the two gunmen held a Colt .45 in his right hand. The shorter, younger-looking one held a rifle.

The tall gunslinger spoke. "Old man, didn't I tell you to stay off the street when me and my friend was around?"

Little glanced fearfully around, as if seeking help or support. None was forthcoming. His wife clutched at his arm.

"Mister," he stammered. "We was just crossing the street."

The gunman grinned, then turned to his companion. "Look like they was just crossing the street to you, Deputy Lake? Seems to me they were threatening us."

Lake nodded. "Yeah . . . threatening us."

"See, even my deputy here thinks you're causing trouble. Can't have that. Looks bad. We represent the law in this town.

Can't have folks disrespecting the law, now can we?"

"You ain't the law. You both are a couple of thugs."

Rage twisted the gunman's face. He took a step toward the old rancher.

"Sheriff! Sheriff Swagger! Easy now!"

Sarah immediately recognized the voice. "Jason!" she gasped.

She looked past Swagger and Lake and saw Neal walking down the street toward them. Small puffs of dust exploded under his boots as he approached. Swagger lowered his pistol.

Molly let out a quiet, "Oh, no."

Neal smiled and raised a hand. "Easy, men. I think these good folks were on their way to see me. Ain't that right, Mr. Little?"

The old rancher tried to speak, but his frail voice refused to respond. Swagger grabbed him. A small group of onlookers had gathered, with Sarah and Molly standing among them.

Trace stepped from the livery stable and surveyed the developing situation. He'd missed most of the altercation. Sarah and Molly stepped back, further blending into the crowd.

"There's no need to harass these kind people. I believe they were coming to sell their ranch to me, at a fair price of course," said Neal, with a sly grin. "Why don't you men escort these good people to my office?"

Sarah turned to Molly and quietly asked, "Sheriff, and Deputy Lake? What's going on?"

"You heard right," an old man next to them said. "They claim to be the law in town now."

Sarah frowned. "I don't understand. We've never had a sheriff before. Never needed one. We've always worked things out between ourselves."

"Well, we do now, or so they claim," the man responded.

Swagger spoke again. "Absolutely, Mr. Neal. We'll bring them to your office right now."

"Why, we never—" exclaimed Mrs. Little. She broke off, shooting a nervous glance at Neal and Swagger.

Lake shoved the woman from behind, nearly knocking her down. Swagger grabbed the old man's arm and pulled him down the street. Sarah gasped at their continued brutality.

"No need for that," Neal called after them. He turned briefly to the onlookers but didn't appear to notice her. "Would suggest you folks move along," he said as he surveyed the crowd. "This is a legal matter." Then he turned and joined the procession moving slowly toward his office.

Sarah stepped forward, alarmed at what she'd just witnessed. She had started to call out when Trace stepped in front of her. "Not now," he whispered. "We gotta get home."

Once the street was cleared, Trace and the women left town with the wagon load of supplies. The bright morning had given way to an afternoon of clouds and pensive silence. Sarah was especially quiet. The sheriff and deputy had treated the Littles so harshly, she was thankful Neal had calmed things. *Who knows what might have happened if Jason hadn't shown up when he did to defuse the situation.*

As they approached the ranch complex, a turkey buzzard drifted overhead. A black and white, mixed-breed dog that normally greeted their arrival with noisy abandon sat quiet and still near the barn, as if even he felt the pall of apprehension that painted the afternoon air.

CHAPTER 8

Smoke rose in a circular pattern from the Meadows chimney and was caught on the wind and swept away. Late afternoon baking using dried peaches from town meant pie for supper. The smell of fresh-baked bread also drifted across the barnyard, but it gave a false sense of goodness. Inside the house, people's feelings were anything but sweet. The news that Jason Neal had stayed in Chugwater was cause for concern.

Trace sipped on a cup of coffee and shared what he'd learned in town. "Word is, Neal rode into town the morning after the party out here. He went to see Agnes McGee about that building of hers. Mrs. McGee was found dead later in the day. Jacob Helms at the stable says the doctor blamed a heart attack. But Neal moved into her building right away, and that's got some folks wondering just how he persuaded Agnes to sell it to him in the first place . . . if something he said or did upset her so much, her heart gave out."

"Why? Why did he stay in Chugwater?" Sarah asked. "Doesn't make sense. I turned down his marriage proposal. He has no reason to stay in town."

Trace shrugged. "And now he's hired a couple of gunmen from Texas, claiming one's the sheriff and the other's his deputy. Folks are getting nervous."

"He has no right to do that," Meadows said. "Who the hell gave him that power?"

Trace looked him in the eye. "Neal put himself in charge.

Nobody dares challenge him."

Sarah let out a breath. "Why such meanness?"

"He's madder'n a hornet about something, I'd guess. Was he like that back in Nebraska?" Trace asked. "You knew him best out there."

"No . . . not at all. At least, not with me," Sarah answered. "He was always so kind, even gentle. I only saw him get moody every now and then, when he mentioned his mother. Mostly, he was a gentleman." She shook her head. "I don't understand. He was so thoughtful when I met him. Then he comes out here and practically demands I marry him. He obviously didn't take my refusal very well. And poor Mrs. McGee. She had a weak heart anyway. What am I going to tell Jake?"

"Tell Jake what?"

Sarah looked toward the front door. Jake stood there with his hat in hand, searching the solemn room for answers.

"What's going on? What's happened?" he asked. "You folks look as if someone just died."

Sarah quickly described their trip to town and explained what they'd learned. "I don't know what to do."

Jake frowned. "Maybe I should go pay him a visit, ask about his intentions."

"No!" Sarah said. "I should talk to him. I know him best."

"Tom and I will go along. I don't want you going alone."

"You can't stay, Jake," Trace said. "I picked up a telegram from Mr. Thompson while I was in town today. He needs all us Box T hands to come home as soon as possible. The work is piling up."

Meadows cleared his throat. "You boys have done all you can here. Most of the stolen cattle have been gathered and sorted. You can't know how much I appreciate all you've done. If Sarah needs help, Tom and Trace and I, and Molly, will be here."

Jake looked worried. "What about Neal, and his so-called

sheriff and deputy? You really think it's okay for me to leave?"

Sarah didn't want him to go but nodded anyway. "We'll stay in touch. I'll send for you if we have problems. I'm sure everything will work out."

Meadows looked at Jake, then at Sarah. "Until we know more, there's nothing you can do. Maybe today was an isolated incident. We'll have to wait and see."

"All right," Jake said quietly. "If you think it's best."

Jake lay awake into the night. Outside he heard cicadas and crickets, and on a distant hill a coyote called for its mate. Cattle bawled in a nearby pasture while horses milled about in the corral. The intensity of Jake's thoughts made all the sounds seem louder. Around him in the bunkhouse, several men snored, and one talked in his sleep about family. Another sucked on his teeth. Jake tossed and turned.

This was his last night on the Meadows ranch, and thoughts of Sarah held him captive. He didn't want to leave, not now. But he was still foreman of the Box T, and he knew there was work to be done. Sleep finally overtook his restless mind a few hours before dawn.

At daybreak, Jake met Sarah outside the barn and gave her a long hug and kiss on the cheek. "Are you sure you want me to leave?" he asked. "Doesn't feel right, somehow."

"I know, but you have work to do. I'll miss you, but, like we said last night, until we know more about Neal and his intentions there's nothing you can do."

Jake gently gripped her shoulders and looked into her eyes. "If you need me, promise you'll send word? I'll come quickly. Next time I get some time off, I'll come check on you and your dad."

She nodded, and reluctantly he let her go. Then he mounted his sorrel gelding and, along with the other Box T hands, said goodbye. At the top of a ridge north of the ranch buildings, he pulled up and looked back, waved at Sarah, then was gone.

In town, Neal hired four more gunmen and made them de facto deputies. He ignored the pungent smell of stale cigar smoke and unwashed bodies in his office that said his newly hired deputies were in need of a bath. From behind a large mahogany desk, sporting a two-day growth of whiskers himself, he gathered his new group of hired guns, along with Swagger and Lake.

"Men, we have work to do. Some in this town need convincing I'm running things around here. That's where you boys come in. Tonight, I want you to go out to the Meadows ranch, find all those cattle they've been collecting, and run them to hell and back. Scatter them so they need to be found and gathered again. And if the old man's bunkhouse should accidently burn down in the process . . . well, things happen, if you know what I mean. Anyone tries to stop you, shoot them down like a mangy dog.

"I know you boys need to be paid for watching over things, so I'm thinking about a protection tax to raise some money . . . seems fair. Tomorrow, we'll start calling on each business here in town and explain it. Let them know how things stand. Now get out of here."

Sunset over the Laramie mountain range was spectacular, the mountains painted against the fiery sky in dark cobalt and navy blues. As the sun dipped behind the rugged peaks it gave off the most brilliant shades of orange Sarah ever remembered seeing.

Sarah and Molly decided to go for a walk along the creek so they could talk. They moved slowly because of Sarah's ankle. Neither spoke until they reached the creek.

"You miss him already, don't you?" said Molly.

"Yes!"

"What about Neal? Why do you think he stayed around?"

"Wish I knew. But it can't be good. He was so angry when he was thrown out of the dance. I'm sure it has everything to do with me. I need to go talk to him, and soon."

They sat on one end of a dead cottonwood log that was partially submerged in the creek. Shade from the trees along with the water created a cool spot, out of the heat. Sarah felt as if she were in the middle of a bad dream. But it was real. Neal was in Chugwater, and apparently up to no good, if the rumors Trace had heard were true. She felt the need to go see him more strongly than ever.

The stream flowed clear and cool, gurgling and splashing over rocks. Sarah and Molly listened without speaking. The sounds calmed Sarah, despite the harsh reality that her one-time love was still in Wyoming. In the distance, she saw her father and Tom riding toward the barn, talking. They looked worn out.

"Let's fix the men some supper. They look beat," said Sarah, turning her thoughts away from Neal.

After supper, they all went outside to have coffee on the front porch. The evening breeze provided some relief from the heat inside the house. Nobody spoke, each lost in his or her own thoughts. Meadows eventually said goodnight and went inside. Molly and Tom soon followed, each going their separate ways. Sarah was left on the dark porch to her own thoughts, a mixture of melancholy and concern.

Finally, she gave up and went to her room. Moonlight stole through her bedroom window and cast a bright glow over everything. Even exhausted, Sarah couldn't sleep. Her mind raced in circles, from her concern about Neal's intentions to the fact Jake had been forced to leave. Despite her brave words earlier in the day, she missed him already.

Time passed. Sarah got up, went to her window, and stared

into the night. Outlines of nearby buildings and a few of the rugged hills beyond were the only things visible. All was still. After a few minutes, she reluctantly returned to bed. Sleep found her soon after. It swept over her like the great waves of some faraway ocean, and she was lost upon its deep, dream-like coming.

She woke suddenly to the sound of bawling cattle and a distant rumbling. Her first thought was a thunderstorm. Then she bolted upright in her bed, abruptly remembering when she'd heard this same sound once before. She scrambled out of bed and ran from her room, shouting, "Stampede! Stampede!"

Her father's bedroom door opened, and he stuck his head out. "What's going on?"

"Stampede! The cattle are running!" Having roused the household, Sarah dashed back to her bedroom to put on her boots.

By the time she, her father, and Molly made it to the porch, steers were crossing the open ground between the house and barn. Tom, Trace, and two other hands ran to the corral to catch their horses. The animals circled in panic, their heads held high.

The cattle overturned an empty wagon, tore through a clothesline, and then a section of fence. Wood cracked as horns and hooves struck it. The cattle ran hard, nostrils flaring and eyes wide, as if late for an appointment in hell.

They climbed over a small rise near the house and plunged in a massive wave down the far side. A pounding mix of beasts and people trying frantically to stop them flowed over the ranch complex, creating patterns of dark shadows across a shifting canvas. Nothing in their path was safe. The ground shook under hundreds of pounding hooves.

Dust rose in clouds, further darkening the pre-dawn blackness. Dishes fell from kitchen shelves and shattered as the herd moved past the ranch house and into the far end of night. Only their own distaste for running would eventually slow them. Even dead and dying beasts among them merely slowed the herd long enough to dodge the carcasses in front of them.

"Stand back!" Meadows shouted. "Stay in the house. There's nothing we can do until they pass." He ran toward the horse corral, where he joined Tom, Trace, and the other ranch hands fighting to catch and calm the frantic horses.

Sarah and Molly huddled together on the porch. Peering into the darkness and chaos, Sarah made out three men chasing the cattle. Two were waving blankets and shouting, while the third man fired a pistol in the air. In the moonlight, she saw all three wore masks. She could only watch as her father and the ranch hands tried to get mounted. But it was too little, too late.

As one of the marauders rode close, Tom dove through the corral fence and ran for the bunkhouse. A steer brushed against him, nearly knocking him down. He dodged two others and reached the door just as two shots rang out. One bullet caught him in the leg and another in the shoulder, pushing him inside the bunkhouse and onto the floor.

Molly screamed as she saw him go down. She started forward, as if to go to him, but Sarah grabbed her arm. "You can't! Those men will shoot you, too. And, if they don't, the cattle will trample you!" she shouted above the melee.

Molly was weeping. "I can't just leave him. He's been shot."

Meadows rushed back toward the house and hurried inside, then came back out with his rifle and cartridges. He aimed at the men who'd stampeded the cattle, but they rode low and slumped over, making it impossible to get a clear shot. One rider suddenly turned from the others, a torch in his hand burning bright. The man threw it through the bunkhouse door. In seconds, the bunkhouse was engulfed in fire and smoke.

"Tom's inside!" Molly screamed. She tore out of Sarah's

grasp and ran toward the burning building.

Meadows charged down the front steps, dodging several steers as he followed in Molly's wake. More shots split the night, but all missed their mark. One of the gunmen shouted at the others, and they rode away, disappearing into the darkness.

Sarah watched in terror as Trace and another hand came running. Meadows passed Molly and reached the wooden door of the bunkhouse first. Smoke and flames swirled around him as he peered into the burning building. The fire and heat forced him to turn aside.

Trace tried to shield himself from the heat and smoke with a hand to his face. "There he is!" he shouted. "He's lying on the floor." He and Meadows fought through the heat and flames, grabbed Tom's legs, and pulled him clear of the building. Molly knelt next to him as the two men gasped for fresh air. His moans carried over the crackling sounds of the fire just as the roof collapsed, still ablaze.

CHAPTER 9

Smoke and dust filled the morning air, thick and heavy throughout the ranch complex. The sound of water flowing in nearby Sybille Creek mixed with the ragged cry of an old rooster announced the arrival of morning, and cattle bawled in the distance. Horses snorted and milled inside the corral. Sarah heard and saw it all from where she sat on the ranch house porch, a rifle across her lap.

All around them lay devastation and destruction, as if a tornado had swept over them. The barn and outhouse located near the bunkhouse had both suffered fire damage. The bunkhouse still smoldered with hot spots. Smoke continued to rise on unseen breezes and drifted away, as if in no obvious hurry to escape this isolated Wyoming outpost. The smell of burnt wood lingered.

Closer to the ranch house, flowerbeds were in ruin, the bright-petaled blossoms smashed and trampled beyond recognition. A small apple tree planted upon Sarah's recent return lay flattened, its bare roots exposed. A section of corral fence where someone had carefully bound lodgepole pine logs together stood broken in the trampled earth.

Tracks and cow manure could be seen everywhere. The stampeding cattle had made no effort to avoid anything. They had run roughshod in wide-eyed fear, their bellowing and bawling filling the night air with a thunderous roar. Now they were scattered for miles, likely too disoriented to find their way home.

Tom Scott clung to life. Molly and Sarah had bandaged his wounds while waiting for the doctor. If Tom lived, the toll of the previous night would surely leave an emotional scar far deeper than any of skin and bone. Still distraught, Molly sat by his bedside, desperately praying.

Nobody had slept while waiting for the cattle to run their course. Sarah's father had not tried to stop them. Now he sat in a rocking chair near Sarah, staring at the distant mountains with a pallid look of shock, his shoulders slumped in defeat.

"Why?" he whispered. "Who would do this? Why?"

"Wish I knew," Sarah said. "Doesn't make any sense. I can't think of anyone. Can you?"

"I have no idea," he answered softly.

Sarah looked at her father as if seeing him for the first time. He'd homesteaded this ranch twenty-two years earlier. And with a high degree of determination, defiance, and downright stubbornness, he'd enjoyed some measure of success. Sarah's mother was buried on a hill within sight of the house. She'd died years before, after giving birth to Sarah, and he still mourned her loss.

Although not a big man, what he lacked in stature was offset by a tough-as-nails nature. Years of manual labor under the hot Wyoming sun had left his skin dry and weathered, his hands and face calloused and dark. He walked with a limp, the result of a horse falling on him as a child. Now he stared blankly at the distant Laramie mountain range. The hopelessness in his face hurt Sarah's heart.

She raised her chin, defiant. "Well I know one thing. We won't be intimidated. We won't let it stop us from building this ranch into something special. I believe in our future here. We'll look back one day and realize this was only a bump in the road."

"I admire your grit," her father said. "But unless we find out who did this, it could happen again."

"I know, and I'm as concerned as you are, but I'm determined to see this through. We'll just need to keep our guard up and be prepared next time."

Sarah and her father eventually met with the few ranch hands they had left, although neither of them was sure what to say. They had no explanation for events of the previous night. Neither did any of the men.

"Going to take days to collect them critters," one older hand offered.

"Hell, we just got 'em gathered. Now this!" said another angry cowpuncher.

Meadows sighed. "Let's take care of the dead and dying. Tomorrow, we'll get started finding those that ran off. Maybe some will drift back this way and make our jobs easier."

"Not likely," mumbled one of the men. "I'd like to know who did this."

"You and me, both." Meadows wiped sweat from his face. "Don't be shy about telling the neighbors. Folks in Chugwater need to know what happened out here." He nodded toward a tall, lanky young hand who'd recently hired on from Utah. The man reportedly liked to spread gossip, so Meadows figured by day's end everyone in the territory would know.

Fire and torment were not new to Meadows. The burned-out bunkhouse was only the most recent. Harold Winston and his henchmen had burned down the Meadows's chicken house. Still, this felt different, more personal somehow.

Meadows and some of the hands took rifles to put down injured cattle they found. Sarah heard one shot, then another as the hurt and dying were put out of their misery. Dead animals were dragged into a nearby ravine and burned, leaving a sickening stench of charred hide and flesh in the air.

The joy that had filled Sarah's recent days was gone. She

recalled seeing Neal in town two days earlier and had a gut-wrenching feeling he was somehow involved in last night's attack. *No. He can't be. He isn't a violent man.* She rose from her seat on the porch, more determined than ever to seek Neal out and learn more about his intentions.

The doctor's arrival a short while later brought a sense of relief as he confirmed Tom's eventual recovery. When he climbed aboard his buggy and headed back toward town, Sarah rode alongside. She'd managed to saddle her buckskin horse and slip away, catching up with the doctor less than a mile from the house. With all the confusion at the ranch, nobody noticed, though she'd left a note for her father and Molly concerning her plans to see Neal.

As Sarah and the doctor traveled together, idle conversation led the doctor to comment on Chugwater's newest citizen, Jason Kelly Neal. "The man has the entire town on edge."

Confused, Sarah asked, "What's he done?"

"He's hard to figure but it's worrisome that he's got such a quick temper. The other morning, that Chinese fellow Kim Sung who owns the laundry was sweeping off the walkway in front of his place. He accidentally swept some dirt on Neal's shiny, black boots. Neal raged at him, like the man did it on purpose. I thought he might shoot Sung and his wife.

"And don't get me started on those two hired thugs, Swagger and Lake. Neal pays them to be the so-called sheriff and deputy in Chugwater. It's getting so ranchers are afraid of coming into town. They might break some crazy, made-up law." The doctor scowled. "Not sure how much more I can take. I'm too old for this. I'm thinking about retirement. Harold Winston was bad enough. Neal and his lawmen may be worse."

Sarah agreed about Lake and Swagger. Neal, though . . . *He's not usually like that,* she wanted to say, but found the whole subject made her uncomfortable. "Doctor, what happened to

Agnes McGee? I heard she died of a heart attack."

"Best I could determine, that's exactly what happened to the poor old woman. Saw no evidence of anything else. But Neal wasted no time moving into her building. Seemed a mite hasty to me. And he was seen leaving her house earlier, on the day she was found dead. Who really knows what happened? Maybe he was involved somehow. Maybe not."

Sarah didn't respond. She thought of Neal's gentlemanly ways back in Nebraska . . . and then how he'd acted the night of the dance, and the fear on Mrs. Little's face two days ago. *Because of that man Swagger,* she told herself.

Word of the stampede and the shooting of Tom Scott had already spread through town by the time Sarah and the doctor arrived. Hushed whispers from passers-by greeted her as she rode down the main street.

Oscar Bloomfeld, owner of the general store, stopped his sweeping and leaned on his broom as she passed. A young cowhand walking toward the feed store slowed to watch her. His quiet "good morning" and tip of his hat went unreturned.

Knowing Neal had moved into the old McGee building, Sarah rode straight for his office. She had good memories of the days when Agnes McGee and her husband ran the store. *They had the best hard candy.* She reached the brick structure and hesitated, looking around before dismounting.

Two tired horses stood tied to the hitch rail in front, switching their tails to keep the horse flies at bay. Wood trim on the red brick building badly needed paint, and caulking between many of the bricks was missing. She stepped down and moved quickly toward the front door, where she paused briefly to look through a small, dirty window in the top half. Unable to see anything, not even her reflection, she went inside.

Unfamiliar voices . . . the laughing voices of men . . . made her hesitate. She couldn't understand their words, only the roughness in it, and that someone—probably more than one person—was having a good time.

She stood silently for another few moments, gathering her nerve, then called out. "Hello!"

The voices broke off abruptly. She caught another low murmur, but no one answered her greeting. She looked around the room where she stood. She saw a single chair in one corner, two three-legged stools, and a pine board bench along one wall. Above the bench hung two worn and faded prints depicting scenes of the French countryside. The frames were dusty and needed cleaning. An old calendar from 1864 still clung to an opposite wall, more than ten years past its usefulness.

A heavy footstep made her turn. The sheriff—Swagger?—stood in front of her, unkempt and smelling unwashed. She fought down an urge to flee.

"Lady, you lost?" he said, not as if he cared.

She squared her shoulders. "I'm here to see Jason."

"Jason?"

"Yes, Jason Neal. Is he here?"

Swagger's grin showed rotting teeth. "Why, for a pretty young thing like yourself . . . stay here!"

He lingered a moment, pinning her with bloodshot, hungry, black eyes. She shivered as she felt his probing stare. He licked his tobacco-stained lips, smiled wider, and turned away.

Sarah's heart pounded as Swagger vanished into a back room. Neal came out a few seconds later, Swagger and Lake right behind him. The sight of Neal brought relief, though not as much as Sarah expected. Why were these rough men here with him?

Neal smiled, as if delighted to see her. "Why don't you boys go get some lunch? This lady and I are old friends. We have a lot of catching up to do. Don't we, sweetheart?"

Both gunmen hesitated. Neal waved his hand toward the

door, urging them to leave. As Swagger and Lake went out, Swagger gave Sarah one last look up and down that made her shift uncomfortably. He glanced from Sarah to Neal, then back to Sarah and gave a nasty grin before leaving.

Neal moved closer to her. "It's wonderful to see you, my dear," he said, his tone sweeter than maple syrup. "To what do I owe the honor of your presence?"

She stiffened. "We need to talk. Why are you in Chugwater? Why are you still here?"

"Because I love this quaint little town. I find it charming and full of opportunities. Besides, staying here keeps me close to you, my dear. You never know, you might need my help one day."

"You hate this country. You told me you wanted to move back East and practice law."

"All true. All true. But that was before I came out here and learned about all the marvelous business opportunities in the territory. I can practice law here as well as anywhere, just like you told me before we parted in Nebraska."

"Really?"

"Of course."

"Jason, I'm sorry about the barn dance. Everything happened so fast. I know it upset you."

"Not at all. Not at all." He paused, as if choosing his words carefully. "Well, maybe a little at first. It was all a big misunderstanding. I realize that now. I hope you will forgive me and we can still be friends. Maybe you can show me around the area. I haven't had much chance to explore beyond Chugwater."

His pleasant demeanor caught Sarah off guard. She had come to see him expecting an argument. This pleasant, even-tempered Neal was the friend she remembered, nothing even close to the angry man Trace and the doctor and others had described. Slowly, she relaxed.

"So you stayed because you like Wyoming?"

"Yes, my dear." He walked over to a window, pulled back dusty, brown curtains, and gazed out toward the Laramie mountain range. "This is a big country, full of potential for a man of vision."

"I'm happy to hear you say that. This is a wonderful country. But . . . but what happened to Agnes McGee? I heard terrible things."

"Yes, the poor woman. I only met her once. After she passed away, I moved in here to watch over her property until we can determine rightful ownership. It seemed like the right thing to do."

"I see." Sarah hesitated before speaking again. "Last night, someone stampeded cattle through our ranch buildings and burned down our bunkhouse. Our ranch foreman was shot. Do you know anything about it?"

His eyes widened. "I did hear some talk in the café about a stampede out your way. Didn't realize it was your place. That's terrible news. Are you all right? How is your father? Is your foreman okay? Tom Scott, isn't it?"

"Yes. The doctor was just out there. Tom will live, but it will take time for him to heal."

"I'm sorry to hear about this. Who would do such a terrible thing? Is there anything I can do to help? Tell you what, I'll have my men ask around. Maybe we can find out who did this. The sheriff and his deputy are good friends of mine. Meanwhile, I'll send some of my men out to help your father rebuild. It's the least I can do."

His calling Swagger and Lake "good friends" made her wary again, though Neal *had* intervened when they roughed up the Littles. "You'll really help us?"

"Yes. I want to make up for my behavior at the dance. Your father must think the worst of me. Now, why don't you go home and rest? You must be exhausted. I'll send some of my men out in the next few days with building supplies. You'll have a new bunkhouse before you know it."

He moved in close and embraced her. Uncomfortable, she stiffened until he stepped away. Not looking the least embarrassed, he took her arm and led her to the front door.

"Everything will be all right," he said, as he gave her a quick kiss on the cheek. "Let's forgive and forget. Let bygones be bygones."

Looking into his eyes, Sarah whispered, "I hope we can."

As they stepped outside, the Cheyenne to Deadwood stage rolled past, flinging dirt from its wheels. Sarah heard wood and heavy leather springs fighting each other as the coach went by. Briefly, she felt heat from the horses and smelled their sweat.

She mounted her own horse and glanced toward Neal. "Thank you. Thank you very much. You're a godsend." She turned her horse toward home, smiling a little as the ever-present Wyoming wind tore at her hat and pushed against her face. *Jason really is a good man. Maybe things aren't as bad as some people say, after all.*

The stagecoach stopped in front of the hotel, and the driver jumped down and opened the door. "Welcome to Chugwater, Wyoming!"

A grey-haired woman stepped out and glanced around. "God help me, this place is filthy . . . and the smell. My God, it stinks!" She dug in her skirt pocket, pulled out a silk scarf, and held it to her nose as she took in her surroundings. Her gaze finally settled on the hotel, and she instructed the driver to make sure her bags were delivered promptly. Dust from a passing freight wagon made her sneeze. As she stepped forward, a feral cat ran in front of her in search of a hidey-hole.

"What an awful place!"

Neal watched from down the street, still standing in the doorway of his building. There was something familiar about the woman. She started down the plank sidewalk, moving in his direction. She wore a brown dress and a dark-brown, small-brimmed hat trimmed in black. He knew that hat, he realized, and the sullen face with piercing, dark eyes beneath it. He gasped, as if he'd just seen a ghost.

"Oh, my God . . . it's Mother!"

CHAPTER 10

Beatrice Neal was not an attractive woman, nor did she possess a gentle manner. Subtle was not in her vocabulary. She said what she thought and meant what she said. Ruthless and roughshod were positive character traits as far as she was concerned, and she didn't much care if anyone liked her or not. She had a sense of humor like dry, seasoned wood.

She was born Beatrice Hammond in a modest home along the Merrimack River, in a county bearing the river's name near Concord, New Hampshire. An only child, she grew up wealthy, provided for by the family business supplying buttons, needles, thread, and thimbles for clothing manufacturers in the area. Her family did not tolerate weakness of any kind, nor did she.

Her father often allowed her to witness his business dealings, many of which were shady or outright dishonest. Her homely appearance left her without many suitors, most of the few she did get only seeking a share of her family's fortune. Young Beatrice knew as much and used their greed to win favors before casting them aside. Even Jason's father, Elmer Neal, a weak banker's assistant she eventually married, had been used up and sent packing.

After abandoning her husband, Beatrice took her only son to New York, and then Chicago. With each stop she left behind corrupt business dealings and social embarrassment that often forced her to engage legal assistance. Upon her son's graduation from school, she'd forced him to study law, even though he preferred business and financial dealings. She knew best and always had.

Now, as she stood in the front room of Neal's modest home in this pit of a town, she felt ready to explode in anger. Her son, her pride and joy, had just described the Meadows dance and how it ended. "I know Sarah still loves me, Mother," he was saying. "But they treated me like some no-account street tramp. They forced me to leave. I was in fear of my life."

"That little hussy was using you, son," Beatrice snapped. "She was just trying to get our money. I tried telling you, but you wouldn't listen. How could you let that uneducated little witch embarrass you like that? She humiliated you in front of all those people."

"They gave me no choice, Mother. They threw me out."

Beatrice flushed deep red. "Nobody treats my son that way . . . nobody! And your sweet Miss Sarah is going to feel my wrath. We'll get even, mark my words! Somehow, some way."

Neal smirked. "I'm already working a plan, Mother. Take it easy."

"Easy? Like hell, easy! Somebody is going to pay for this. Nobody treats my boy like trash. Think how it slanders our good name. I won't stand for it. Not at all."

Her face crunched in anger, and her grip on her cup of coffee was so tight her fingers whitened. A sip of the coffee only made her angrier. The stuff had gone cold!

With considerable effort, Neal persuaded her to calm down while he explained his plans for controlling the town and getting even with the Meadows family. "Scattering their cattle and burning their bunkhouse is only the beginning. I will get revenge. Why do you think I stayed out here?"

For the first time in the two hours since her arrival, Beatrice relaxed and smiled. "I like your thinking. But, just the same, I'd better not see that little tramp anytime soon."

"Sarah came to see me late this morning. I offered to help her find out who was responsible for stampeding their cattle and starting that fire. She believed me. I've set my plan in motion, Mother, and anyone who gets in my way will pay a heavy price."

"Wonderful! How can I help?"

"First, I'm thinking we need to find you some way to be my eyes and ears, keep track of what people are saying."

"What do you have in mind?" She scowled. "I didn't come out here to work. I have my standards and reputation to think of."

"Relax, Mother." He grinned at her. "How would you like to run the general store?"

"Well, I don't know. I might enjoy that."

"Leave the details to me. Welcome to Wyoming, Mother. Everything is going to be just fine."

A short time later, Beatrice Neal entered the general store. Oscar Bloomfeld was helping an elderly woman with some cloth. Two little girls close by, presumably her granddaughters, were trying to decide between colors of hard candy. After the woman and children left, each girl holding a piece of yellow hard candy, Bloomfeld turned to Beatrice. "Can I help you find something, ma'am?"

"Yes, you can, as a matter of fact. I want to buy your store."

"Excuse me, ma'am?"

"You can help me by selling me your store."

He frowned. "Lady, my store ain't for sale."

"I intend to make this store my own. Thinking I'll change the name to Beatrice's Haberdashery."

Bloomfeld laughed, uncertainly, then wiped one hand across his grease-laden brown hair. He peered over his large, wire-rimmed glasses as if trying to gauge just how serious she might be. "It ain't for sale, lady. Now if you need something else, I'll help you. Otherwise, I've got work to do."

Beatrice kept silent and looked around some more.

The storekeeper turned his back on her and adjusted cans of fruit along a back shelf. Labels on each can depicted yellow-orange peaches from various suppliers. Stacks of dry goods, more canned fruits and vegetables, glass jars filled with hard candy, clothing, boots, and ranching supplies crammed the store. The hardwood floor was well worn, with a few boards needing replacement. Black flies buzzed near some uncovered slabs of bacon and a couple of chickens devoid of their insides, and feathers lay near a block of mold-covered yellow cheese. The store smelled of old wood, rotten food, and livestock feed.

Beatrice figured she'd amused herself long enough. "Mister, maybe I didn't make myself clear, or perhaps you're just a little slow witted. I'm buying your store."

Bloomfeld turned quickly to face her again. "Listen, lady, I'm not selling. I own this store. It's all I got. You can't pay me enough. Now, if you want to buy something, I'll help you. Otherwise, I suggest you move along."

Beatrice moved closer. "There are two ways we can do this," she said. "Either you sell to me right now, or I'll get my son involved. Your choice."

"Lady, you and your son, whoever he is, can take a long walk off one of those bison jumps along Chugwater Creek for all I care. I ain't selling, now or never. Now get out of here before I throw you out."

"I warned you," said Beatrice, with a sarcastic smile. "Looks like you've left me no choice. My son won't like this."

"Who the hell is your son? He needs to teach his mother better manners."

"Jason Kelly Neal." She paused while the name sank in. "Maybe you've heard of him. He recently moved into town."

Bloomfeld's face turned ashen white. Beatrice thought she saw beads of cold sweat break out on the man's forehead. "Neal's your son?"

"Good . . . you *have* heard of him. Now we can talk business."

"Lady, I can't—" His voice trailed off as Neal walked through the front door with Swagger and Lake close behind.

"Any problems, Mother?" Neal said.

Beatrice put on her best innocent look. "Son, this man refuses to sell me his store, and I'm just heartbroken."

"That a fact?" Neal stepped closer to Bloomfeld, waving his men toward the counter. Swagger stepped behind it on one end, while Lake moved to the other side, blocking the store owner's escape. "Is that true, storekeeper? You not being nice to my mother?"

A young boy and his dog entered the store, unaware of what was happening. Neal turned, grabbed the boy by the collar, and pushed him outside. "Store is temporarily closed, boy. Now stay out." The dog growled softly but followed the boy onto the plank walkway.

Neal stepped back inside and confronted the store owner again. "Well?"

Bloomfeld was sweating profusely now. "Mister Neal, I don't want to sell my store. It's all I got. How would I survive?"

"I really don't care. But I tell you what I'll do. There's a bay gelding tied out front." Neal pulled some papers from his jacket. "Sign this deed selling these premises to Beatrice Neal, clear out your cash register, and I will let you ride out of here. Otherwise, I may let these two boys try to convince you to sell. Up to you."

"Please, I beg you!"

Neal didn't budge. Beatrice said nothing but stood nearby smiling.

The store owner looked around, his shoulders sagging as he understood his hopeless situation. "May I pack some food?"

"Sure . . . sure. We're good folks. Never want to see anyone go hungry."

While everyone watched, the storekeeper threw a few basic food items in a burlap sack—some canned tomatoes, some bacon, and a few small bags of sugar and salt. Next, he reached for an old pistol he kept close for protection.

Fire exploded from the barrel of Swagger's Colt .45. The bullet hit the storekeeper in the chest. He slumped forward. The sack slipped from his hand, its contents spilling onto the floor. He grasped for the counter with his other hand and missed. Air escaped from his lungs in a rush, and he fell to the floor dead.

Slowly, Neal shook his head. "Shame! A real shame," he said. "Why would he go for his gun like that, with us being so peaceable? Swagger, Lake, take his body out on the prairie somewhere and leave him for the wolves and coyotes." He turned toward Beatrice. "Mother, it looks like you've got yourself a store. Time to start making a profit."

The shot had drawn onlookers. Two men came running from the street and stopped in the doorway. Others were gathering just outside, each trying to find out what happened.

"Come on in," Neal said, beckoning with a laugh. "Welcome to Neal's General Store."

Beatrice smiled wider. "How about Beatrice's General Store and Haberdashery?"

"I like it," Neal said. He eyed the still-warm body of the previous owner, sprawled behind the counter with blood still oozing from his mortal wound. "Beatrice's Haberdashery it is. If we ain't got it, you don't need it."

He turned to the group of curiosity seekers who'd gathered at the door. "Spread the word how Mr. Bloomfeld refused to negotiate with me. He went for his pistol, and the sheriff had to

basic items had doubled, tripled in some cases. And, while nobody was going hungry, Neal and his mother held a vise-like grip on everyone. Yet nobody dared say anything, at least not very loud.

The letter closed with her saying how much she missed Jake and hoped to see him again soon. A postscript mentioned that recent events were taking a heavy toll on her father's health, and that things had become increasingly difficult with Tom laid up. She stopped short of asking Jake to come back and help, but he read a plea between the lines.

Jake leaned back on his bunk and stared at the kerosene lantern that provided his reading light. Smoke from a dozen cigarettes drifted by, creating a fog-like haze. His mind spun with the many decisions he needed to make.

An angry shout from across the room broke Jake's melancholy spell. "You cheat! You lousy cheat!"

Ben Gentry, a long-time Box T hand with several days' whisker growth on his face, jumped to his feet. One hand rested on the butt of his still-holstered pistol. The laughter had stopped, all eyes glued on the card table. Men standing nearby backed away. A young man Jake recognized as Fred Dunwoody faced his accuser, struggling to find words. Before him lay two aces . . . both spades. The boy was blushing a bright red that nearly matched his hair color and a crimson vest he was wearing.

Jake got to his feet and started across the room. "Hold on, men. No gunplay in here. What happened?"

Gentry had been drinking heavily and losing all evening long. He pulled his pistol and pointed it at Dunwoody. "The boy was cheating," said Gentry. "Look at them cards."

"Put the gun down. We will settle this peaceable."

"But—"

"You heard me. Put the gun down."

Gentry slowly lowered his pistol but didn't return it to his holster. He stared at Jake, who had turned his attention to Dunwoody. "The boy was cheating. Not just me, but everyone in the game. What are you going to do 'bout it?"

Two others at the table mumbled in agreement, their hands flat on top of the table.

Dunwoody tried to stand. Two men standing behind him each grabbed a shoulder and shoved him back down in his chair. Jake saw he was unarmed.

"You been cheating?" Jake asked.

Before the boy could answer, Gentry spoke. "Hell, yes! Look at them aces."

Once more Jake asked, "Boy, have you been cheating?"

Dunwoody stammered a reply. "Yes, but—"

"Told you!" shouted Gentry, stepping forward for emphasis. "We should string him up right now."

Jake stepped between Gentry and the boy. All eyes were on the Box T foreman. Nobody said a word.

"Get up, boy, and leave your money on the table," Jake said. "Gather up your stuff and get out. You're fired. Somebody go saddle his horse. Boy, you leave this territory tonight and never come back."

Gentry started to protest, but stopped short as Jake continued. "Everyone get your money. That's the end of it. Dunwoody, you're getting off easy. Anywhere else and you'd be dead by now. Now, grab your particulars and get out."

Dunwoody was sweating heavily. Jake guessed him to be about seventeen. "What am I going to do? Where will I go?" stammered the boy. "Can't I stay? I know I was wrong. It won't ever happen again, I promise." His lower lip trembled. The men watched in silence, each glancing at Jake to see what he might say.

"Gentry, it's up to you. You willing to give him a second

chance?" Jake asked.

The older man looked at the boy and then turned to survey the room, as if trying to evaluate the mood. "No! Hell, no! He knew better. We should string him up."

Jake turned toward Dunwoody. "Boy, you'd better go. Things won't be healthy for you around here if you stay. I hope you've learned your lesson."

"But—"

"Your horse is saddled. Get moving."

Dunwoody gathered up his few belongings and left the bunkhouse. His face reflected a mixture of embarrassment and angry submission.

Jake turned to the hands. "Lights out, men. We have work tomorrow."

He went back to his bunk and found Sarah's letter again. He carefully folded the thin sheets of paper and tucked them in a leather bag near his boots. His decision was made. Tomorrow he would resign as Box T foreman and ride out for Chugwater.

A mixture of orange and yellow clouds stretched along the eastern horizon just after sunrise, as Jake rode from the ranch complex for the last time. In his pocket was a letter of recommendation from William Thompson and a couple of sourdough biscuits.

Jake decided to follow much the same trail he and Tom had followed some weeks earlier on their first trip to the Chugwater area. He crossed several creeks and rode through stands of mountain mahogany and then into areas of conifer and aspen as the trail took him still higher. He saw signs of elk but didn't spot any animals. As he crossed higher mountain streams, he found considerable beaver signs.

As Jake rode, he thought about a new beginning with Sarah and the chance to see his old friend Tom again. That evening he camped by a mountain lake, and not even the yip of coyotes nearby could spoil the night. Every now and then wolves howled in the distance. Somehow the stars seemed brighter, and he felt more alive and excited. He was up early the next morning, riding in the darkness before daybreak.

As the morning light overtook him, he sensed a change in the land. The lack of rain in recent weeks had left the native prairie grasses brittle, and the constant hot, dry wind sucked precious moisture out of everything. Short vegetation consisting of blue grama, buffalo grass, wheatgrass, and some bluestem gave way to sagebrush. All were dry. Further north on the Box T, occasional rains still kept things green, but not here. Only along creek banks did any degree of green remain. This once lush valley along Chugwater Creek was a mixture of yellows, creams, and browns. Water holes along the trail were also dry or near dry, with muddy bottoms surrounded by the tracks of wildlife seeking water.

By mid-morning the air was already hot. Sweat ran down his back as he followed a meandering path around several rocky outcroppings that soon dropped into a series of grassy ravines and swales. Toward noon he found himself on familiar ground.

We searched for some of the stolen cattle up here, he thought. *Old man Meadows must really be in a fix if his cattle have nothing to graze but this stuff. And, if Sarah is correct about prices in town, the cost of feed must be through the roof.*

Jake pulled up under a stand of cottonwoods to get some shade. In the distance, where only a few weeks earlier open range pastures sloped down toward an unnamed creek, he spied barbed wire fencing. Four strands of wire nailed to wooden boards posing as fence posts stretched along the creek, denying cattle access to precious water. "What the—? Who would do this?"

This wasn't the work of homesteaders, but obviously

something different. Someone was trying to prevent the Meadows cattle from reaching water. Who?

He rode on toward the creek, then pulled up on a sage-covered rise. From there, he spotted a small group of cows and calves trying to find an opening in the fence so they could reach water. A couple of cows brushed against the barbed wire, then backed off.

A weak cry caught his attention, and he saw a white-faced black calf caught a little ways further off. The barbed points tore into its young hide as it struggled to get free. Blood flowed down one leg in a red stream, and one shoulder lay raw and exposed. The calf's anxious mother stood nearby, bawling to her baby.

Jake spurred his horse toward them. He drew up and dismounted, keeping a careful eye on the unhappy mother, whose wide eyes were born of fear and concern. His good intentions be damned if she felt her calf was threatened.

He found wire cutters in his saddlebags and approached the struggling calf. The other cattle stood off to one side, nervously watching. "Easy, fella. Give me a minute here."

The calf stopped lunging against the wire and watched Jake as he began to cut the barbed metal strands. As Jake got even closer, the frightened animal began struggling again.

"Take it easy, little guy. Just a minute more."

A few more snips, and the calf was free. After a few uncertain steps, it went running to its mother. She began to lick him before glancing at Jake.

Jake sighed with relief and satisfaction and started for his horse. His efforts had created a big hole in the barbed wire fence. Whoever built it here wouldn't like that, but as far as Jake was concerned, there was no decision. Thirsty cattle should have water.

He mounted his horse and started to leave but found two

men blocking his way. One of them held a rifle. The other rested a hand on his still-holstered pistol. They had hard faces, and their grim expressions promised trouble.

The rifleman spoke. "Mister, you cut our fence. Now you're going to fix it."

"Not in my lifetime," answered Jake. "Calf was caught. I cut him free. Besides, these cattle need water."

"Stranger, we don't care a tinker's dam about no baby calf, but we do care about this here fence. We get paid to make sure it stays put. Get my meaning?"

Jake sensed things were about to get ugly. Before he could react, the second man pulled the pistol and pointed it at him. "Now get down from that nag and fix our fence."

Jake turned his horse back toward the opening in the fence, then pulled his own Colt as he swiftly dismounted on the right side. Using his mount as a shield, he fired at the rifleman, knocking him from his saddle.

In the sudden confusion the second man fired two quick shots at Jake. One hit his saddle, but the next one missed. The man's horse shied wildly. Jake reached under his own horse's neck and fired, hitting his attacker's leg. The man screamed and reached for his bloodied thigh while his terrified horse circled. Jake's next shot caught him in the chest.

Jake holstered his pistol, then tied each dead assailant over their saddles and led them toward Chugwater. He looked back to see the cattle scrambling through the opening toward the water, and he smiled.

Outside of town, he set the horses free to find their way. Whoever was responsible for the fence wouldn't be happy to find out about the deaths of his men. Clearly, Jake had ridden into the middle of a firestorm he was now helping flame. This wasn't the time to meet anyone new in town or try explaining what happened to the wrong people. It was time to make for the Meadows ranch.

CHAPTER 12

The office was empty except for the silence, which filled every crevice and corner. Shattered glass covered one end of the room near a beer-stained, still-wet wall. The initial roar of Neal's outrage after learning two of his men were dead had subsided. After Neal's tirade, he'd gone to the saloon to have a drink and calm his nerves.

Exactly who shot his men was a subject of considerable conjecture and debate. All anyone seemed to know was, two horses had wandered into town, each with a dead man tied neatly across the saddle. Swagger had identified both corpses.

Neal had hired them only days earlier to string barbed wire. They were also told to make sure nobody objected to or tampered with the fence. The fact that neither man was a ranch hand didn't matter. They could take orders and handle a gun. That was enough for Neal.

Much of the land in Wyoming was open range, miles of grassland broken up by ravines, bluffs, swales, and rugged terrain stretching toward the foothills of the Laramie Mountains. Ranchers in the area had an unwritten rule that livestock should have free access to water and grass.

Neal didn't own any of the land being fenced, so he fully expected trouble. Enforcement would come at a price and no doubt would require more gun hands to assure success. However, other than the usual quiet rumblings of discontent, there had been no serious objections . . . until now.

"I want somebody's head on a plate. Find out who did this!" he'd shouted at Swagger and Lake. "I want answers. I want answers *now*. I'm paying you sorry excuses to protect my interests. I expect results. Those horses drifted in from the north end of town. Ride out that way along our fences. See if you can learn anything. But don't do anything stupid. If you find anything, report back to me. Now get out of here! Damn, I want somebody's blood for this."

Swagger and Lake followed the fence along South Sybille Creek northwest of Chugwater. They found where someone had cut the wire and left it open for the Meadows cattle to reach water. Several cows grazed near the creek, and it took considerable effort to get them back through the fence. Once clear, the men repaired the fence.

"That should do it," Swagger grumbled.

They rode back to town and found Neal in his office. "Boss, there was a gunfight," Swagger told him. "We found spent cartridges on the ground, and someone cut a hole in the fence."

His face red with anger, Neal glared out the window.

"One more thing. Them was Meadows cattle by the creek," said Lake.

Neal turned to face his men. "You sure about that?" he asked. "It's hard to believe that addled old man would shoot anyone. And that foreman of his, Tom somebody, is still laid up. Couldn't have been him."

"What about that girl?" Lake asked.

"Sarah? I can't imagine her outshooting two armed men, then tying them over their saddles. No, somebody else had a hand in this. We gotta find out who and teach him a lesson . . . and soon!"

"Maybe they've hired themselves a gun," Swagger offered.

"Not likely! They have no money for anything like that. I saw to it when I told the old man he'd bought all those building supplies. Charged them double the going rate. I thought he'd pass out. Chances are, some Meadows cowhand got a conscience and felt bad about a few thirsty cows, then got the jump on those two drifters. Doesn't matter; somebody's gotta pay."

Sarah finished feeding the chickens and gathered several brown eggs before spotting a rider coming toward the ranch buildings. She put a hand above her eyes, shielding them from the morning sun. The rider looked familiar somehow.

A moment later, surprise and excitement spread over her. "Jake! Jake!"

She dropped the freshly gathered eggs and left them in a scrambled mess on the ground as she hurried toward him. An old dog found the eggs and started lapping them up, dirt and all. Two other dogs started barking as Jake headed toward the house. Chickens searching for insects in the barnyard scattered as he rode among them.

Jake dismounted and caught Sarah in mid-stride, lifted her from the ground, and hugged her long and hard. She put her arms around his neck and squeezed. After a few moments they separated. "Guess you missed me," he said.

Sarah laughed, blinking happy tears from her eyes. She took him by the hand, and they walked together toward the barn. "Yes, I've missed you. But why are you here?"

"I got your letter. After reading about what happened and Tom getting shot, I decided to come back. Maybe I can help somehow."

"How long can you stay?"

"I've left the Box T. I'm here for as long as you and your father need me, or at least until Tom is back on his feet. Will that work?"

She squeezed his hand. "Good for a start," she said. "Tom

will be so excited. Maybe not as much as me, but seeing you will be a tonic for him."

As they neared the ranch house, Molly called from the porch. "Welcome back, stranger! Tom's sure going to be glad to see you. He's been depressed lately. You'd better get in here."

The smile on Tom's face stretched from one ear to the other as Jake walked into his room. "Hey, pard. I leave town, and you go and get yourself shot," Jake said. "Can't leave you alone for a minute."

Near the doorway, Sarah glanced at Molly. Tom was clearly trying to find the right words, but the expression on his face said everything.

That evening at dinner, Meadows, Sarah, Tom, and Molly sat quietly listening to Jake recount details of how he'd been attacked and forced to defend himself. He told them about the calf caught in the barbed wire, and how the Meadows cattle were being kept from water.

"Barbed wire?" Meadows looked incredulous. "Why? Who?"

"Cattle won't last long without water. Six days is about it," said Jake. "I don't understand why someone would deliberately put up a fence to keep them away from water. And why your cattle?"

Tom sipped coffee, then said, "I suspect Jason Kelly Neal is behind it somehow. Trace says rumors are going 'round that Neal's been fencing off land lately. Trace saw several rolls of barbed wire in town the other day."

"This area is open range. Nobody should be putting up fences," said Meadows, frowning. He chewed on a piece of steak. "Doesn't make sense. Maybe we should contact John Hunton up near Bordeaux and see if he's had any problems. Or George Rainsford over at the Diamond Ranch, or other ranchers in the area."

"Tom, why would you say that about Jason, especially after he helped rebuild the bunkhouse? He's been very kind," said Sarah, standing up for Neal.

Jake gave her a long, uncomfortable look before turning his gaze back to the old man.

"Some kindness," said Meadows. "He helped rebuild the bunkhouse, then billed us at prices we may never be able to pay. That's an expense we can't afford right now, and he knows it. He's got us in a bind. I'm not convinced it wasn't his men who burned it down in the first place."

"Dad, I didn't know about this. Why didn't you tell me? Are we really that bad off financially?"

He patted her hand. "I didn't want to worry you. I'm sure Neal knows our money situation. He seems to know everything."

"Is that true?" Jake turned toward Sarah. "Did he bill you for the materials to rebuild after offering to help?"

She felt flustered. "I'm sure it's just a big misunderstanding. I can't believe Neal would do that. Maybe it's his men, raising the prices and stealing the difference for themselves? We'll work it out. I mean, why burn down our bunkhouse and then offer to help rebuild it? That doesn't make sense."

Meadows shook his head. "I'd like to give him the benefit of the doubt. But something doesn't seem right.

"Honestly, I don't see any misunderstanding. We're hurting financially. We haven't been able to sell any cattle since last year. We can't even afford to buy feed for our chickens anymore. Prices at the store he owns have gone so high that, if we don't pay him, he'll likely take our ranch. He seems to be trying to take everything in the area."

Jake glanced at Tom, then at Sarah. "Maybe I should pay him a visit. If your friend is behind all this, someone needs to confront him."

"No," Sarah said. "If anyone talks to him, it should be me."

"If those two dead men worked for him, he's not going to be happy. We need to be on our guard," said Jake.

Meadows broke in. "We need to get those cattle to water, and soon. I'm thinking we should move them away from Sybille Creek and up along Mule Creek, or maybe those meadows along Deadhead Creek. It's higher up and further from the ranch. The grazing won't be as good, but there's plenty of water."

"Okay. Let's start at daylight tomorrow. Once they smell water up that way, moving them should be easy," said Jake.

Sarah said nothing. She quietly decided it was time to go see Neal again and clarify everything. She found it hard to believe Neal was behind all their trouble. In the distance, she thought she heard a thirsty cow bawling, knowing the smell of water nearby would taunt the animal's senses. A memory of wolves in the area made her shiver.

In Chugwater, Neal watched as the last few rolls of barbed wire were loaded on a wagon in front of the general store. His mother stood nearby. He had special ordered the wire from Iowa, a Shinn Locked four point. It had two twisted strands with a four-point barb on one strand. One leg of the barb overlapped the other leg.

"Those barbs are dangerous if you get too close. But then, that's the point." He grinned at his own joke. "Get it, the point?"

Nobody laughed. Swagger and Lake looked at each other but said nothing. Neal's mother scowled. He knew she didn't understand what the wire represented, but he'd explain later.

"Swagger, pick some men and send them up along South Sybille Creek tomorrow to finish building that fence. Next week, we'll fence things off up along Mule Creek. Sooner or later, old man Meadows will be forced to sell his place to me—I mean, give me his ranch—to pay off his debts." The thought made him snicker.

The sun slid behind the Laramie range, blending blues and purples with bright oranges and yellows as the sun reflected off the clouds. The air was cool and the sunset spectacular. Neal glanced at it, then turned to his mother. "Let's go have some dinner. I have a hunch my plans are going to start bearing delicious fruit real soon, and I'm suddenly very hungry."

CHAPTER 13

Sounds of creaking wood and leather filled the morning air as the Cheyenne to Deadwood stage climbed a steep slope south of Chugwater. The stage driver's shouts urging his team of horses onward blended with the songs of meadowlarks and other songbirds, breaking the quiet of this Wyoming morning. Daybreak was at hand.

After conquering the steep roadway, the stage stopped on a level stretch of road to let the winded horses catch their breath. "Stretch your legs, gents," the driver shouted down to the passengers inside.

Two men in dust-covered black suits emerged from the coach and took advantage of the brief interlude. They welcomed the chance to fill their lungs with fresh air and feel the early morning wind on their faces. The sun was rising, and they could see for miles in every direction. "Where are we?" asked Alexander Swan as he gazed over the grass-covered prairie.

"Wyoming Territory just south of Chugwater," answered the driver as he checked one horse's harness. His long, grey hair hung to his shoulders. A matching untrimmed beard was stained with wet tobacco and held the remains of saltine crackers the man had eaten for breakfast. "We'll be in Chugwater by noon."

"Looks like great grass country. Many cattle ranches out here?" Swan asked.

"Some . . . mostly small places and a few homesteaders moving in, trying to farm. This is really open range country for as far as you can see in every direction."

Swan hailed from Pennsylvania and had influential and wealthy friends in Scotland looking to invest in the American West. His companion, J. A. Epperson, looked at the broad expanse of land rolling out before them. In the distance, a small group of antelope grazed.

"What do you think?" Swan asked.

"I see opportunities, especially if there's water," Epperson answered. "Looks like good grass and lots of it. We can build a Swan Land and Cattle Company out here."

Swan nodded. "I'm thinking the same thing. This country looks like it could carry several head of cows. Say, driver, are there any water sources out here?"

The driver shrugged. "Few small streams here and there . . . more and bigger the closer you get to the mountains."

Swan pulled a small black notebook from his shirt pocket and wrote down a few words. "What about in the summer? Do they dry up?"

"The smaller ones, yes," answered the driver as he adjusted a second horse's harness. "Dry weather can play havoc on anyone trying to raise cattle out here. But if they have the space and can move their animals closer to streams up in the mountains, it might work."

"Why the mountains?"

"Water in the mountains is more protected from any kind of dry off."

"What are the winters like?"

"Damn rough if you aren't prepared. Firewood is precious out here."

"Can cattle survive the winters?"

"Sure," said the driver. "We have lots of cattle now. When it snows, the ranchers keep them in more sheltered areas. I'm no cattleman, but some of my passengers talk about doing things like putting up hay for winter feeding. Not so much in these parts yet."

"Something to consider," Epperson said. "It would add more labor cost, especially in winter."

Swan turned his attention toward the eastern horizon, shielding his eyes from the sun with one hand. "Why aren't there any trees out here? Back in Pennsylvania, we have lots of trees."

"Two main reasons," the driver said as he shoved a wad of chewing tobacco in his mouth. "First, the bison. Used to be thick as flies on a gut wagon. Hunters have pretty much cleaned them out. Kind of a shame, really. A buffer steak was mighty good. Second, prairie fires. Once a fire starts burning out here, especially in dry weather, ain't nothing to stop the burn until it reaches a water source or comes a heavy rain. Sometimes even them things ain't enough.

"A prairie fire is a sight to behold, especially at night, but don't get close. They can burn faster than a scalded rabbit can run. You can't outrun one. Them things leave the prairie black and scorched. But come spring there's all sorts of new grass sprouting up. Guess you could say they're good to have now and then. They keep the trees and brush burned off, along with any dead grasses."

"That a fact?" Swan assumed the driver's comments were somewhat exaggerated . . . but it might be worth talking to a few local ranchers, whichever of them were most prominent hereabouts.

"Get back inside," the driver called as he climbed back on top of the coach. "We still got a ways to go."

As the stage lurched forward and the horses snorted, Swan wrote in his notebook. Epperson quietly looked through the stage window, as if trying to envision great herds of cattle where bison once roamed.

★ ★ ★ ★ ★

Jake and two other hands from the Meadows ranch were up early and moving. They rode out before daybreak with plans to move about fifty cows, calves, and a few bulls away from Sybille Creek and up into a small meadow along Mule Creek several miles from Neal's—or whoever's—barbed wire. *We can't keep running and moving cattle every time someone puts up a fence,* thought Jake. *Sooner or later, someone must be confronted.*

The cool morning air felt good going into their lungs. A slight breeze blew from the southwest along the creek. Higher up in any open areas, the winds would be blowing harder.

Jake and his men crossed a couple of small dry creeks and started for where they suspected the cattle would be gathered. They found the thirsty cattle along Neal's fence only yards from water. Several animals bore small, bloody wounds where they'd tested the fence.

Nearby, an antelope had gotten caught and died struggling against the sharp barbs in the twisted wire. Jake looked away with a sick dislike for the fence and all it represented. The days of the open range were disappearing. He knew it, but at what cost to freedom in this vast land?

The thirsty cattle didn't want to leave with the smell of water so close. It took considerable effort to move them toward Mule Creek, several miles away and higher up in the Laramie range foothills. Several kept trying to turn back. "Kinda like trying to herd a bunch of cats," Jake joked. It would take time, but he knew once the cattle smelled water in Mule Creek, they would move without any problems. The sun was growing warmer, and they rode easy.

His mind drifted back to the previous evening, when he and Sarah had gone for a walk together along the creek near the Meadows home. They had talked for what seemed like hours.

"Tom doesn't look so good," he remembered telling Sarah.

"He should be healing faster."

"I know," Sarah said. "The doctor thinks he should go to Denver or St. Louis and see a specialist. He doesn't want to go without Molly. And he's worried about Dad and the ranch. Maybe with you here, he'll feel different."

"Those two should just get married and go together," said Jake.

"Once you get Dad's cattle moved, maybe you can talk to him. I'm worried about him, too. He can't remember things that happened just last week. That's not like him."

"What do you mean?"

"Jake, he forgets things, and he seems confused. He's having mood swings. I'm having to help him take care of himself, and it's getting worse. He didn't even know who I was the other day. I haven't said anything to anyone because so much has been happening. Maybe it's just all the stress, but it seems like more than that."

"Have you told the doctor?"

"Yes. He blames it on stress and lack of sleep. Also, Dad is getting older. The doctor doesn't know what's causing the problems, not really. Apparently, there's no cure for whatever it is."

A shout by one of the Meadows hands broke Jake's trance and brought him back to the present. A small brindle cow was trying to turn back toward Sybille Creek. Jake wheeled his horse to one side, to cut off the cow's escape, and nearly lost his seat in the process. He quickly recovered as they chased the cow back into the herd through a stand of sagebrush and juniper. A sage grouse ran ahead, disappearing into the bushes.

Ahead stood some ponderosa pine and the opening into a small canyon leading to Mule Creek, which eventually flowed back to Sybille Creek. The cattle sensed water ahead and moved faster.

Several miles behind, three men Neal had sent to put up more fence started working, but they weren't happy. After a few hours, they stopped to rest.

"I ain't no nester," complained Ben Childers. "Neal hired us to run cows and do his gun work, not build fence."

"He ain't paying me enough to get poked by this damn wire. I've shed a pint of blood and been scratched enough. Looks like I've been attacked by a crazed cat," grumbled Chester Headwright. Like Childers, he'd recently drifted into the area from southern Arizona.

The men each rolled a cigarette from their own makings and then took a long swallow of whiskey Childers had brought along in a canteen. The sun was hot, and the dry wind carried away their cigarette smoke. Now and then large, puffy white clouds passed between the sun and valley floor, creating huge shadows that drifted over the landscape as the clouds quickly moved and changed shapes.

"I hate fences, but let's get this done and get back into town," Childers said.

All three men hauled themselves upright and started back to the task at hand. Childers tossed his unfinished cigarette on the ground and went to mount his horse. Headwright walked toward the half loaded wagon of wire. The third man, Marcus Knox, went to the creek to fetch water.

A gust of wind caught Childers's cigarette and sent it into a dry stand of sagebrush, where it smoldered and then ignited. By the time Headwright saw the smoke and flames, it was too late. The fire was spreading. Childers shouted to Headwright and turned his horse toward town. Headwright climbed into the wagon, slapped the reins across the wild-eyed team's backs, and followed Childers.

Knox screamed, trapped between the fire and a rocky bluff. He made frantic efforts to climb it but failed to get a foothold. Again and again he tried as the flames raced toward him.

"Help me!" he shrieked. "Help me!"

Childers pulled up his horse and looked back as the wagon and Headwright raced past. He hesitated, then continued toward town. The wind caught the crackling sounds of burning sagebrush and the screams of a dying man and sent them out over an unsuspecting landscape. A day of fire and fury was born.

CHAPTER 14

Cold is the heart that cannot be warmed by a child's smile. But such was the case with Jason Kelly Neal. On this morning, two young boys were tossing a ball in the street, and it got away from them. One boy went to retrieve it and ran in front of Neal, who was walking to the bank along with Swagger and Lake. Neal nearly tripped over the boy. "Get out of my way!" he shouted.

The boy froze in fear. Neal grabbed him by the arm and tossed him aside like a rag doll. "Get off the street!"

The boy started to say he was sorry but saw Swagger staring at him and hushed. Lake picked up their ball and shoved it in his pocket. "Get out of here or else," he said, echoing Neal's warning. Both boys ran away down the street.

Neal continued toward the bank. He realized controlling the town would require more than brute force. The key to financial control as well was the bank's owner, Gabriel Swanson.

Inside the bank, he motioned for his sheriff and deputy to remain in the small lobby, while he passed by the bank's only teller without comment. The surprised teller started to object, then saw Swagger and Lake watching him and thought better of the idea.

Neal strode into Swanson's office without knocking. "What the—" Swanson stammered from behind a pile of papers on his desk.

"Mr. Swanson, I think it's time we came to an agreement on

how things should run in this town. As the sole attorney in Chugwater, I'm sure you know what influence I have on the legal side of things. I believe it's time I got involved in the money side of things as well."

The banker had regained his composure. "Neal, why in the world should I work with you? I'm not a helpless old woman like Agnes McGee, or a mere storekeeper like poor Oscar Bloomfeld. I'm a wealthy man. I don't need your involvement in my affairs. And as to 'the legal side of things,' I'm not breaking any laws."

"Now that's all true. Very true. Except . . . in case you haven't noticed, I run this damn town, and that includes you and this bank."

"You can't talk to me that way."

"No?" Neal smiled. "Here's how things are going to work from now on. No loans to anybody will be made unless I approve them. Nobody borrows money or gets any credit unless I say so. We'll begin by increasing the number of foreclosures, especially on ranch land. Homesteaders are to get nothing."

"What in blazes are you talking about? Get out of my office!"

Neal didn't budge. "Work with me, and you'll get a cut of the profits. Cross me, and you'll end up dead. I'm sure Sheriff Swagger and Deputy Lake can come up with something you've done wrong enough to be punished for. Get my drift?"

The ashen-faced Swanson was more greedy than brave. He'd begun sweating through his neatly starched white shirt, and perspiration clung in heavy, wet droplets on his forehead. "I don't—"

"Don't what? You mean you don't see a problem with what I'm proposing? Is that what you're trying to say?"

Swanson nodded and wiped his wet brow with the sleeve of his expensive black frock coat. The heat plus moisture made his wire-rimmed glasses fog over.

"Mighty fine. Mighty fine. Good doing business with you," said Neal. "I'll be back to look at the books later. Just remember. Never cross me."

Neal and his lawmen left the bank and headed for the saloon, where the smell just inside the front door nearly took his breath away. The room reeked of tobacco smoke, chewing tobacco, spit, and sweaty men. While Swagger and Lake went to the bar for something cold to drink, Neal surveyed the place. In one corner three old cowhands long past their prime sat at a table swapping stories. At another table, Neal spotted two more down-and-out hands.

He recognized one of them from stories overheard at the saloon and café. Charles Mann had punched cows for George Rainsford at the nearby Diamond Ranch but was recently fired. Failure to follow orders was given as the reason for letting him go, but rumor claimed he had an unsavory disposition. Mann sought any chance to square things with area ranchers who refused to hire him. He didn't much care how ugly or mean spirited the task.

Neal sized him up. Mann was older and clean shaven, exposing numerous scars on both jaws. His clothes were well worn but clean. Three front teeth were missing, the result of too many fights. He wore two guns that didn't match. Alongside him at the table was a younger man, who gave his name as Nelson Elliott.

The younger man wore a dusty, black, felt hat over light-brown hair. His pale-blue shirt sported holes in both elbows, and his dark-brown leather vest and pants looked so dirty, they might have stood on their own. A Colt .45 pistol rode low on his right hip, and he constantly touched its handle as if to remind himself it was there. A ragged, untrimmed excuse for a beard covered the lower half of his face, as if he hadn't shaved in days. An unlit cigarette hung from lips stained by chewing tobacco, and his teeth were dark yellow.

Loose cannon, thought Neal. *Might have to have him shot someday.*

Neal pulled a chair out, parked one foot on it, and leaned forward. "Understand you boys might be looking for work."

"Might be," answered Mann. "What's the job?"

"Nothing happens in this town unless it goes through me," Neal said.

"So what? We understand it's your town. But what's that got to do with us?"

"I'm looking for a few more good men who can take orders. Keep their mouths shut and be willing to shoot and kill to protect my interests. You interested?"

Elliott stood up. "What's it pay?"

"Double what you're getting now."

"We're barely working now," the man stammered. "Just mucking stalls at the livery for meals and beer money."

Neal grinned. "So—we got a deal or not?"

"We gotta get something," Elliott muttered. "I ain't working for nothing."

"I'll pay you," said Neal. "How about it?"

Mann stood as well. "Just tell us what you want done."

"I don't know," Elliot said.

"That's right, you don't know because you're an idiot," Mann barked. "We gotta eat."

Neal nodded. "The sheriff and his deputy will be in touch. Until then, have a big steak and a few beers on me. Be ready to move when I need you."

The stage from Cheyenne pulled up in front of the hotel. Alexander Swan and J. A. Epperson stepped into the dusty street and looked around. Swan stopped a man riding by on his horse. "Who do we see about buying land around here?"

"Down there." The man pointed toward a brick office building at the far end of the plank walkway. "Man named Neal. He ain't there, though . . . just saw him over at the saloon."

"Thank you, mister." Turning to Epperson, Swan suggested they get settled into the hotel and have a good meal before meeting with anyone. "I'm hungry and covered with enough dirt and dust to plant a good garden. We can see this fellow Neal later. Land isn't going anywhere."

The two-story hotel was an eclectic mix of furnishings attempting to claim some semblance of style and elegance, failing at both. A well-worn, brown leather couch sat along one wall, a wooden rocking chair near the front door. A seldom-used spittoon was nearby, and the floor around it was wet. Old calendar prints hung randomly on the walls. The unpleasant smells of cheap perfume and old cigars lingered.

The elderly clerk was a frail, unflinching monotone of a man. He wore a black vest over a sweat-stained white shirt long in need of washing. Surly and disinterested, he checked them into separate rooms at the top of the stairs. When they asked about a good meal, he grunted, "Ain't but one place" and pointed them toward the café. With that, he turned back to a dime novel about Kit Carson and said nothing more.

Having finished his hiring of Mann and Elliot, Neal left the saloon, followed by Swagger and Lake. They went straight to Neal's office, and he was surprised to find two well-dressed strangers sitting in the front room.

"Gentlemen, good afternoon. How may I help you?"

Both men stood up. "Mr. Neal, I presume?" one of them said as he offered a handshake. "I am Alexander Swan, and this is my associate, Mr. Epperson. We are interested in possibly purchasing land in this area, maybe several ranches. We've already corresponded with the Box T Ranch near here. But we understand you're really the man with whom we should be discussing such matters."

"Why . . . why, of course." Neal immediately sensed a chance for making a profit . . . perhaps a nice big one. "I'm your man when it comes to finding and buying land in this part of Wyoming. I represent most of the cattlemen hereabouts and can provide you with all the land you might need. Why, just this morning I was discussing such opportunities with our local banker." He nodded at Swagger and Lake to leave, then gestured toward Swan and Epperson. "Come into my office. May I get you something to drink or eat?"

The newcomers gladly accepted water, and Neal settled in behind his desk. "Opportunities . . . opportunities," he continued. "This land is full of opportunities for men of vision. Why, there's talk of a railroad coming through Chugwater. Rumor has it the Cheyenne and Northern Railroad has been chartered and will one day stretch across eastern Wyoming and into Montana. We can have cattle pens right here in town. There's a perfect location just this side of Chugwater Creek."

The three men spent the afternoon talking about the countryside and its potential for raising vast herds of cattle. Swan and Epperson left the meeting with positive opinions about the area and its potential, although they appeared unsure about Neal and his role in their future dealings. Neal figured it wouldn't take him long to talk these wealthy strangers around.

Ben Childers rode into town on his sweat-lathered horse. Headwright followed in the wagon, its remaining rolls of barbed wire rolling and bumping as the wagon swayed.

A quick glance backward showed smoke towering into the sky, like a storm cloud against the gathering darkness. Several townspeople gathered in a small group, pointing toward the rising smoke in the foothills. The smoke rose higher and billowed outward as it was caught by the wind. "Prairie fire," someone murmured. "And it's spreading!"

Childers and Headwright stared at the distant smoke and swallowed hard, both knowing full well the fire's origin.

"We should have—" Headwright said.

"We should have what?" Childers whispered fiercely. "You need to shut up. We know nothing. Don't forget that. Let's go to the saloon. I'm thirsty."

"But Knox died out there," Headwright muttered.

Childers stared him down. "I said, forget it! Nothing we can do now. Not another word. We don't know anything about this. Besides we don't know for sure he's dead."

"Well, if he ain't dead he's going to be mighty pissed at us for leaving him. Can't say as I'd blame him."

Childers said nothing more as he stepped inside the noisy saloon. Such unpleasant work made him thirsty. He felt a twinge of guilt that they'd done nothing to save Knox but suppressed it. Nothing mattered except that his throat was dry . . . extremely dry.

CHAPTER 15

A crackling, popping sound rose on the wind and followed the thick smoke. As night turned the sky black, the horizon glowed a brilliant yellow-orange. A torn seam of dancing flames with ragged edges told of a massive fire burning in the distance.

Mountain wildlife of nearly every species sought escape from the inferno as the wind pushed the ravenous fire toward the Laramie mountains foothills. A ground squirrel outran a field mouse, only for both to be swallowed in flame and crackling fury. The voracious fire devoured great gulps of grass, brush, and trees as it spread over the dry landscape.

Sarah looked toward the smoke-filled sky in the east and shuddered. The fire was still several miles from the Meadows ranch but burned ominous in its potential. Prairie and forest fires raced with the wind and tugged at the mind, beautiful and terrifying. Sarah knew of such things. On her trip home from Nebraska, she'd barely survived a prairie fire. She'd managed to reach the Platte River just in time.

Remembering the stagecoach driver's shouts at the frightened team of horses sent a chill down her back. Huge fireballs had flown past the coach as the fire swept over the ground, igniting the grass ahead of them. Wild animals ran alongside the stage, also seeking shelter.

Even inside the coach Sarah had felt the tremendous heat. The horses had run to near exhaustion, pushing onward out of sheer panic. Smoke had filled the coach and blowing embers touched her face as the flames gulped up great chunks of grass.

Suddenly, the coach plunged down a riverbank into lifesaving waters of the Platte. The driver had shouted for Sarah to get out. "Stay under the water. Protect your head from the sparks."

She'd lain in the shallow river for a long time, lowering her head below its surface as burning embers fell into the water and sizzled. Various species of wildlife, some badly burned, shared the wet space around her. A sickening smell of burnt hair and flesh mixed with the smoke and made her vomit, adding to the growing stench. She dimly recalled the driver throwing buckets of water on the coach to keep it from burning.

A shout from nearby brought her back to the present. "Are you okay?" Jake asked as he stepped up beside her. "You looked like you're in a daze."

"Just reliving another fire," she answered. "What's our chances?"

"As long as the wind stays out of the southwest, we should be okay. But if the wind turns during the night, it may head in this direction. Come morning we may need to build a backfire. We should make plans to get your father, Tom, and Molly out of the house and farther away, just in case."

"Tom won't want to go. And if he won't go, neither will Molly."

"They have no choice. They can't help us. If the fire turns, we'll be busy with backfires and keeping ourselves alive. We can't be worrying about them. Tom and Molly will understand, and so will your dad."

Just after midnight, Tom, Molly, and Meadows reluctantly got into a wagon. One of the hands drove it from the ranch complex toward an area higher up and further west.

Throughout the night, Sarah and everyone left at the ranch watched as the wall of flame continued to consume everything in its path. The fire created its own light and changed the atmosphere, driving thick, suffocating smoke ahead of it. Within the fire itself, the dry sagebrush and grass crackled, sending small orange embers into the sky.

Blankly staring at the horrific scene unfolding before her, fear threatened to overwhelm Sarah. Yet she also found beauty in this towering wall of fire. Framed by the black night, its fierce light drew everyone's focus.

Anyone who lived on the prairie or even close had at some time seen such a spectacle. A prairie fire would burn until rain fell or until it reached a river too wide to jump, devouring everything ahead of it and sometimes moving faster than a running horse.

Come morning the sky was dark with smoke, and the fire was much closer now. Just as Jake feared, the wind had turned in the night and pushed the fire toward the Meadows complex. The blaze followed both sides of Sybille Creek, the Meadows ranch buildings directly in its path. High bluffs on each side of the creek forced it to narrow as it advanced.

Sarah joined Jake, Trace, and the two remaining ranch hands building backfires as swiftly as they could. Ashes fell around them. Crackling and popping sounds filled the air as the approaching fire bellowed its impatience and power. The fire sucked up everything, creating its own energy. Burning embers fell into the creek, creating puffs of steam that rose to blend with the fire as it swept ever forward, pushed by the wind. Left unstopped, it would soon sweep over them.

The bandana over Sarah's face did little to keep her from breathing smoke. Fighting terror and the relentless wind that threatened to turn the backfires, she kept working even as she coughed and gasped for fresh air that no longer existed. Red hot embers filled the air, stinging where they struck bare skin.

Sarah brushed hot ash from her hair and blinked sweat from her eyes. She saw horses still in the Meadows corral circling in panic, their loud snorts and wide-eyed fear clearly evident. Jake shouted for Trace to saddle them, ready for a run to safety. The frightened animals were hard to catch and control. Even as Sarah watched, one bolted from the corral and escaped.

Smoke blotted out the sun. The fire was coming fast, the flames jumping ten feet or more per second. Huge fireballs hurtled in front of the inferno, igniting the dry grasses and sagebrush. One fireball landed near the barn but was quickly brought under control.

Wild animals raced ahead, trying to reach safety. Rabbits and coyotes ran shoulder to shoulder, along with antelope and mule deer and large numbers of smaller animals. Many were caught in the blaze's deadly grip. On the wind, the odor of burnt hair and flesh mixed with the overpowering smell of smoke.

Exhausted, her face blackened and sweat-smeared, Sarah stood paralyzed by the fire's immense power. The sky disappeared, lost in a twisting blend of flame and smoke. The roar was deafening, the heat intense. She felt nauseous but fought down the urge to throw up.

They'd already waited too late to escape. Running now would be futile. Their only hope for survival was to stop the fire's advance. The backfires had to starve the main fire of fuel.

"Sarah!" Jake shouted. "Get out of here. Take one of the horses and run for it. Go join your father up on the ridge."

"No!" she shouted back. "I'm staying here with you and the men. This is my home."

"Sarah, please go!"

"No! I'm staying." She picked up the axe she'd let fall and jogged toward a stand of brush the fire hadn't yet reached. Around her, the sounds of more axes cutting down trees and brush rang out against the roar of the main fire. Working alongside Jake and the other men, she lost track of time. Soon, the heat and smoke became too intense, and they had to withdraw.

"We'll make a run down the valley and Sybille Creek if we have to," Jake said, even though a successful escape was unlikely given the speed of the fire.

As they reached the corral, the main fire met the backfires head on. They converged in a twisting mix of flames, a massive column rising together in an erotic dance of fire. Then it was over. The backfires had destroyed all the fuel, and the main fire began to die of starvation.

Jake and Sarah sat on the ground near the ranch house and watched the last remnant of the fire burn itself out. Where it had swept across the landscape, the ground lay black and burned beyond recognition.

Jake looked at Sarah and quietly asked, "Are you okay?"

"Yes, but I'm still shaking. That was close . . . too close."

Jake moved over and took her in his arms. They held each other, both providing comfort.

"Makes you appreciate your life and those around you," said Sarah. "So many things and people in our lives each day we just take for granted."

Jake looked toward the still smoldering fire. "I agree. Too often we get caught up in staying alive and fail to actually live."

They stepped apart, still holding hands. Jake spoke first. "We need to check on everyone. They'll be worried about us. Trace and the other two hands can handle the hot spots and other small fires that may still flame up."

Sarah nodded, then looked at Jake's soot- and ash-covered face. She spent a moment gazing at the man she'd come to know so well during difficult and trying times. *Jake Summers is a good man. He's always been there for me. I hope he knows how much I care.*

"Wonder how it started?" asked Jake, breaking the mood.

"We might know one day," said Sarah. "All I know right now is, we're alive, and I'm exhausted."

The real meaning of what they'd experienced overcame her, and she felt a wave of despair. They had escaped death, but how much had they lost? She wanted to cry but fought down the tears and started toward the house.

The valley floor still smoldered with pockets of burning vegetation. The valley once full of sagebrush and prairie grasses was a wasteland. Come spring it would return, but not until then.

What else could possibly happen? Jake thought as he gazed toward the Laramie mountain range. *Winter will be here soon enough. Already there's snow in some of the mountain passes, and there's a chill in the mornings now. What else can go wrong?*

Turkey buzzards glided over the charred valley floor, sensing a source of easy food. The remains of animals unable to escape lay along a wide, blackened path. The Wyoming wind caught the leftover smoke and carried it away. But turmoil and tragedy had bound themselves to the Meadows family, and Jake felt as if nothing would ever be the same again.

In the Chugwater saloon, Neal smoked a cigar, with several of his men sitting nearby. "Wonder just how that fire got started?" He looked around, not expecting an answer, then noticed Headwright looking at Childers.

"You two were up that way building fence. You wouldn't happen to know anything about this?"

Headwright lowered his head and said nothing. Childers took a long swallow of whiskey.

"Well?" asked Neal. "I think you both know something. What is it?"

Childers glanced at Headwright. "It was an accident. I dropped a cigarette, and next thing we knew, the whole damn area was on fire. We ran for our lives."

Neal took a long draw on his cigar. "That's mighty interesting. Now why didn't I think of that?" He grinned and shouted to the barkeep. "Get these two gents another whiskey, on me. Maybe your fire burned old man Meadows out. Now, wouldn't that be a pleasant tragedy? Drinks on me for everyone! Time to celebrate."

Charles Mann spoke up. "Boss, this might be a good time to recoup some of your investments by rustling the old man's cattle, assuming any survived. I know where we could take them for some quick money."

"Now, now, we can't be talking of cattle rustling. We are law abiding citizens. However . . ." Neal paused. "We might collect some of his stock as payment for monies owed me, with the support of Sheriff Swagger, of course." Neal laughed, holding his whiskey glass high.

CHAPTER 16

The days melted into autumn, and, in the mountain areas not lost to the fire, leaves on the aspens turned yellow against a backdrop of dark-green pines and juniper trees. Even the cottonwood leaves changed to a mix of yellows, oranges, and reds. The air was chilly, and wood smoke from fireplaces and stoves in the Meadows home drifted on the wind.

Three weeks had passed since the fire burned its way down the valley, and some sense of normalcy had returned. Still, everyone remained on alert. Rumor had it Neal was handling some kind of major land deal involving investors from Scotland. No one knew what land he owned, or might be claiming, or what he'd do to get it.

Jake and Sarah spent much of their free time together. Each evening they walked along the river, or just sat on the front porch talking. They often went riding late in the day to watch the sun set behind the Laramie range.

Meanwhile, Tom's health improved, and he and Molly made wedding plans. They would get married in early October, then travel to St. Louis, where Tom could see a specialist about his wounded leg and also meet Molly's mother.

Sarah seized the chance to help plan the wedding, which all agreed would be small, with the ceremony held in the Meadows home. The opportunity to help Molly occupied her mind, keeping it free of Neal and the ranch's worsening financial situation.

The Meadows family was running out of money at an alarming rate.

Once the special day arrived, the sun was shining, but the air was near freezing. Molly and Tom didn't notice anything but each other. A traveling preacher making his monthly circuit performed a brief and simple ceremony, accompanied by one of the Meadows hands on an old fiddle. The music was long and sober, better fitting a funeral. Afterward, the new bride and groom said their goodbyes and headed for town, where they planned to catch the stage to Cheyenne, then board a train east. Both admonished Sarah and Jake to make their own wedding plans. Jake blushed, and Sarah smiled.

A few days later, Jake asked Sarah to go riding and have a picnic lunch. She agreed, saying it sounded like fun.

Morning broke cool on the day of their picnic, but it was clear with a startling blue sky. A warm, gentle breeze filled the idyllic autumn day. Jake and Sarah rode side by side, each caught up in the moment. Although they had recently spent considerable time together, this day was different, and both sensed as much.

The horses were in no hurry. The couple rode toward a spot Jake had found weeks earlier, its exact location kept secret for this day. They watched some birds sent flying by an unseen source. A sage grouse scurried out of their way, while a couple of ground squirrels watched at a distance as they rode past.

"Where are we going?" asked Sarah, with a mischievous smile.

"A special place I found a few weeks ago."

She laughed. "Okay . . . can you give me a clue?"

Jake smiled from behind a well-trimmed mustache and looked at the young woman riding beside him. His brown eyes twinkled with mischief. "We're almost there."

A few minutes later they rode past a stand of ponderosa pine and into a group of aspens with brilliant yellow leaves. They were higher in the mountains now, but the temperature was getting warmer. Jake led them past downed logs and around rocky boulders before descending into a small mountain meadow. Nearby, a stream flowed over some rocks, gurgling as it coursed its way across the meadow.

They laid out a blanket near the stream and had their picnic. They shared fried chicken and potato salad, followed by chocolate cake washed down with cold water from the stream. Time had no meaning for them. Only the moment held their attention, passing as if in slow motion. Both Sarah and Jake wanted it to last.

As idle chatter gave way to moments of silence, Jake looked into Sarah's blue eyes and was overwhelmed with emotions. She touched his cheek, and he took her in his arms.

"This moment is like none I've ever known," said Jake.

"I feel the same. This place and this time . . . I never want it to end."

Sarah touched his lips. A warmth flowed over her, and she felt her heart racing. A meadowlark sang in the distance, and a hawk drifted overhead as the horses grazed nearby, but the young couple paid little heed to any of that.

Jake looked at Sarah. Their lips met in a soft embrace and the sensual expression of love. They would know love at its most basic physical and emotional levels. Their bodies came together in love's embrace, witnessed only by a few puffy, white clouds. The meadow grasses swayed as if some orchestra were playing a timeless symphony waiting for its final crescendo. Meadowlarks and other birds offered up solos, each song blending in perfect harmony. A bald eagle swept from his lofty perch on a distant, rocky podium to lead the final chord.

When they later relaxed and looked at each other, Sarah reached out and touched Jake's shoulder. But it was Jake who spoke first. "You're so beautiful."

"Thank you." She smiled and kissed him.

They spent the afternoon talking, laughing, and sharing love's embrace once more. Jake proposed marriage but admitted he had little tangible to offer except his love. Sarah accepted and told him what he had to offer—his love and respect—was more precious than money.

As afternoon turned to evening, they rode side –by side toward the ranch. Neither said anything, but their glances spoke volumes. They held hands at times, both realizing their futures would be forever bound together. They shared not only a love for each other, but for the land and wide-open spaces around them. Jake promised he would talk to her father soon. Back at the ranch, they parted after a long hug and kiss, followed by a promise to meet later.

Jake returned to the bunkhouse, forgetting to unsaddle and cool down their horses. His lapse was not lost on the other hands. Trace Johnson, who took care of the horses, was among the first to comment. "How was your picnic?" he asked, with a sly grin.

Jake didn't answer. His mind was a mixture of emotions and memories of his afternoon with Sarah. Life for the young cowhand had been difficult at times, but now things were changing. His early life in Texas, then on the Harry Haythornwaite cattle drive north, and even his work on the Box T had been hard, but good. Now things would be even better.

In recent months he'd felt lost, not in the physical sense, but lost in a conflicting maze of self-doubt and confusion about his future. By most standards he was considered too old to work as a ranch hand. Jake knew that well. His days riding sunrise to sundown for someone else's brand were nearly at an end. Life was good, and he enjoyed his work, yet he felt something of value was lacking.

Loneliness was the lot of most hands. Most accepted it as a

condition of the job, but Jake felt different. Often, deep in the night, he could hear an inner voice asking more from life. That quiet voice spoke to his soul, giving off a heartfelt pain.

Then Sarah came along, and everything seemed clear. Opportunities for a family and his own ranch glimmered. His old boss William Thompson had offered to help him get a start with a section of ground along the Laramie River and even a small herd of cattle. Nothing was impossible.

"Say, Jake! You okay? Jake?"

"What?"

"Nothing," Trace answered with a grin. "The look on your face says it all."

Sarah entered the house and, without a word, walked past her father toward her bedroom. "How was your picnic?" Meadows asked as she passed. She didn't answer.

A few minutes, later she returned and sat on a chair opposite him. "Dad?"

"Yes, Sarah?"

"I'm in love. Crazy as it seems, I'm in love with Jake Summers."

Meadows smiled. "And who didn't know that? Not after watching you both the last few weeks."

"He's going to talk to you soon about us. I hope you approve."

"Don't worry. Jake is an outstanding young man. And with Tom gone, I'd like him to be my new foreman if he's interested."

Outside, the sun found its way behind the Laramie mountain range. The sky was a mix of dark blues and purples. Along the mountain tops, several shades of yellow defined the horizon. Shades of white faded into greys and then into deep blues and blacks. Canada geese in a broken V formation flew in front of the lighter-colored clouds, making them easier to see as they headed to some feeding area farther south. The day would eventually fade to memory, but Sarah would never forget it.

CHAPTER 17

Meadows stared into the valley before him, watching Jake and Trace ride among some cattle in the distance. The ridge where he sat rolled off into a series of small hills off to his left. To his right, a steep incline rose roughly toward the mountains. Behind him lay a region called Iron Mountain, where several smaller ranchers were trying to get a foothold.

In spite of his recent streak of bad luck, the decision to move the herd away from Neal's barbed wire had been a stroke of good fortune. Because the stock had been moved to this secluded valley deeper in the mountains along Mule Creek, they hadn't been affected by the prairie fire.

"All accounted for," Jake said as he and Trace rode up. "There are a couple of brindle cows with bite marks on them . . . wolves might have been in the area. Something we need to watch."

"Why are we here?" Meadows asked. "Why did we ride up here?"

Jake glanced at Trace, then turned back to Meadows. "You wanted to check on your cattle. Make sure they're okay."

"Oh! Guess I forgot." Meadows shook his head as if trying to clear the cobwebs. "Those are my cattle?"

"Yes, all yours. And they're in great shape up here," said Jake.

Sarah had mentioned her father seemed more confused lately, often going somewhere and forgetting why. Jake had also noticed the change in recent weeks. John Meadows often forgot important dates and events and was having problems reading and managing money. Two days earlier, he didn't recognize Trace Johnson and had to be reminded the former Box T hand now worked for him.

Meadows gave him a bewildered look. "Jake, for the life of me, I don't think I know how to get home from here. Can you lead the way? We should try to get back before noon."

Jake's heart sank. "Sir, it's already late afternoon. We should head back now if we want to be home before dark."

The men rode in silence, often crossing small creeks and through stands of ponderosa pine. After almost an hour, Meadows said, "We should be home in time for lunch. Are we going to the bank first?"

"No . . . we're headed home, Mr. Meadows. Sounds like you're a little confused."

Meadows didn't answer. Jake was concerned the man might drift off the trail and get separated from the group and then get lost. He asked Trace to ride drag and watch the old rancher. They reached the barn and corrals as the sun was sliding behind the Laramie range.

After dinner, Jake asked Sarah to join him on the front porch, where he recounted the day's activities.

"I'm worried about your father. Something more is wrong than just stress from recent happenings. Someone needs to start keeping a close eye on him," Jake said as he sat in a rocking chair. "I'm afraid he might ride off one day and not be able to find his way home. I'll ask the hands to alert us if he tries to leave."

Sarah twisted her fingers in her lap. "Jake, I'm scared. The doctor doesn't seem to know what to do or even how to diagnose Dad. And his health is going downhill fast. Not only that, we're broke. We're out of money to run this place."

"You're out of money?"

"Yes. We have only the cattle and this ranch. Dad tried to get a bank loan, but Gabriel Swanson said no. I don't know why. He didn't tell my father much, or Dad just didn't remember. Since we couldn't drive any cattle to market last spring, we have no money to pay our bills, much less buy food and supplies."

"I was wondering when that was coming," Jake said quietly. "There must be some way."

Darkness covered the ranch buildings like a blanket. A coyote yipped in the distance. They sat in silence, both deep in thought, searching for answers.

Come morning, Jake told Sarah he was taking a couple of men to check on the cattle again and do some evaluating.

"If we cull out some of the older animals and those without calves, we might have enough to drive to Cheyenne or even Denver. I've heard rumors of railroad construction north of Cheyenne working its way toward Chugwater. If that's true, it means hungry workers who need feeding. Selling even a few head might help pay for winter supplies. Might be worth a try."

The idea gave Sarah a shot of hope. Buoyed by it, she decided today was the perfect time to go into town and talk to Neal. After Jake's departure, she saddled her horse and headed for Chugwater. Before leaving, she made sure someone watched her father. "If he tries leaving, you go with him," she told a young cowhand left behind to do the chores.

She nudged her horse in the ribs, and the animal moved out at an easy lope. She knew Jake wouldn't approve of this trip, so she hadn't mentioned it. Neal had been so nice during their last meeting . . . she still couldn't believe he'd meant to overcharge them for rebuilding their bunkhouse, since he'd kept his promise to send men to do it.

I'm sure it was all a mistake by someone else. She frowned as an uneasy thought surfaced. *He volunteered to check on the details. But maybe he got too busy.*

Once in town, Sarah rode directly to Neal's office. A shiver climbed her back as she rode up and saw Swagger sitting in a chair outside the building, staring at her. He said nothing until she dismounted and started inside. Then, "He ain't here."

She stopped short with her hand on the door knob. "Where is he?"

"Beats me. I'm not his mother."

"I need to see him. It's important."

"You can sit here and keep me company till he comes back, Miss Meadows," he said. A dribble of chewing tobacco spit escaped from the left side of his mouth, and he wiped a dirty hand across his lips. "We should get to know each other."

"That idea thoroughly disgusts me. I need to see Jason. Where is he?"

Swagger answered slowly. "If I had to guess, lady, I'd say he would be at the general store with his momma. But then, maybe not. There's a new girl working in the saloon, and the boss wants her to feel welcome . . . if you know what I mean."

Revolted by the man's lewd remark, Sarah quickly turned and started for the general store. Jason's mother was here? She braced herself for a much-dreaded meeting with Beatrice Neal instead of the pleasant meeting with Jason that she'd planned. Sarah and Beatrice hadn't been friends in Nebraska, and she had no reason to believe things would be any different in Wyoming.

She entered the store and glanced around, hoping to find Neal before Beatrice spotted her. She saw a young man looking at a plaid wool shirt pulled from a stack of them, but nobody else. *Maybe she's not here*, she thought with a touch of hope.

Beatrice emerged from a room in back of the store and headed toward her customer. She glanced at Sarah, looked away without saying anything, and continued toward the man wanting a shirt. Then she halted, nearly tripping over a small barrel of nails and into a container of weevil-infested flour.

"Sarah Meadows! As I live and breathe," she gasped.

Sarah forced a smile. "Hello, Mrs. Neal. How are you? I'm looking for Jason."

"Hold on . . . hold on! He isn't here, but we need to talk." The woman hurriedly finished selling the man his shirt and turned her attention to Sarah. "Been a long time," she said. "A lot has happened since I saw you last."

Sarah looked away. "Yes, a lot has happened."

"I understand there was a cattle stampede and fire out at your place recently, and someone was shot. Then that big prairie fire destroyed much of your ranch and stock. Lots of bad luck. Are you all right? How are you and your father making out?"

Beatrice's interest made Sarah wary. The woman had made no secret of her dislike back in Nebraska. Why did she care how Sarah and her father were faring now? "We're okay. Jason was kind enough to help us rebuild our bunkhouse. He's been very supportive."

Beatrice gave a twisted grin. "That's my Jason."

"That's why I'm here. I need to talk to him about some things. Do you know where I might find him?"

"No, I don't, dear. Maybe over at the café or down at the saloon discussing politics. He's been very busy lately, talking land deals and the coming railroad. He also says there's a problem with sheep moving into the area."

Sarah could only nod in agreement. She knew little of such things. She had her own problems. "Thank you." She turned to leave.

Beatrice called after her, "We'll talk again soon. We have lots of catching up to do."

Sarah left the store and stepped onto the wooden plank walkway. *Catching up? As if either of us wants to.* She had an uneasy premonition that Beatrice Neal was going to be a thorn in her side in the coming months. Then she spotted Jason leaving the saloon and heading toward his office. She hurried to catch up.

When she reached him, Neal greeted her with an upraised hand and a welcoming smile. "Sarah, my dear. What's brought you to town on this beautiful autumn day?"

"I've come to see you. I'm hoping you can explain a few things, and maybe help me."

"Well, of course. You know I'll help if I can."

They walked the remaining distance to the brick building that housed his office. A new sign near the front door announced *Jason Kelly Neal, Attorney-at-Law*. Distracted by Swagger, she hadn't noticed it earlier. Swagger still sat in front of the place, and once again she felt his stare as if she were a piece of meat and he was a hungry dog.

Once inside his office, Neal sat behind his desk and gestured Sarah into a chair in front of it. "Now, what's this about my explaining a few things?"

Sarah brought up the shocking cost of the bunkhouse building supplies. Neal shook his head, frowning. "I'm sorry, Sarah. I meant to keep better track of things. You just let me sort that out, and don't worry about it. How else can I be of assistance?"

Sarah drew a breath, then told him of her father's deteriorating health and their financial straits. "That's part of the problem with those bills for the bunkhouse. We can't afford to pay them, much less buy almost everything else we need . . ."

"Oh, my dear. I had no idea your situation was so grave."

His sympathy made her cry a little. "I don't know what to do."

"Desperate times sometimes call for desperate measures," Neal said softly. "Perhaps there is a way I could help."

He offered her a handkerchief, and she wiped away the tears that had gathered in the corners of each eye. "How, Jason? I'd be ever so grateful."

He sat back. "Would your father consider selling his ranch to me? You both could still live there, but it would relieve you of all financial obligations. Of course, I would also take ownership of any livestock . . . cattle, horses, and such."

She bit her lip. "My father is a proud man. He homesteaded our ranch. He's worked all his life there . . . more than twenty years trying to make a go of it. My father survived drought, blizzards, locusts, rustlers, and even the Indian Wars out there. Each struggle only made him stronger and drove his roots deeper into that soil. He built all those buildings with his bare hands, the corrals, everything. My mother is buried out there, and he visits her grave nearly every day. That place is his life. He will never sell his home, Jason."

"Well, it's one option."

"I know . . . and I appreciate the thought."

"There's a second." He paused.

Sarah looked up, sensing what Neal was about to suggest.

"Marry me. As my wife, all your troubles would be taken care of. We could afford to give your father the best of care. Your father's ranch would stay in the family, and he could live out there. I'm going to be a very important man in this territory soon, when a land deal I'm working pays off. I would take good care of you and your father."

Sarah blushed. She couldn't immediately find the right words. She thought of Jake and their idyllic afternoon together in the mountains. "Jason, I'm not ready to get married. I sincerely appreciate your offer—I really do—but for now I need some other solution. Jake may have one. It's a long shot, but maybe."

"Who's Jake?"

"Jake Summers, our new foreman. He once worked at the Box T north of here. He and Tom Scott helped get our ranch back from Harold Winston. Jake's been a big help."

"What's this solution of his?"

"He thinks if we can gather enough old stock and cows without calves, we can drive them somewhere and sell them. It could give us the money we need to make it through until the spring roundup."

Neal stood and walked to the window that overlooked Chugwater's main street. After a moment, he turned back toward Sarah.

"It might work. But can you gather enough stock to make a difference? By the time you hire some help and get the herd moving, the grass along any trail this time of year will be scarce, especially with all the dry weather. What about buyers? The big buyers out of Chicago aren't out here this time of year."

"I know, but Jake heard they're building a railroad this side of Cheyenne. Word is, the railroad will come through Chugwater. They'll need beef to feed the workers."

"That's true. I've heard the same stories. I tell you what. My offer to buy your father's ranch still stands, as well as my proposal of marriage. Gather up your cattle. I'll send a couple of men to help you. We'll make something work. Don't you worry."

Sarah relaxed and took a deep breath. This was the caring man she'd known in Nebraska. Relief spread throughout her body, and for the first time in days, she felt hopeful.

Sharing her troubles with Jake was important; Sarah knew that.

But what can he do except try and help sell a few of our cattle? Jake doesn't have any money. I know it's wrong not sharing my problems with the man I love. But it will only frustrate him. He has enough to worry about. Jason will help us, and once things are better I'll explain everything. Jake will understand.

She rode home feeling better. *Everything will be okay,* she told herself.

Neal called Swagger into his office. "Find Lake and some of the other men. Old man Meadows seems to think he can gather some stock, push them down to Cheyenne, and find a buyer, make enough money to survive the winter. Not going to happen.

"I've got that old man by the throat. No Meadows cattle are going to reach Cheyenne or anywhere else. Send a few of our men out there to help with their roundup. Have them report to me when they're ready to start any kind of drive. I have plans for those cattle, and for a certain new ranch foreman."

After Swagger left, Neal sat in his office awhile and watched the twilight gather. Outside, lantern lights burned brightly, giving off an almost festive glow. A few riders drifted into town from nearby ranches for an evening of poker and beer. A dog barked at the far end of town. Neal took it all in and sighed. More and more, things were finally turning in his favor. Now, it was time for some supper.

CHAPTER 18

Smoke from two early morning campfires hung heavy in a narrow canyon formed by Mule Creek. A towering bluff overhead cast a dark shadow across the campsite. Jake watched the three men with him shake the morning dew from their bedrolls and stretch their aching bones. They coughed or cussed, sometimes both, in the thick, cold air. Darkness still covered the canyon floor, but, through the smoke and up past the rimrock, Jake could see sunlight edging its way between the mountaintops, giving promise of a new day. The air's chill made it hard to breathe.

A strong smell of wood smoke and boiling coffee reached him. Two men rolled cigarettes. One pulled a match from his wool coat, struck it, and watched it flicker brightly in the early morning gloom. Light from the small flame bounced off those nearby. The second man pulled a burning twig from the campfire and set the end of his cigarette ablaze before tossing the stick back in the fire.

Horses nickered anxious pleas to be gone from this place, free of the freezing air stinging their lungs. Their breath created a white fog, soon carried away on the morning wind. The animals were restless and wanted to move, despite dry winter grasses all around them.

Jake glanced at the distant mountains and recognized the need to start soon, even with his grouchy, irritable crew. They were following a small herd of missing Meadows cattle. More than a hundred head had been culled from what remained of the Meadows herd and were being readied for a trip south to Cheyenne, where potential buyers might be found. Word spread about their plans; it wasn't a secret. Now the selected cattle were gone.

Stolen, thought Jake. *Somebody is driving them southwest toward Iron Mountain.* He and the three other men had followed the cattle most of the previous day through rugged terrain and rocky foothills. The going was slow, but they were gaining on the rustlers.

They finished breakfast, mounted up, and rode most of the morning. Signs showed the rustlers were no longer trying to conceal their escape, making their trail easier to follow. *Almost too easy.*

"We should catch up to them by early afternoon," Jake told the others.

Sam Davis, a grizzled old puncher originally from Texas, reined up near Jake. Davis had showed up in Chugwater recently, and Jake knew little about the man. But he needed help gathering the cattle and driving them to Cheyenne, so he'd hired him along with two others.

"Boss," Davis called out.

Jake pulled up short. "What's up?"

"Bawling cattle! Off that way." Davis gestured toward a series of rock covered ridges off to his right.

Jake frowned. "You sure? I don't hear anything."

Davis pointed with a gloved hand. "Off there . . . a rumbling sound. Might not carry quite this far." He turned toward another new hire who rode a short distance away. "Ain't that right, Breman?"

Jackson Breman nodded. "Yes, sir. Bet we can see them from that bluff up there."

"Let's ride cautious," said Jake as he turned his horse. "They may be closer than we think."

They rode slowly toward the bluff through scattered large boulders and ponderosa pines. Jake still heard nothing. Aspens clung to lower slopes as they rode above a small canyon through which a fast-moving stream was flowing. The stream bubbled and gurgled over several large rocks in the riverbed before disappearing farther down. In the distance Jake could see a small valley, but no cattle.

A rifle shot rang out. The third rider, a young cowhand Jake only knew as Arizona, slumped and fell dead from his saddle. Jake froze, his mind screaming *Ambush!* as he heard a second shot and felt the bullet enter his side. A second bullet exploded against his head. He fell from his horse against a pile of rocks as darkness claimed him.

"Why'd you shoot the kid?" Davis shouted at Breman. "We was just supposed to kill Summers."

Breman grinned. "We don't need witnesses. Them rustlers did this, remember? The kid would have been a problem."

"Talk about a problem, we gotta get rid of the bodies. Get down and help me," said Davis as he swung off his horse.

"I ain't burying nobody," said Breman. "This ground is too rocky and frozen. Best we leave them for the wolves. Day or two, nobody'll recognize their bones."

"Neal told us to leave no evidence behind."

"Let's throw them off the bluff and into the river, then. Let the river swallow them up. What the river doesn't claim, the wolves will."

"All right," Davis said. "Neal wants proof Summers is dead. We'll take his gun belt and his horse."

As Davis and Breman carried Jake's lifeless body to the cliff's edge, a mixture of snow and freezing rain began to fall. They tossed his body over and watched it land among boulders along the river.

Davis scowled. "Damn, he didn't hit the water."

"Well, I ain't going down there and put him in it. It's getting colder and snowing. I'm getting out of here," said Breman.

Quickly, they dropped Arizona's body over the escarpment and watched it splash into the rushing stream. The corpse bobbed up once, then disappeared.

They gathered up both of their victims' horses and led them away. The snow fell harder now. "Let's ride!" shouted Davis. "Too damn cold up here."

"Well done, boys. Well done," Neal said as he struck a match, lit a fresh cigar, and slapped his left hand on his desk. "Did you bring me some proof?"

"Got his gun belt, his horse, and his saddle covered with blood," answered Davis.

"Left his body up in the mountains along with the boy for the wolves," Breman added. "Way it was snowing up there, won't be any sign of any bodies until spring . . . if then."

"Good job. Go to the café and get yourselves a couple of big steaks and put them on my account," said Neal.

As Davis and Breman left his office, Neal turned and stared through the window into the street beyond. *I've got the Meadows family just where I want them. They have no money. The old man is nuts. And they have nobody left who can make any kind of decisions. They're ripe for the picking. Sarah Meadows will come crawling.*

The late afternoon sky darkened, and snow began to fall. He put on his heavy wool coat and headed for the saloon. There was planning to be done, but first he needed a good stiff drink.

CHAPTER 19

The morning after Jake's shooting broke icy and uncomfortable, like a clinging wet blanket. Morning sunlight stayed hidden behind grey clouds drifting over nearby mountains. Water born in some distant source flowed free, wild, and cold down a rock-strewn stream through a series of canyons and ravines with high bluffs along each side. Nearby, among a pile of boulders, lay Jake's nearly lifeless, snow-covered body.

The familiar songs of native birds in this high mountain setting painted an auditory canvas of winter's cold. Cottonwoods, aspens, and other native plants growing along the stream showed scant signs of life. There was little wind, but the temperature hovered near freezing.

The body stirred. The injured man opened his right eye just wide enough to capture a sliver of gloomy, greyish light, then closed it just as quickly, returning to total darkness. He couldn't open his left eye . . . it was crusted shut with something. Blood? He could taste that in his mouth. Again he opened his right eye just enough to see the snow-covered landscape around him. His vision was blurred and foggy, making it hard to see details.

Movement of any kind sent pain throughout his body, although it was numbed by the cold. He tried moving his right arm, but it barely functioned. His left arm wasn't much better. His head hurt, and he guessed he had several broken bones. He vaguely recalled a bullet, the impact in his side. Blood from the wound there no longer flowed, although he felt so weak, he must have lost a substantial amount.

He reached out with his left hand, managed to grab the base of a small tree, and tried pulling himself forward. The attempt sent massive pain shooting throughout his body and cost him considerable energy. He lay still for quite a while before trying again. Conscious enough to realize he couldn't remain among the rocks, he chose to try for what looked like a clearing not too far away.

After nearly four hours he'd managed to move about fifteen feet, leaving a bloody path in the pristine mountain snow. The wound to his head made him dizzy and confused. He had trouble determining the direction of the stream, and its loud splashing became a torturous backdrop when silence would have been welcome. He couldn't think clearly. Every movement, no matter how small, brought pain and stole more than its share of precious energy. He was thirsty, but the stream seemed far away and unreachable. He faded in and out of consciousness.

Darker clouds drifted into the canyon, and toward mid-afternoon it began to snow. The wind rose, sending the temperature well below freezing. Big flakes filled the air and touched his cheeks.

Again he tried moving, but a stabbing pain pushed through his head and down his spine. Some part of his clothing had caught on a rock, holding him captive. He relaxed and stayed still for the moment. Eventually, he rolled onto his side, freeing himself. The effort took considerable time and energy and sapped what little strength he had.

His limited movement had warmed him enough so he felt more pain now. Breathing was difficult, due to what he assumed were broken ribs. Each time he moved, he moaned. Still, he was making progress. The clearing, with a stream running through it, lay only a few feet distant. He felt so exhausted, it might as well have been miles away.

Thirst consumed him. He managed to roll onto his back and watched the falling snow against a backdrop of dull grey. Each flake danced and taunted him, swirling on the wind instead of falling into his mouth where their melting might give him some relief. He closed his good eye and tried to imagine sunlight and warmer weather. He tried remembering what had happened to him, but found nothing . . . not even his name.

He drifted into a state of blind depression. His body floated, and illusions fought reality for control of his mind. The cold ceased to exist. Each snowflake became a miniature angel come to take him home. Then he heard voices, or perhaps a bell, and was briefly unconscious again.

Something touched his face . . . some type of animal was standing over him. He sensed several animals surrounding him, and his first thought was wolves or coyotes. There was a gamey, pungent smell he couldn't identify. Then he heard a bell and the bleating of sheep, filling the air with a continuous call of *baa . . . baaaaa!* He heard voices next, more than one.

Confusion gripped him. Were the sounds real? *What is happening to me?*

Snowflakes landed on his face, soft and cool, quickly melting. The wetness ran into his one good eye and worsened the haze of his surroundings. Again, he heard the bleats of sheep. He tried turning to see, but his body refused to respond. Even his arms, worn out from the arduous task of pulling himself away from the boulders, didn't want to move.

Consciousness came and went. The sky filled with swirling flakes, mixing with the sounds of sheep, then more voices, close enough now to make out words.

"Pa is going to kick our butts if we don't get these ewes home soon." A young voice, a boy's.

"It's all your fault they wandered off in the first place," came a second young voice. "It was your turn to watch them."

"Wasn't either! I was just supposed—"

"What's that? Over there."

Silence for a moment. Then the first voice spoke, closer now. "Looks like a body!"

"Is he dead?"

"Don't know. Can't tell."

A boot poked his leg. He tried moving, even tried speaking, but his battered body wouldn't allow for more than a small shrug and a twitch of his left arm. He could just make out two boys, who both jumped back when they saw him move.

"Looks near dead," said the shorter boy, his voice quivering.

The taller boy turned to him. "Willie, you go fetch Pa. Tell him we found a man out here along the river, and he's near dead. He needs help bad."

Willie hesitated. "But Pa said—"

"Git outta here! He could die!" the boy shouted. Willie turned and dashed away through the snow.

The taller boy knelt within touching distance. "Mister, you alive?"

He tried to focus on the boy's vague shape. Had the boy really spoken, or were the snowflakes talking to him?

A hand brushed his shoulder. "Mister, can you move? Willie's gone to fetch help."

Ten-year-old Willie Lincoln didn't slow down until he was within sight of his family's makeshift cabin. What the Lincoln family called home was a roughly constructed shack at the base of a high mountain bluff. A rocky outcropping overhead provided some semblance of a roof. They had used cottonwood logs to build three additional walls. Where the outcropping didn't quite reach the front wall, they had added more logs and covered them with sod and branches. The place offered some warmth in winter and was cool in summer.

"Pa . . . Pa . . . Pa!" shouted Willie, out of breath, as he ran toward the house.

A tall, stoic man with a full black beard stepped from a makeshift lean-to used in the spring for lambing and shearing. "Boy . . . what's going on? Where's Patrick? I thought I told you both to find those ewes and wethers and get 'em back here before dark."

Willie explained how they'd found a stranger by the river. "He's still alive, but he's in really bad shape."

"I'll hitch the horses to the wagon. Go tell your ma we may need her help with some doctoring. Hurry, now!"

For what seemed like an eternity, Mister—it seemed as good a name as any—heard the sheep and Patrick's occasional question. He struggled to stay awake, fearful sleep would bring death. He couldn't answer the boy, his throat too parched for anything but guttural sounds.

"They're coming, mister. Hang on," Patrick told him. "Won't be long now."

He had no sense of time. Minutes passed that might have been hours. Finally, he heard an older voice he guessed to be an adult. "Looks like he's hurt bad. Gotta be careful moving him or we'll hurt him worse, maybe even kill him."

With some effort, they got him loaded into the sheep wagon. The numbing effect of the cold dulled what would have been unbearable pain, but he gasped as they moved him. One of the boys nearly dropped him and had to grab him a second time. He cried out but was too weak for more than a loud moan.

The boys' father, whose name was James Lincoln, said, "Easy now. We'll have you looked after soon."

Icy sleet fell from dark grey clouds over the valley as James and his sons carefully drove the wagon back toward the Lincoln home. Once there, James's wife, Martha, ordered everyone outside except her daughters, Catherine and Marie. As water heated in the fireplace, she cleaned the injured man's wounds and prepared a poultice of dried, powdered herbs to reduce swelling and pain, then a second one to prevent infection.

"We need to change this one every two or three hours," she told the girls. "We may need to use a compress or fix a decoction of some type."

One of the girls asked, "Will he live?"

"God only knows," answered her mother. "All we can do is pray. We've done all I know to do. It's in God's hands now."

Later, he listened to the family discuss the day's events over a meal of mutton, beans, dried apples, and strong tea. They sat at a large, hand-hewn wooden table still marked with axe cuts. The cabin walls were sparsely decorated with children's drawings and an old dried flower wreath. Coats and hats hung on hooks near the front door. Herbs used for cooking and healing hung along one wall and from beams in the ceiling. A pile of wood lay near the fireplace, which didn't draw well and allowed smoke to make its way into the living area.

He drifted in and out of consciousness as light from a nearby kerosene lantern created shadows across the wall, and likely his bandaged head. The lantern flame flickered now and then as air from outside found its way through the cottonwood walls. He could hear voices from time to time, but efforts to recall what happened to him were futile and frustrating. He couldn't remember anything.

"Any identification on him?" James asked.

"None I could find," answered Martha. "Not sure any of his clothes are worth saving. If he survives, we may need to let him use some of yours. He's about your size."

"Suppose he's from one of the cattle operations around here? Maybe he spotted the boys herding those strays and got hurt waiting to ambush them?"

"No," said Martha. "He was shot at least twice. Somebody wanted him dead. And from the looks of him, they came awfully close."

"Well, if someone tried killing him, we need to be careful. Could be if they find out he's still alive, we're in danger ourselves. If any of you find someone poking around and asking questions, don't say anything. Next time I go into Iron Mountain or Horse Creek, I'll ask around and see if anyone's missing. Of course, it may be weeks before I make it into town again now winter's come."

Outside, a howling, mournful gale whipped the sleet into a fresh snowstorm. Now and then a burst of wind found its way through the walls, carrying a few flakes of blowing snow with it. Inside, the warm room smelled of wood smoke, wet wool, and human sweat. Light from the fireplace created ever-moving shadows on the ceiling. Mister gave up trying to remember who he was and how he'd been hurt, closed his eyes, and found sleep.

CHAPTER 20

As dark grey clouds spread a heavy blanket over the morning hour, Neal rode up to the Meadows ranch house and dismounted. Swagger and Lake remained on their horses. Sarah heard them arrive and came onto the front porch.

"Jason! What a surprise . . . why the visit?"

Neal took off his hat. His face was tight, and he glanced down at the ground before looking at her. "I'm afraid I have bad news. You told me in town a few days ago about your plans to gather up some cattle and drive them to Cheyenne."

"That's correct," said Sarah. "Somebody stole them. Jake took a few men and went after them."

"That's why I'm here. A couple of my men were hunting up near Iron Mountain, and . . ." He sighed heavily. "They found the body of your foreman and another man. Sarah, I'm sorry, but they were both dead, and there was no sign of your cattle."

"That can't be. It just can't." Sarah slumped into a nearby chair and started to cry. "It can't be true. Jake can't be dead. Oh my God, no!"

The screen door swung open, and her father shuffled out. "What's wrong?" he asked her, then glanced at Neal in confusion. "Who are you? What did you say to my daughter?"

"I'm Jason Neal. You obviously don't remember me. I'm a friend of Sarah's, and I've been forced to share some bad news."

Sarah fought to regain her composure. "How do you know for sure it was Jake? I mean, three other men went with him."

Neal turned to Swagger, who handed him Jake's bloody gun belt. "I believe this belonged to your foreman."

Sarah sobbed uncontrollably. Tears streamed down her face. Her father touched her shoulder and stared blankly at the scene before him.

"That gun belt belonged to Jake, all right." Trace said, as he walked up to the house. "I recognize the holster. What happened?"

"Couple of my men found your foreman's body and another man's up in the mountains, along with their horses. There was no sign of anybody else, or any cattle. The wolves had gotten to Summers already, so my men buried him. But they brought me his gun belt, and his horse and saddle." He turned to Sarah. "I'm sorry to be the one to tell you this. You obviously cared for the man. If there's anything I can do—"

"What about the rustlers and cattle they were following? The other men who rode with him? Your boys find any of them?" Trace asked, sarcasm and anger in his voice.

Neal stared at Trace. "I understand this is hard, losing your friend and everything. I already told you, there was no sign of any cattle or rustlers up there. We can only assume your friend came upon the rustlers, who shot him and left him for dead. There's no evidence to the contrary."

"Of course not," said Trace.

"What's that supposed to mean?" asked Neal as Swagger and Lake turned their horses toward Trace. "What are you trying to say?"

"Nothing . . . nothing. Just peculiar there were no other signs of anything else up there, especially a hundred head of cattle. That's all."

"My men said it was snowing hard. Another hour or so and they wouldn't have found anything. Even the bodies."

Sarah choked back sobs, struggling again to compose herself.

Finally, she managed to stand and took hold of the porch railing. "Thank you for coming, Jason. That was kind of you. I'd like to be alone now. Maybe . . . maybe in a few days, we can talk . . ."

"Of course, I understand. Just remember, I'm here if you need me." Neal swung back up on his horse. "Men, let's head back. Sarah, if there's anything I can do, please let me know. Somebody can pick up your men's horses and saddles in town." With a polite wave of his hand, Neal and his men turned and rode off toward Chugwater.

Sarah slumped back into the chair and held her head with both hands. "Jake dead! Jake gone! I can't believe it. It can't be true. What am I going to do now?"

As the days passed, Sarah found it harder and harder to concentrate. *Must move on,* she kept telling herself. *This brooding and self-pity has lasted long enough.*

Neal continued to offer his condolences, often stopping by the ranch to visit and provide encouragement. She felt grateful for his kindness in a tough situation. Fate had dealt her a mortal blow. He didn't mention his offer to buy the ranch, or his marriage proposal, but she thought of it more than once. She rejected the idea each time, finding it distasteful, but what real choice did she have?

Marriage to the young attorney would be her last chance to keep the ranch and provide for her father as his health failed. And sometimes she couldn't help wondering if that special afternoon with Jake had produced more than memories.

I can't lose this ranch, she thought.

She wrote to Molly and Tom, explaining recent events and Jake's death. Alone and without hope, she poured out her heart to her distant friends . . . but the choice in front of her stayed the same.

"Think I'll go for a short ride before the weather turns bad," she told her father one day. "I need to clear my head about some things."

Sarah asked Trace to watch her father, saddled her horse, and rode east away from the ranch. Short-stem grasses and snow-covered sagebrush soon surrounded her. She gazed at the grasslands stretching for miles as they rolled across eastern Wyoming toward Nebraska. After about two hours of riding, she saw a small herd of antelope watching her, ready to run at the slightest threat.

Life wasn't always fair, especially for the timid and weak. Sarah knew as much. She gazed at the vast snow-covered prairie and saw the blades of grass sticking up through the snow. The weight of the snow kept the grass from swaying much in the timeless and unforgiving wind.

A turkey buzzard caught the midday currents and drifted overhead. She had never felt so alone in her life. Her world was caving in around her. Even her love of this vast land wavered, as if the wind itself could carry her away like a feather before a storm.

I'm out of options. If I'm going to save our ranch, provide for my father and take care of myself, my only choice is to marry Jason.

With a quick turn, she realized her brief morning ride had brought her far from home. The landscape was white as far as she could see. Only the Laramie Mountains behind her offered any sense of a landmark. She shivered at the thought of being lost and decided to turn back. As she urged her horse forward, in the distance she could make out a lone rider, moving without discernable haste in her direction.

Maybe I should hide! Wonder if he saw me?

She looked around, then headed into a nearby ravine, hoping the strange rider hadn't seen her stop. Watching closely from her refuge, she realized she was being tracked in the snow. The rider was getting closer and would soon follow the tracks right into her hiding place.

Need to move. Find somewhere else. But where?

She pulled her dad's rifle from its scabbard and waited. Then she stepped from the ravine directly into the rider's path. Only then did she recognize Neal. "Oh, my goodness!"

His startled horse lunged sideways, nearly throwing Neal from his saddle. "Sarah! What are you doing?" he asked, regaining his composure with effort.

"You had me worried. Why are you following me?"

"I was riding out to check on you and saw you leave the ranch. Thought I'd catch up. But you got well ahead of me. Please put that rifle down."

She settled the gun back in the scabbard. "You scared me, following me like that."

"I'm sorry. Never meant to alarm you. Just wanted to make sure you're okay."

"I just needed to get away and clear my head. I meant to come see you later anyway."

"Let's ride together," said Neal. "We aren't that far from town. We can talk."

They turned their horses southwest toward Chugwater. For several minutes, neither of them spoke. The only noises were the wind, their horses' hooves, and creaking leather. Now and then a shod hoof hit a rock under the snow with a loud pinging sound.

"Jason?" Sarah asked quietly.

"Yes," he answered.

"Do you still want to marry me?"

"Yes . . . yes, of course I do."

Sarah sighed and squinted her eyes to hold back the tears. "And you'll help me save our ranch and care for my father?"

"What are you saying, Sarah? Have you decided to accept my proposal?"

"Yes, Jason. I'll marry you."

Standing just inside the saloon doors, an attractive, young woman with long, blond hair watched with interest as Jason Neal and Sarah Meadows rode together into town. Cheyenne Mitchell was only nineteen and new in Chugwater. But, privately, she had laid claim to Neal and the power and wealth he possessed.

Cheyenne had spent most of her life drifting on the winds of fate and opportunity. Forced from home at thirteen by her drunken stepfather, she was often homeless and penniles, but eventually found work in various brothels and saloons around Denver where she grew up. The life was distasteful to her, but it was better than going hungry.

Before long, she discovered she could use her long, blond hair and deep blue eyes as tools to meet her needs. A smitten forty-year-old Arizona gambler named Harper Cox, who'd found her in back of a popular roadhouse situated on Cherry Creek, taught her to target potential marks and ply them with drinks. He'd shared his winnings as well as his bed with her, until he got tired of her demanding more money and flirting with other men.

One night, Cox offered her up to pay off a gambling debt to a railroad executive from Cheyenne. In a drunken stupor, the man accepted, but, once sober, he realized his mistake. He was married, and having a young woman on his hands placed him in an awkward situation. The executive bought her a one-way ticket on the Cheyenne to Deadwood stage and sent her packing.

When the stage stopped in Chugwater for a change of horses, she got off and literally stumbled into Neal, who happened to be walking past. After a brief exchange of embarrassed pleasantries, Neal offered to buy her a meal at the café. The stage left without her. Cheyenne Mitchell had become a good judge of men, especially those with money and power. Harper Cox had taught her well.

With Neal's help, she got work at the saloon and developed her own plans for the future. Watching her man ride down the street with Sarah Meadows didn't fit into those plans. No rancher's daughter, no matter how pretty, was going to take what belonged to Cheyenne without a fight.

Beatrice Neal was in the general store when her son and Sarah came inside and shared their news. It was all Beatrice could do to swallow her anger and welcome Sarah to the family. Her pulse pounded in her veins, and her blood pressure raced higher. She gave Sarah a cold, cursory hug while seething with resentment. *You wicked little hussy. You will never have my son.*

After a brief stay in town, Sarah decided to ride home before the weather worsened. Big snowflakes were already falling and gathering on the street. "Best you stay in town," Neal told her, taking hold of the horse's bridle. "There's a big snowstorm coming. I can feel it."

On most days, Sarah might have agreed. She had a long way to ride, and the weather might be worse closer to the mountains and home. Today, though, she needed to get back where things were safe and familiar.

"No, I have to get home," she told him, trying to back her horse away. "My father will worry and wonder where I am. Someone needs to fix him something to eat."

"Stay in town," Neal insisted. "I'll get you a room at the hotel."

"If I don't make it home, everyone will worry. I'll be fine if I leave now."

Neal's face darkened, and his voice rose. "I told you to stay in town. I don't want you going anyplace alone in this weather. If I'm going to be your husband, you'd better start listening to me."

Alarmed at his tone and attitude, she yanked hard on the reins. The buckskin lunged backward, free of Neal's grip. She turned the animal sideways and kicked him hard with both heels.

"I'll be all right," she yelled as the horse ran down the street. "We'll talk soon. If the weather is too bad, I'll come back to town."

Angry and embarrassed, Neal glanced around to see if anyone had witnessed the exchange with his bride-to-be. Swagger stood nearby, grinning. "Woman problems, boss? Need some advice?"

"Go to hell!" Neal shouted as he headed for the saloon in search of a stiff drink and a more willing and docile companion.

As Sarah rode home through the worsening storm, her thoughts swirled like the snow on the wind around her. The heated exchange with Neal had caught her off guard. She'd seen him angry before, at the barn dance and when she'd turned him down back in Nebraska, but, both of those times, he'd been struggling to master injured feelings.

I just agreed to marry him, she reminded herself. *Have I made a mistake? How am I going to explain this to Dad? He won't like me marrying Jason.*

Big snowflakes were still falling in the fading light of early evening as she approached the ranch house. In the distance, she saw wood smoke rising from the chimney. She pulled up on a ridge and watched Trace carry firewood toward the house while José closed the barn doors. The wind was rising, and she could feel icy pellets mixed with snow hitting her face.

She urged her horse off the ridge. With snow clinging to her clothing and hat, she rode to tell her father the not-so-good news. The icy wind sent a shiver through her body and mirrored the feelings in her heart.

CHAPTER 21

The sound of carriages and freight wagons rattling by on the streets of St. Louis woke Tom Scott, although there was some question whether he'd ever been asleep. Shod hooves striking the cobblestone streets added to the eclectic mix of sounds outside his window in the Roughneck Bar and Gaming House.

A shaft of light from a gas lamp along the street below penetrated the early morning darkness of his room. The yellow light passed through the window, where it reflected off a dresser mirror before striking a nearby wall. Beside him, Molly was still asleep.

Tom got out of bed, walked to the dresser, and picked up Sarah's letter. He went to the window for better lighting and once more read the words he still couldn't bring himself to believe. *Jake is dead, killed by cattle rustlers.* He shivered and felt a chill born of emotions, not the winter winds outside.

Down the street he saw huge chunks of ice bobbing in the Missouri River, all with rounded edges from bumping into each other as they floated downstream toward the Mississippi. An old alley cat dashed across the sidewalk. Icy patches where snow had melted the previous day and frozen anew in the night were everywhere. Snow clung to rooftops and in shaded areas along the street.

In the glow of the lantern and street lamps, Tom saw coal smoke rising from several chimneys. Barges and steamboats were tied up along the riverbank, unable to move through the ice in the river. Only railroad boxcars moved as they were loaded and then shifted from one track to another, awaiting an engine and shipment date.

Warehouses lined the river, filled with assorted items, many eventually bound for upriver shipping: dry goods, guns, gunpowder, barbed wire, leather shoes and boots, clothing, and various foodstuffs.

A freight wagon rolled past, headed for one of the warehouses, followed by a milk wagon on its daily rounds. Tom turned his attention back to his sleeping wife. Their bedroom was one of many in this combination saloon and boardinghouse where Molly had once lived, and where her mother still plied her trade dealing in the pleasures of men.

As he watched Molly sleep, he thought how the death of his good friend had shaken him, almost as much as Sarah's news that she would marry Jason Neal. Molly had gasped when she read that part of Sarah's letter, shocked and disbelieving on both accounts.

Afterward, she and Tom had talked deep into the night. Sometime after midnight, they agreed to return to Wyoming come spring. The winter weather made traveling any sooner all but impossible. Molly vowed to write her friend and share news of her own . . . she was with child. Tom urged her to suggest Sarah hold off getting married so they could attend the wedding.

Neither Tom nor Molly had been happy since their arrival in St. Louis. Meeting Molly's mother had gone well enough. But city life wore on him, chafing his normally pleasant personality. He didn't like the icy streets and the smell of burning coal, the unpleasant mix of city air and manmade filth they couldn't escape.

Even rides into the surrounding countryside could not clear his mind or his nostrils of the ever-present stench. He missed the wide-open spaces and mountains. Even Molly admitted she missed the clean, pure air of Wyoming.

Work was hard to find. Tom had met with several local cattle buyers and packing plant representatives to discuss employment, but without success. He'd hoped his background in the cattle industry might prove useful to someone. A couple of companies showed interest in having him coordinate cattle shipments from Wyoming and Colorado, but so far no offer of work had been forthcoming.

Nights echoed with an unhealthy mix of bar fights and shootings, though Tom and Molly managed to avoid both. The days passed slowly. Molly spent much of the time visiting old friends and bar patrons she'd known.

"Little has changed," she had told him.

Neal heard arguing in the saloon downstairs, then a gunshot. He climbed out of Cheyenne's bed. "Come back and keep me warm. Don't go," she begged. He ignored her as he opened the door and peered out over the railing into the smoke-filled room below.

Swagger and Lake stood over a man Neal didn't immediately recognize. The man moaned. Blood oozed from a chest wound, and his shirt had turned dark red. He clutched his wound with bloodied fingers and grunted.

"Let that be a lesson," Swagger shouted to everyone in the room. "Nobody cheats me at cards or anything else. When I want something, I don't ask; I take. Now somebody get that body outta here and bring me another bottle. Don't let him die in here."

Another loud moan, followed by a gasp of precious air, and the man's body went still. Four men picked him up and tossed him onto the plank walkway outside. Someone else went for the doctor, though there hardly seemed any point. Swagger sat down and whispered something to Lake, who laughed. Others in the saloon returned to their own activities, each in their own way wary of Swagger.

Uneasily, Neal noticed two men in dusty suits sitting together at the far end of the room. They hadn't moved during the altercation but had watched intently as it unfolded. *Gotta get Swagger under control. The man is a loose cannon and getting worse. He's going to ruin my chances of getting rich out here,* Neal thought.

He shut the door and lit a kerosene lantern near the bed, then threaded his arms into a dark-blue, wool suit jacket.

"Come back to bed, sugar," whispered Cheyenne. "I'm getting cold."

"Later . . . I've got to go." He tugged his trousers on. "Tomorrow's my wedding day. I need to get some things done first."

"You still plan to marry that woman? She'll never treat you as good as me!"

"Baby, it's all business . . . part of a bigger plan. Probably bigger than your little brain can comprehend. Nothing is going to change between you and me. You're still my woman. Now I've got to clean up a mess downstairs. That Swagger is getting on my last nerve."

He left the room, hurried downstairs, and went straight over to Swagger. "What the hell are you doing?" he said, his voice low and hard. "You can't just start shooting people when you feel like it. What's the matter with you?" He nodded toward the two men in suits. "Those men over there represent the Swan Land and Cattle Company. Didn't you see them before you pulled your gun? If you want to get rich, you need to be a little more cautious. We can't blow this."

Swagger glared. "I understand," he muttered. "I understand."

"Good." Neal crossed the smoky room to join Alexander Swan and J. A. Epperson. He offered to buy them a round of drinks. "I'm sorry you had to witness such a brutal act. It's rare for such a terrible thing to happen here in Chugwater. Though it does show we demand law and order. That should be good news for someone wanting to settle here or start a business. We take law and order very seriously."

"We've seen worse in cow towns across the West," said Swan. "But you should know we haven't settled on Chugwater to be our headquarters just yet. We've learned a railroad line already exists west of here in the town of Iron Mountain."

"Iron deposits were found in that area back in the 'fifties and mined until about 1870," Epperson said. The railroad extended a line into the area, expecting heavy use from mining concerns. That never happened, but remnants of the line are still there."

Swan continued, "The hills and valleys up there are covered with excellent grass, along with stands of box elder and other native plants. There's plenty of water in Horse Creek, Chugwater Creek, and several other smaller streams. We just came from up that way."

Neal hid his concern as best he could. If Swan and Epperson chose Iron Mountain as their cattle shipping center, it would affect his own ambitions and interests. Somehow, he must convince them to locate their headquarters in Chugwater. Hopefully, Swagger's outburst wouldn't discourage them from making Chugwater the hub of their operation. Neal had already made inroads in discussions with Swan. Now it was a matter of sealing the deal.

Still angry and drunker by the minute, Swagger watched Neal talking to the land company men. He said nothing himself, but he was thinking plenty. *Damn you, Jason Neal. I should shoot you right now. Nobody dresses me down like that in front of my friends and stays alive. You and me are going to have it out one day. I'm not putting up with your disrespect much longer. Just you wait.*

And I'm going to have that tramp Meadows woman of yours as well.

An icy winter rain fell softly without fanfare sometime in the night. Cold and penetrating, it drove deep into Sarah's soul. She lay in bed, feeling each chill raindrop as if it were meant solely for her. Although she was warm and dry, the night covered her like a soggy blanket, drowning her spirit.

Sarah couldn't sleep. She tried to convince herself it was excitement that kept her wakeful, but it felt like apprehension. She got up, and, with the light of a candle reflecting off her face and the surrounding walls, she sat with her mother's wedding dress in her hands.

Memories of better days and nights stole the moment. She smiled, recalling her youth and growing up on the ranch. She thought of her Aunt Ruby and Uncle Lewis back in Nebraska, with whom she'd lived while teaching school. Then she recalled meeting Neal for the first time. *Fresh lemonade. We shared lemonade at the church social. He looked so handsome standing alone in the shade of that old oak tree. He seemed so shy, gentle, even a little bashful when I first saw him.*

Now everyone is telling me how cruel and hard he's become. I don't know. Agnes McGee dead after selling him her building, that she swore she never would. Everyone scared of him. It doesn't make sense.

He was so handsome and so kind. He was nothing like what he's apparently become since arriving in Wyoming.

She sighed, and tears welled up in her eyes.

Tomorrow is the day I've dreamed about my entire life. I so wanted to marry Jake. I love him so much, always will. Now he's dead. She swallowed hard and choked back her misery. *Nothing turns out like we plan, I guess. Jason's not all bad. Maybe I can smooth his rough edges and make him a more understanding man. The man I knew is good. I just know he is. He must be.*

Sarah carefully hung the wedding dress up again, then moved to her bedroom window and looked out at the sleet-turned-snow as she thought of her future and that of her father, snoring in the adjoining bedroom. Outside by the barn, a thirsty horse whinnied and stomped on the wet, frozen ground. It was so cold, the water in the horse trough was frozen.

A coyote yipped on a nearby ridge. A rusty hinge on an old gate wailed like a banshee as it was tested again and again by the snow-laden wind. It was going to be a long night and still longer day tomorrow. Sarah sighed, fearing the cold weather might be an omen of things to come.

Chapter 22

Days gave way to weeks. The weather grew worse, making it difficult for the Lincoln family to keep their flock healthy. The December wind blew hard out of the north, and snow fell heavy throughout the valley. All the Lincolns took turns going outside and building extra windbreaks to protect the sheep from the winter storms.

Meanwhile, their guest became increasingly aware of his surroundings as his wounds and body healed. His nostrils adapted to the smell of sheep, but their constant bleating sounds made it hard to think. Unable to remember anything about his past, he found it frustrating he didn't even know his name. The Lincolns called him Amos, after a shepherd in the Old Testament of the Bible.

On this morning, Amos felt well enough to be up and moving. He sat with James Lincoln, having coffee by the fireplace, and listened as the elder Lincoln talked about sheep.

"Sheep can keep warm during the winter. They do have wool coats, you know. They handle the cold better than most livestock, and some breeds even prefer it. Even if you see them covered with snow and ice, their wool insulates them, holding in body heat and helping resist moisture. At night, they bed down together and stay warm that way. Sometimes their wool freezes to the ground, and we have to help the little ones get up.

"The one thing they can't handle is drafts. We worked all fall to build a windbreak along a natural tree line near here, but this weather is worse than we expected, so we need to build more."

"What kind of sheep you got?" Amos asked.

"Navajo-Churros from Mexico, mostly. We also have a few merino sheep, and we plan to add more. They have better-quality wool come shearing time."

"So how come you keep 'em outside in winter, not in a barn or a shed?"

Lincoln gestured to his wife for more coffee. "Fresh air even in winter is better for sheep, long as we keep their water unfrozen." He turned to the two boys, who were sitting close by. "Willie and Patrick, you check their water every day. Your main chore this winter is to break ice in the streams. Sheep can eat snow if things get real bad, but if the snow is covered with ice and the streams freeze over, they're in trouble. You boys understand?"

The brothers nodded.

"How can I help?" Amos asked. "There must be something I can do to earn my keep around here."

"Can you handle a rifle?"

"I don't know. I suppose so."

"Tell you what. While we work on a better windbreak, we could use some help watching out for predators, especially wolves and coyotes. When it snows like this, they find it easier to kill sheep than chase down deer, elk, beaver, rabbits, and rodents."

Amos nodded. "I can handle that."

"Come better weather, we could have another kind of prey around here," Patrick whispered.

"You boys hush," admonished their mother. Amos ignored Patrick's comment without thinking what it might mean.

Coffee finished, Martha Lincoln gave him clothes belonging to James, including a heavy, black, wool coat and hat. From a distance he looked much like the elder Lincoln. The clothing gave off a strong smell of sheep, so much so at first that he found it hard to breathe.

Though extremely cold and windy, the fresh air felt good in his lungs. Something about seeing the nearby snow-covered mountains lifted his spirits. He couldn't explain why, but he had a feeling of being home. A borrowed rifle in hand, he moved toward the sheep flock, grateful for the strength and ease that had returned to his limbs over the past several weeks.

Shortly after noon, Amos noticed a restless stirring in part of the flock, which huddled near a stand of ponderosa pine well north of where the family was working on the windbreaks. Nobody else seemed to notice, nor did the family's two border collies, Blackie and Hank.

Still, he decided to walk in that direction. The snow was still falling, though more slowly now, and in places the wind was creating deep drifts. Walking without snowshoes was difficult and slow. He found a rocky outcropping with a good vantage point near but above the flock. The Lincolns' cabin sat in the distance, and the flock slowly drifted in that direction. The wind kept the rocks clear of snow. Amos found a spot shielded by large boulders, out of the wind. He sat, propped the rifle nearby, and took out a piece of sourdough bread Martha had baked that morning.

After a period of watching and waiting, he saw a black streak moving against the white landscape. He shook his head to make sure he wasn't seeing things. No . . . there it was again. Then something else moved, dark grey, and he realized two wolves were attacking a young wether that had strayed from the flock.

A black wolf had one of the wether's hind legs in its mouth and was pulling it further from the flock. The bleating cry of the captured sheep rose above the wind. The second wolf tried grabbing the wether's throat to secure the kill.

Jake stood. His sourdough bread fell into the snow at his feet.

He grabbed the rifle, quickly brought it to his shoulder, and sighted on the black. The sound of the shot echoed down the valley. The black wolf fell backwards, dead.

A hurried second shot missed the grey, who made one last lunge for the neck of the freed wether. The wolf missed, ran off a short distance, and halted as if not sure of what had just happened. Amos's third shot caught him in the hindquarter and sent the wolf spinning into a snowbank with a mournful cry of pain. A fourth shot ended all doubt of the outcome.

Red stained the pristine white snow near both dead wolves. Within minutes, a fresh layer covered the bodies. The embattled wether limped away to join the flock, which had drifted farther south. He continued to bleat, but the other sheep ignored him.

Amos reloaded his rifle and surveyed the area for signs of other predators. Seeing none, he followed the retreating flock toward the cabin and the newly created section of windbreak.

The rest of the day proved uneventful, and by nightfall the snow stopped, and the wind subsided. Dark came cold, well below zero, and clear. Amos stepped outside to join James, who was smoking a pipe and watching the moonlight that reflected off the white landscape. The flock had bedded down for the night, although Amos could still hear an occasional bleat.

"Came from Pennsylvania," James said.

"What?"

"My family lived in Pennsylvania when I was a boy. My parents came out here with six ornery kids, including me, in the 'sixties, trying to escape the war. Settled in Colorado." He drew on the pipe, which glowed in the darkness. "With cotton hard to come by in those days, raising sheep for their wool was a way to make some money. A man could make a living for his family back then. I grew up in Colorado, mostly. When me and Martha married, we came up here to this place. Decided to stay and raise young'uns and sheep."

"Seems to be working out for you," said Amos.

"I don't know anymore," said Lincoln, with a long, deep sigh. "Since the war ended, wool prices have been falling almost every year. Many growers are switching from just wool production to selling mutton for meat. You once could get $3.50 to $4.50 a hundredweight for wool alone, and that would make you money, but things are changing.

"We've always been able to raise sheep, pound for pound, as well as any cattleman. But this territory is filling up, and the demand for open-range grazing is growing. Things are getting tense.

"We always try to move the flock to better grazing each summer, then back here in the winter. It's a lonely, difficult life. Especially now."

Amos shrugged. "Can't say I know much about raising sheep, or cattle either for that matter. Then again, I can't say I don't, either."

"Cattlemen hate us! Want us out of this country. They don't believe there's a place for sheep out here." James was getting agitated now. "But honestly, predators can be just as bad. We face our share of wolves, coyotes, bears, and mountain lions."

He took a long draw from his pipe and suggested they go inside by the fireplace. The fire felt good after the bitter cold outdoors.

"Sounds like raising sheep can be a good business if it's done properly," Amos said.

"Lonely at times," James answered. "I'm fortunate to have my family with me. Many sheepherders don't. Before Martha joined me up here, I stayed with my flock and a couple of good dogs. Once we exhausted the grass in one area we'd move to another area. Could go days, weeks or more, without seeing another soul."

"Sounds tough. I can't imagine."

"I heard tell of herders who went insane tending to their flocks. Some forgot their own names and had trouble speaking after listening to bleating sheep all day and night for months. One man was found on his hands and knees among the sheep, bleating along with them. Crazy, huh?"

Martha called out from the back of the room. "You men better get to bed, or I know of one in particular who might be sleeping with the boys in the sheep wagon tonight."

James winked at Amos, emptied his pipe in the fireplace, and headed for bed. Amos had been sleeping on the floor near the fireplace, so he found his wool blanket and rolled up snug in it. Sleep wouldn't come at first. He tried counting sheep but had to stop and laugh at himself. *Counting sheep . . . can't seem to get away from those woolies anymore.*

Chapter 23

The marriage of Jason Kelly Neal and Sarah Alicia Meadows was not the social event of the season. The day was cold, windy, and threatening snow. Only a few townspeople showed up, along with Sheriff Swagger, Deputy Lake, and most of Neal's other hired gun hands. Some stood outside, watching to make sure everything went as planned. Neal wanted no interruptions or objections.

The wedding was held in the Neal home, the parlor decorated with a few silk flowers offering neither joy nor promise of happiness.

Neal's mother remained aloof and sullen throughout the brief ceremony. The look on her face spoke of a mood befitting the day, grey and ice cold. Beatrice planned to continue living with her son and his new bride. Neal doubted she'd make life easy for Sarah, but that was all right with him.

Meadows was there as tradition demanded and reluctantly gave Sarah away. His mind was fading more each day.

Neal knew old man Meadows didn't like him, had even tried to talk Sarah out of marrying him, but he kept quiet. After the marriage, he planned to do away with the old rancher. He would make sure of it. He'd have to get around Trace Johnson, who'd agreed to keep working at the Meadows ranch along with some of Neal's handpicked men. Sarah had insisted he stay, quietly and emotionally linking him to Jake Summers. Had there been something between her and the dead foreman? If there was, she should pay for that.

Neal had intended a brief honeymoon in Denver, but the day gave way to heavy snow blowing down from the Laramie mountain range and out over the foothills. The snowstorm prevented them from leaving town, so they postponed any kind of celebration.

By the next morning, everything was back to normal. After a silent breakfast with Sarah, Neal met Swan and Epperson in his office to discuss land purchases, available ranches for sale, and future opportunities in the cattle industry for the Swan Land and Cattle Company.

"Most of Wyoming is wide-open range with free grass. And there seems to be plenty of water," said Swan. "There are opportunities here for tremendous profits, perhaps a hundred, even one hundred fifty percent or more."

"The Union Pacific Railroad must agree," Epperson added. "Railroad surveyors made the route into Cheyenne, not Denver. We need only to get a rail line into this area. And with cattle prices running about five dollars a hundredweight, we stand to make a nice little profit."

"Hell, some cattle have brought as much as seven dollars a hundred," said Swan. "We've researched this thoroughly. Demand for beef is growing worldwide, and we need to take advantage of it. However, it's not going to be easy. Cattle prices won't stay high forever."

Neal leaned across his desk toward them. "Everything is going to be just fine. There's plenty of money to be made out here."

"We agree. But we do have concerns," said Swan. "Not all is good."

"What do you mean? How can I help?"

"Homesteaders and sheep herders," answered Epperson. "People are filing claims everywhere. Why, in 1870 there were less than ten thousand people in the entire Wyoming Territory. Now there's more than sixty thousand. Homesteaders and sheep herders are moving into this country and claiming some of the best grazing land. Right here in Chugwater you have farmers moving up on the plateau east of town, trying to grow crops. And we see sheep everywhere. They're ruining the grassland for cattle production."

"I know what you mean," Neal said. "Let me and my men address those issues for you. This is cattle country, always will be."

"Let's hope so!" said Swan. "I plan to invest a lot of money in this territory. It would be a shame if anything kept me from making money on this investment."

Neal smiled. "I understand completely."

After Swan and Epperson left for the hotel, Neal called Swagger and Lake into his office. "We have work to do. Take some men and go up on the Iowa Plateau and emphasize to those homesteaders this may not be a healthy place to settle, much less grow crops. Get my meaning? I've been nice long enough."

"Loud and clear boss," said Swagger.

"And boys, don't leave any evidence we were involved."

Swagger smiled and touched his pistol.

Lake nodded in agreement. "Let's get to work."

"One more thing, men," said Neal. "After Christmas, we'll start visiting sheepherders. They need to hear the same message. I can't stand those smelly woolies."

Neal's reputation grew with each incident, and soon everyone in the area knew his name. He demanded respect, whether earned or not. More than one innocent bystander was swept up in his malicious intimidation campaigns.

"The man is out of his mind," whispered Felix Newman, one afternoon in the saloon. Newman owned a small ranch near town. He'd stopped in for a beer and found two old friends.

"Winston was bad enough. This guy may be worse," added Mitchell Stevens, another rancher.

"You got that right," said the third man, a rancher named Martin Jones. "Claims he's an attorney. Claims he has the law on his side. What law?"

"What can we do?" asked Newman. "We're ranchers, not gunmen."

"Ain't nothing can be done right now," Stevens said. "I'm still trying to get my ranch back. That no-account Harold Winston and his men ran me off. I moved back out there after Winston got killed, but now this Neal guy says I don't have a legal right. Something about how it belongs to Winston's estate, which he claims to be handling."

"That's a bunch of BS," said Newman. "I don't have all my cattle back, either. Meadows and the hands out at his place are trying to sort the herds. But because the brands on most were altered, Neal says I don't have a right to any cattle unless I can clearly show they were mine."

Stevens sighed. "Right now, it's his word against the rest of us, but if Neal goes out and hires more gun hands to back his claims, we may be screwed. Yep, things could get worse."

An hour or so later, Neal heard a loud commotion in the hallway, and his office door flew open. A middle-aged man in clean, well-worn work clothes and a heavy overcoat fell on the floor in front of his desk. The man's boots were worn from hours of working in his fields on foot. *Homesteader*, thought Neal.

Swagger stepped into the room and tossed a dirty, brown, wide-brimmed hat at the man on the floor. Then he grinned at Neal. "Brought you a gift, boss."

"Gentlemen, why this intrusion? What's going on, sheriff?"

171

"This dirt farmer was in the general store complaining about prices and creating a nuisance of himself. He knocked over a stack of canned tomatoes and refused to pick them up. Your mother was very upset."

"Oh my," said Neal. "Is that true?"

From his knees, the farmer braced one hand on the top of Neal's desk and tried standing. As he started to pull himself up, Swagger grabbed his shoulders and shoved him back on the floor.

"What's your name?" asked Neal.

"McCord . . . Luther McCord."

"You one of those homesteaders trying to farm up on the plateau?"

The man hesitated. "My family—"

Swagger kicked McCord in the back. The farmer fell forward, breaking his nose on the edge of Neal's desk.

"Sheriff Swagger, let's let the man speak," Neal said, with exaggerated calm. "Pardon the sheriff's impatience, Mr. McCord. Now answer my question."

"We grow some corn and wheat up there." McCord touched his broken nose. Blood dripped from it onto the floorboards.

"What the—" Neal leaned forward in his leather chair. "You're bleeding all over my floor!"

McCord started to respond but thought better of it.

Neal leaned back and took a cigar from a box on his desk. He struck a match but didn't light the cigar. Instead, he held the burning match in front of his face and stared at the flame until it nearly burned his fingers before he shook it out.

"Well, Mr. McCord . . . Luther, is it? I see that country more suited for raising cattle, not crops. Maybe you and your neighbors made a mistake settling here. Maybe you should consider another area . . . say, California, Oregon . . . or maybe you should go back where you came from."

Watching Swagger carefully, McCord managed to stand. He held his hat with both hands and looked straight at Neal. Bright red blood covered most of his nose and continued to drip slowly onto his shirt.

"That's our business. We homesteaded that open range legally. Built on the hundred-sixty acres the government gave us under the Homestead Act of 1862, planning to live on it for five years just like the law says. That land belongs to us now, and we ain't going nowhere. Now if you and your goons will let me leave."

Swagger grabbed the man's shoulder. "Who you calling a goon?"

McCord twisted away. "You people have no right to be threatening me!"

Swagger cocked a fist, but Neal held up a hand. "Living on a piece of ground for five years can be very difficult." He struck a second match and watched it burn. "Things can happen, Mr. McCord. Tragic, terrible things. I'd hate to see anything happen to you and your family. I hope for your sake you understand." Neal pinched the match flame between his left index finger and thumb and squeezed. The flame went out.

"Remember that, Luther. Things can happen. Now get out of here."

Neal spent a little while longer alone in his office, finally smoking his cigar. He felt the need to stop at the saloon for a drink before going home to Sarah. He found Cheyenne Mitchell waiting for him at the bar, got a bottle of whiskey, and they went upstairs.

Sarah sat in the bedroom of the home she shared with her husband and his mother. Making her marriage work despite its rocky foundation might not be easy, but she intended to accomplish it. Being Neal's wife hadn't been part of her hopes and dreams, but she meant to make the best of a bad situation. Her father would move into town where she could watch over him. *Everything will be all right,* she told herself and hoped it was true.

Beatrice Neal had other ideas, of course. From the way Neal's mother had acted in Nebraska, Sarah doubted any woman would be good enough for her son, especially a poor rancher's daughter. So far, she'd done all she could to make Sarah's life miserable. Sarah stood, her jaw set in determination. *It won't work. Beatrice Neal will just have to accept that I'm here to stay.*

She went down to the kitchen and began preparing a meal of beef steaks, fried potatoes, beans, and fresh-baked sourdough bread with honey. They would have cold buttermilk and fresh spring water to drink, and dried-apple pie for dessert. Her father would join them for dinner. Trace Johnson had promised to bring him before stopping by the saloon.

Beatrice came home early and wasted no time giving orders for exactly how Sarah should prepare supper for Neal. None of it appealed to Sarah. Her stomach was so touchy these days. She stood still briefly, the bread pan in her hands, as an obvious reason for feeling nauseous struck her. She and Neal had been married just about long enough . . . she thought of Jake suddenly, and tears stung her eyes.

She welcomed her father with relief when he and Trace showed up at the front door. After Trace left again, the three of them sat near the fireplace, drinking coffee and awaiting Neal's arrival. All was ready and waiting on the table.

Down the street, Neal slipped out of Cheyenne's bed. "Later, darling. I'm late for dinner."

Up on the Iowa Plateau, a homesteader named Franklin Lawrence lay dead near a small shed where he had just finished milking the family's Jersey cow. The milk bucket lay nearby, its contents running onto the cold, thirsty ground.

Lawrence's wife and two young boys huddled together next to the corral gate in shock and fear. The six masked men who'd brought death to the family ignored her. They shot one of the two sorrel mules the Lawrence family used to farm the one hundred-sixty acres surrounding their one-room cabin, then dispatched the second mule. The first one lay dead while the second jerked through the final motions of life. Blood flowed freely from the animal's sliced throat.

The men had ridden to the homestead without warning just after dark and started shooting. Lawrence had no chance to use the squirrel rifle still leaning against the fence.

After killing the mules, the men set the cabin on fire and held the woman and boys at gunpoint while the flames caught and consumed their home. Dried corn shucks and stalks piled near the house for winter feed exploded as a stray ember found them, followed in short order by a stack of hay.

Then the marauders turned and rode away just as quickly as they'd come, heading east toward the Luther McCord homestead. The evening was young, and the night would be long.

CHAPTER 24

Smoke settled into the Chugwater Valley as fires continued to smolder on top of the plateaus east of town. The morning air, thick and dark, made breathing difficult. At least ten homesteads torched during the previous night were still orange hot in places. Sheds of corn, oats, and wheat stored for winter feeding continued to burn along with piles of cornstalks and hay. At least six men and two women were killed trying to defend their homes. Another two men and one woman were wounded, with the woman not likely to survive the day. Six children of various ages had sustained injuries.

Residents of the town and surrounding area were outraged as word of the fires spread. The streets filled with ranchers, cowhands, freighters, merchants, and a few down-on-their-luck drifters. They were soon joined by homestead survivors seeking medical help and supplies.

The most often asked questions involved *who* and *why*. Who would inflict such devastation on the innocent? Why would anyone commit such horrific acts? The townspeople of Chugwater stood in small groups discussing the terrible events of the previous night. Most suspected Neal and his men were involved, but few dared say so.

From the window of the Neals' front parlor, Sarah watched in disbelief as the surviving homesteaders came down off the plateau and into town. Men, women, and children, all with blackened, ash-covered faces and some with burned skin raw and peeling. Most walked, their mules and horses shot dead to keep them from working their fields. Only a lucky few managed to still possess a wagon and team.

A wounded mule pulling a cart, with a man, a woman, and two small boys in it, collapsed and died in the middle of the main street. Blood from the animal's wounds mixed with mud, manure, and melting snow.

Sarah started towards the door, feeling the need to provide some type of assistance. Neal intercepted her and grabbed her arm. "Stay in the house. No wife of mine is going to help a bunch of worthless sodbusters. They got what they deserved."

Shocked, she stared at him. "You can't mean that, Jason. Those people are human beings. They need our help."

"Those people are worthless, hardly fit to breathe the same air as us decent folk. They should be run clear out of the territory!" Neal shouted.

She tried to pull out of his grip. "Jason, please!"

"You heard me! I said, let them be. I'm warning you. Stay away from that riffraff."

Beatrice joined them in the front room, a satisfied smile on her face. Clearly, she enjoyed seeing her son put his "uppity" new bride in her place.

"Jason is right, Sarah. Those worthless farmers should have stayed in Iowa, Ohio, or wherever they came from. They don't belong out here." She put on her hat, preparing to leave and open up the general store for the day.

Sick at heart, Sarah glared at them both. "I can't believe either one of you. Those people need our help."

Beatrice gave Neal a quick peck on the cheek and opened the front door. On her way out, she looked back. "They got what they deserve. Maybe others should listen and learn from this."

Insulted and angry, Sarah started after her. The insinuation she should behave or else was obvious and condescending.

177

"Easy now," said Neal, grabbing her arm again. "Mother didn't mean you, I'm sure."

Sarah knew better, but there had been enough arguing. "Your breakfast is getting cold," she said, roughly pulling away and turning toward the kitchen.

"I'm not hungry. Got things to do. You stay here. I'll see you later."

Sarah watched him leave. Her hands trembled, and her face was flushed with anger.

Jason was always so kind to me before. He's my husband. I don't understand why he won't let me help those people.

She stayed in the front hallway a moment longer, fists clenched at her sides. She had to do something, and not even Neal would stand in her way.

As the sun reached its noon peak and shadows virtually disappeared, the street filled with more burned-out homesteaders and others passing through town on their way out of the area before they were forced out. Entire families sat atop wagons loaded with furniture, clothing, and other personal items. In some cases, caged chickens rode in the wagon bed, and the family milk cow was tied behind. Dogs barked and snarled. Chugwater's main street was bedlam, intense and loud.

Sarah slipped from the back of her house and into a narrow alleyway. She chose a route that kept her behind a few other homes and ramshackle cabins and managed to reach her friend Missy Fernsmith's house without being seen.

Missy and her husband, Robert, owned the only blacksmith shop in town. Sarah knew they had openly opposed Neal and more than likely would be willing to help the homesteaders. Rumor had it that Sheriff Swagger and some of Neal's gunmen had threatened Robert Fernsmith more than once, but Neal had put a stop to it. He realized the town needed a blacksmith, even one on borrowed time.

Missy opened her back door to a breathless Sarah. "Come in quick, before someone sees you."

Sarah ducked inside. "Thank you! Jason has gone wild. He forbade me to help the homesteaders. He threatened me. But I don't care. We have to do something for them."

"Dorothy Helms will be here soon along with her two teenage boys," Missy said. "They'll bring some of their horses from the stable. Help me gather food and supplies. We can give them to anyone who needs them. I've also sent Ramona to get Victoria Swanson and Emily Goodrich. Victoria and Emily might be able to provide temporary shelter in that big house of theirs." Ramona was Missy's fourteen-year-old daughter.

By mid-afternoon, they'd set up a makeshift infirmary and morgue in the back of the Helms's stable. The town doctor was kept busy running between his own office and the temporary hay-filled hospital.

Sarah wiped the ash-covered face of ten-year-old Levi McCord while watching the boy's six-year-old sister Lisa eat a sugar cookie. Their father, Luther McCord, was dead, their mother beaten so badly she was not expected to live. Another homesteader family had already offered to take the boy and girl if their mother didn't survive.

The doctor told her he was running low on supplies, so she volunteered to go to the general store for more ointment and other medical items. She knew there was a chance she'd run into Neal, but it was a chance she had to take.

As she neared the store, she saw a group of homesteaders talking.

"We can't put our families in danger," said a tall farmer standing next to his loaded wagon. "They can have my land."

The man wore a large, flat-brimmed hat and a heavy, black coat pulled up tight around his neck to shield him from the cold December wind. His boots still held tightly to pieces of the soil he'd tried to farm. He told his wife and four little girls to stay outside while he went in the store for items they would need for leaving town. Sarah followed him inside.

Beatrice had recognized the strong demand for flour, bacon, sugar, salt, beans, and other staples and decided it was a good time to raise her prices. Deputy Lake stood nearby to deter any objections.

When the farmer complained that she'd charged him double, Lake hit him across the face with his rifle butt, knocking the man down. Sarah rushed to his side, glaring at Lake.

"You know who I am. Don't even think of hitting me," she shouted at him. "All this man wants is a few supplies so he and his family can leave town. There's no need for such brutality."

"You should mind your own business," Beatrice snapped from behind the counter. "Deputy Lake was doing his job."

Lake started to speak but backed down as Neal entered the store, followed by Swagger. Beatrice told him what happened, being sure to mention Sarah's involvement, while others in the store stood back and watched.

"Get your supplies and get out of here!" Neal shouted at the farmer.

"What about your precious Miss Sarah?" Beatrice asked. "She wants more ointment and bandages and whatnot so the good doctor can keep treating those filthy sodbusters."

"Give her what she needs." He turned and glared at Sarah with eyes as cold as ice. "I'll settle with my good wife later."

By nightfall, things in town calmed considerably. The homeless and injured were accounted for and treated. Up on the plateau, men and women prepared to spend another long, cold night ready to defend their property and themselves. There would be no more surprise attacks.

Neal came home and found Sarah in the kitchen baking sourdough bread. His mother stood nearby. "Mother, would you please leave us for a few minutes? Sarah and I need to talk."

Beatrice left, and Sarah turned to face her husband. His face was bright red from anger, his fists clenched so tight his knuckles turned white.

"This morning I told you to stay away from those homesteaders. I told you not to help or encourage them. You ignored me. You disobeyed me. You made a fool of me."

"Listen, Jason. I know you're angry. But I did what any decent person—"

"Stop right there. I don't want to hear your excuses." He stepped forward, grabbed her by the throat, and shoved her against the wall. "Listen to me. There will be no second chance. Next time I tell you not to do something, you will obey. Do you understand me?"

Sarah choked from his tight grip on her neck. She pulled at his arms, trying to free herself.

"Do you understand? I won't say it again." Neal pushed hard against her, his face inches from hers. "You will do as I tell you!" he shouted. Spit from his mouth struck her face. Then he shoved her onto the floor.

"I'm . . . I'm sorry," she said, gasping for air. She touched her throat. "Please don't hurt the baby," she whispered. "I beg you, don't hurt the baby."

Abruptly, Neal stepped back. "What? What did you say?"

"I'm with child, Jason. I didn't know how to tell you. When I saw those little kids, I couldn't help myself. I thought of my baby, and I had to do something."

Neal looked blank faced. "Oh, my God. A baby?"

"Yes."

"How? When? Oh, my God. I need a drink." He turned and stalked out of the kitchen. A moment later, she heard the front door slam shut. Neal was heading for the saloon.

181

As she pulled herself up off the floor and sat in the closest chair, Beatrice came into the room. "Everything all right?" she asked, sarcasm in her voice. The woman poured herself a cup of coffee from the warm pot on the stove and smiled. "What did you say this time to make my son so angry?"

Sarah looked up. "He was upset because I tried helping those farmers who were injured." She hesitated. "And—"

"And what?" Beatrice glared.

"I told him I was having a baby."

"Really? Whose is it?"

Shocked, Sarah found no words to respond.

"Are you sure it's my son's baby?" Beatrice asked, then turned away without waiting for an answer. She left the room, and Sarah heard her going into her bedroom.

The days that followed were quiet and uneventful. Snow fell more often now, leaving the streets a muddy mix of dirty snow, ice, and manure. Christmas wasn't far off, but Sarah felt no sense of celebration. Her father grew worse, his mind all but gone. News of his death came on a cold, grey morning, four days before Christmas.

The funeral was simple and brief. A few friends and townspeople came and went. John Meadows was buried next to his wife on the ranch where he had homesteaded and raised his daughter. Once everyone had gone, Sarah, dressed in black, stood near the grave alone and stared down at the heaped earth that covered his wooden coffin. Neal had been too busy to attend, so she grieved in silence. There was no eulogy, no other tear-stained faces. Snow covered much of the landscape, the only blemish the freshly dug soil where her father would lie for eternity. By nightfall, even this small island of earth would be covered with snow.

On a cold, clear morning two days later, Sarah rode back out to the Meadows ranch. The temperature was just above zero. She could hear squeaking saddle leather and the crunch of snow with each step her horse took. Chill winter air found its way into her lungs, and she expelled a foggy breath as she rode.

Once she reached her secret place above the ranch house, she dismounted, built a small fire for warmth, and sat down to evaluate her life. *Why have things turned out so badly? Just months ago we were all so happy. The future looked so bright, so wonderful. Then Jason showed up, and nothing has been the same since. He's ruined us. And Jake . . . my precious Jake . . . and my father are both gone now.*

God, I'm praying here. I'm scared of Jason, but what can I do? I know I must be strong for my baby. I must be!

In the distance, the sun slid toward the Laramie mountain range. The sky along the mountain tops was already turning a deep, cobalt blue with streaks of orange. Nightfall would come soon, and it was getting colder. She put out the fire and remounted her horse.

Down by the ranch buildings, she spotted some of Neal's gun hands standing around, smoking cigarettes and talking. She couldn't hear what they were saying. Jake's sorrel gelding stood alone in the corral. She shuddered at the thought of the gunmen neglecting it and decided to have the horse brought to town where she could care for the animal herself.

Sarah turned her head and gazed at the mountains and felt a strength of purpose wash over her. *I must be strong, not back down from doing what's right no matter the consequences,* she told herself.

A bald eagle swept down off a distant ridge. She watched its powerful motion, its massive wing span and strength. Perhaps it was an omen. She rode home with renewed faith that God had a plan for her life, and it was important she not give up.

It was long after dark before she reached town, and the streets were empty. She could see a few Christmas decorations tied to some buildings along Main Street. The wind was biting cold, and she feared frostbite on her face. Still, she had found new strength and vowed to keep fighting.

CHAPTER 25

Christmas came at last, and so did another snow, falling during the night. The flakes came thick and heavy and by morning had spread throughout the mountains. Each flake drifted through the cold air bound for its special place on the pristine, white valley floor. The sheep huddled behind a rugged windbreak of trees and branches, leaving behind a frozen mix of mud, manure, ice, and wasted hay.

After breakfast, Amos went with the Lincoln boys to hay the flock and make sure the sheep had water. The ewes wouldn't lamb until spring, but it was critical they be kept well watered and fed. They crowded close together and seemed to accept the falling snow as normal. Dust from the hay mixed with the snowflakes, making it difficult to see.

The boys rushed to finish feeding and get back inside. Waiting for them all was a Christmas meal being prepared by Martha Lincoln and the girls. They would have a baked Canada goose along with boiled ham and sausage links. Their mouths watered at the aroma of freshly baked sourdough bread to be spread with newly churned butter and huckleberry jelly. Canned corn and tomatoes along with beans would round out the meal, all of which would be washed down with copious quantities of coffee, water, and cold goat's milk.

The family settled into a day of laughter and games, while Amos sat near the fireplace and wondered about his past and his future. Would he one day have his own family? Or perhaps

185

he already did, and they were having Christmas without him?

The next morning, James Lincoln made the decision to move half the flock about three miles farther up the valley, where hay had been stored the previous summer.

"If we're to survive the winter, we need to separate the flock and use the hay we have up there," he told the family. "Amos here has volunteered to watch over them. He can take the sheep wagon, and he'll have all the comforts of home. He'll also take Hank with him . . . he'll need a good dog. We'll move the boys back into the cabin."

The canvas-covered wagon was about eleven feet long and six-and-a-half feet wide. The Lincolns had purchased it in Rawlins, Wyoming, two years earlier. The canvas top stretched over hickory bows in three layers, insulated with wool blankets. Inside, the bunk sat about four feet off the floor on the wagon's tongue end. A small window above the bunk provided cross-ventilation.

The wagon had several cabinets and a small wood-burning stove along the right side. The stove would also burn coal or cow chips. There was a bench with more cabinets underneath along the left side. A pull-out table and washbasin completed the interior. Kerosene lanterns provided the lighting, along with two large candles.

"The wagon will keep you from being exposed to the bone-chilling winds we get up there," said Lincoln. "You'll need to melt snow to take a bath and have drinking water. And your food will no doubt freeze, so keep that in mind. Me and the boys will help move the flock and wagon and help you get settled. We'll show you where the hay is stacked. And you'll need to make sure the stream up there doesn't freeze over.

"There's a good windbreak for a small flock, which is why we won't take all of them. Don't worry if snow gets on them . . . the oil in their heavy wool fleece protects them from moisture and keeps them warm. The snow won't necessarily melt on their backs, because the wool is holding their body heat inside."

Amos nodded in understanding. The wagon would be well stocked, and Lincoln promised to check on him from time to time.

"Your main job will be to keep predators out of the flock. The worse the weather, the more likely wolves and such will seek an easy meal. Hank will be a great help, but he's young, so you'll need to watch carefully."

As the sun climbed over the valley floor the next morning, they set out, and by evening Amos and Hank had settled into their new home. Amos had brought two rifles and plenty of ammunition to hold off an army of mutton-hungry predators. He fixed some soup on his stove, lit one of the lanterns, and rolled himself a cigarette. After eating, he took Hank and checked the flock, then turned in for the night. The job would require constant vigilance.

"You ready for this?" he asked the dog, not really expecting an answer.

Several days passed. Amos saw no evidence of predators, although each night he heard coyotes yipping and wolves howling in the distance. One morning he came across what looked like mountain lion tracks, but they were old, and he wasn't sure. The only fresh tracks he found were those of birds, squirrels, and rabbits. The weather remained clear with temperatures below zero.

Calm before the storm, he kept telling himself.

As the days went by, the sheep drifted into a wider area, but he didn't mind. The exercise warmed his muscles. After a week, he and Hank had developed a regular routine with the dog keeping watch at night and Amos during the day.

Before sunrise one morning, he heard a cry from near the timberline where the sheep used the thick trees as a windbreak.

Hank was barking at something. He grabbed a rifle and went to check. In the distance, he saw a solitary dark-grey wolf dragging a young wether from the main flock. Hank had gone to the wether's aid but stayed back as he barked.

Still some distance away, Amos decided to take a shot before the wolf could get the wether into the trees. He missed, but the cold morning air magnified the sound and got the wolf's attention. The wolf dropped the sheep, cowered, and looked around. He started snarling at Hank, and Amos was suddenly fearful he might lose the dog.

His second shot exploded off the trunk of a cottonwood tree just behind the wolf. As the animal turned and ran, tree bark hit it in the back.

Good thing Hank raised an alarm. Need to mention that to James or one of the boys next time I see them, Amos thought. *That wolf will probably be back, and more than likely not alone next time.*

Snow showers occurred daily, sometimes followed by a heavy snowfall, and the wind never ceased. Temperatures often fell well below zero, so Amos made his trips outside brief. One night the wind shook the wagon with such force, he feared it might tip over. The next day he tied it securely to some nearby trees.

He positioned the wagon where he could sit in the back out of the wind and still see the flock in the distance. As the days kept passing, a deep loneliness came over him. Even brief visits by the Lincoln boys didn't seem to help. Something was missing, a major part of his life gone, and he felt frustrated. In the long, lonely hours of watching the sheep, those missing parts of his life began to haunt him. He was a man with no past, no life.

January slipped into February, and he grew more and more melancholy. He tried to stay busy beyond watching the sheep and keeping predators away. Now and then he had to chase away coyotes and wolves, killing a few.

On one clear, cold morning, he decided to walk upstream to learn more about the stream's source, perhaps find a spring. After struggling through the snow for what seemed like hours and not finding anything, he decided to head back for the wagon. Following the stream over snow-covered boulders and through dense trees had been difficult, leaving him tired and hungry.

Suddenly he heard shots coming from the valley. His first thought was that the boys had come calling and seen a coyote or wolf, maybe a mountain lion. Bears would still be in their winter dens. He hurried toward the sounds, fearful of a stray bullet finding its way to him through the trees.

Amos reached a clearing along the stream, about three hundred yards from the valley, and saw three men on horseback crossing the water. They all held rifles.

"Let's get the hell out of here!" yelled one man on a bay mare. His horse was working to reach the far bank. A second man rode behind him, whipping his horse, trying to make it move faster in the water.

The third rider's dapple grey gelding didn't want to enter the fast-moving stream. The horse shied away, pulled back, and turned sideways. The rider spurred the horse hard and tried turning its head back toward the stream. The animal's front hooves hit an icy spot on the bank, and he slid into the water. He lunged forward, nearly unseating his rider.

"Dunwoody, come on, or we're gonna leave your sorry butt!" shouted the first rider, already on the other side of the stream.

"Leave him!" the second man said as his own horse climbed the far bank. "Never should have brought him."

The young man they'd called Dunwoody finally got his horse moving through the cold, rushing water. Then the animal stepped into a hole and stumbled, and the rider lost his hat. He had bright-red hair and an equally red face as he struggled to gain control of his horse. It took some effort, but horse and rider managed to reach the other side and the two waiting riders.

"You're a fool, Dunwoody,!" shouted the second man. "Where'd you learn to ride?"

Before Amos could move any closer, the three men wheeled their horses, rode into some underbrush, and were gone. Amos hurried along the stream and into the valley. What he found made him sick. Blood was everywhere, and twenty pregnant ewes were dead. Several more wounded ewes would need to be put down. A wounded Hank lay near the sheep wagon.

Motion made Amos look up. James Lincoln on horseback, followed by Patrick and Willie on foot, was coming up the valley toward the carnage. "You all right?" shouted James as he pulled up next to Amos. "What happened here?"

Amos explained how he'd left the flock for a couple of hours to check the area upstream and heard rifle fire on his way back. "I saw three men ride away. They crossed Horse Creek about three hundred yards north of here. One of them called another Dunwoody. We could go after them. Their tracks would be easy to follow in the snow."

"No," James said. "They're long gone, most likely. This has happened before. Cattlemen trying to send us a message to move on . . . get out of this country. So far it's only been some sheep, but one day it might be one of the boys . . . or one of us."

Amos shook his head. "Who would do such a thing?"

"That's a cattleman for you. Could be any of them. Maybe Victor Miller or somebody else. Last fall, rumor had it some guy over in Chugwater was trying to push sheep ranchers and homesteaders out of the area using gun hands and rustlers. Let's gather up these dead ewes and check the others. Make sure they're okay."

James picked up a hand shear and a knife. "We can salvage the wool not stained with blood and much of the meat, but we need to hurry before all that blood and the carcasses attract predators. Amos, you, Willie, and Patrick pile the damaged wool and bodies downwind and burn them."

The smell of burning flesh and wool soon grew overpowering as the flames climbed higher, sending smoke into mountains.

"You gonna be okay if we leave you alone up here with a wounded dog?" James asked, looking into Amos's eyes for any sign of doubt or fear.

"Yeah. I just need to be more guarded from now on. I'm sorry. I shouldn't have left them alone."

"I should have warned you something like this could happen. But, honestly, I didn't expect any trouble before spring. Somebody must want this valley pretty bad for their cattle come summer."

James and the boys left, heading for home as the sun set. Deep shadows cast by the trees and mountains stretched over the valley floor, making the blood-stained snow look darker and more ominous. Amos took a look around, mindful that the smell of fresh blood would attract hungry night visitors. He ducked into the sheep wagon, fixed a meal of bean soup and biscuits made in his Dutch oven, and decided to spend the night outdoors watching for trouble.

He took care of Hank's wounds and got him settled in the wagon. Luckily, the dog's injuries weren't life threatening. Then he took both rifles and found a spot behind several boulders out of the wind where he could watch the flock. A full moon reflecting off the snow lit up the area, making it easy to see the sheep.

Deep in the night, his mind wandered. He thought back on events of the previous afternoon, and from somewhere he remembered a quote:

"As a stream meanders down a distant slope, its course often forced to change by even the smallest of obstacles, so it is in our own lives. We are influenced by even the smallest events, so we walk through life choosing the path of least resistance. But happiness is often found on the mountains we dare to climb and the barriers we choose to break down . . . daily obstacles holding us back from our true path."

Was that a glimmer of his past? Remembering the quote provided him with the hope that other memories would soon follow. He leaned back against a granite boulder and looked up at the bright moon just sliding behind a distant mountain peak. The night air was cold and crisp in his lungs, and there was little wind. The stars were hard to see in the bright moonlight.

"Dunwoody. The man called him Dunwoody," Amos said, recalling the boy's red hair. "That name. It's familiar." He paused, groping for more. "There was a card game, and he was cheating. But where? When? We were in a bunkhouse somewhere."

He struggled to remember, but his mind went blank. Yet he was sure the name Dunwoody offered some clue to his past. He just couldn't remember why.

Amos dozed occasionally, never for long. Near morning, he spotted a coyote sniffing the blood-stained snow. With its tongue hanging out, the animal moved toward the sleeping flock. Amos blew on his cold hands and took careful aim with his rifle. The crack of the shot shattered the night, and sent the coyote howling into the trees. When morning came, Amos found blood spots and tracks, but no body.

He sensed the days were getting longer. And his nights were filled with images he couldn't explain. He dreamed of family on a Texas ranch . . . working on a cattle drive. Did that make him a cattleman? He still had no recollection of his name or how he'd found his way into this area of Wyoming.

Something deep inside told him he hadn't seen the last of the men trying to run the Lincoln family from the territory. He knew he would do his best to stop anyone trying to hurt this family. Memory or no memory, it was the right thing to do. They had saved his life.

CHAPTER 26

As the winter dragged on, Neal grew colder and more aloof toward Sarah every day, with his temper on a hair trigger. She sensed the emotional chasm between them was widening, yet there was little she could do. Most days, she tried to keep out of his way. Friends she'd known for years also stayed away, fearful of Neal's wrath.

Burned out homesteaders openly blamed Neal's men for the brutal attacks upon them. Many were pulling up stakes and moving rather than fight back. There would be no spring planting for them. Others lived in constant fear that one night the gunmen would return.

"The killing of my friends and neighbors will forever be on Jason Neal's conscience, if he has one," said one bitter farmer leaving town. "May he rot in hell."

Word soon spread that anyone raising sheep was in danger. Rumors raced through town that one rancher's entire flock had been killed, his dog shot, his herder hung, and the man's sheep wagon burned. Others faced intimidation in various ways each day. Sarah didn't want to believe Neal was involved—and accepted his protests to the contrary on the rare occasions she dared raise questions—but she couldn't quiet her doubts.

Neal had not threatened her since the shoving incident back in December, but she lived in fear he might. He often scolded her for some trivial matter, his words cutting and cold like the weather outside. As days passed into weeks, his look and

194

demeanor left her concerned. She often caught him just staring at her.

Beatrice was no help, often showing delight when her son berated Sarah. The woman likewise enjoyed hearing about incidents of homesteaders or sheep herders being harassed. Sarah's only joy came from knowing sometime in the summer she would have a child. Even that happiness was muted by Neal's apparent lack of interest, usually followed by a trip to the saloon. Sarah wondered what his mother might be whispering in his ear, and whether he believed her.

In early February, she received a letter from Tom and Molly. They were still in St. Louis, and Sarah was excited to learn Molly was also expecting a baby. They planned to return to Chugwater sometime in the spring but weren't exactly sure when. It depended on the weather and Molly's health.

Sarah planned to suggest they stay at the Meadows ranch upon their return. She would need Neal's permission, even though she considered herself the legal owner. Asking him would have to be handled carefully. She secretly hoped Neal would put Tom in charge of the old home place.

The day came when a Chinook wind blew more frequently through the Chugwater Valley, coming down from the north and through the town. Chugwater residents smiled and prayed for an early spring. Sarah missed having flowers and being outside with the warm breeze in her hair and the sun on her face. She learned to sew and handle more domestic duties, hoping her diligence at being a good wife to Neal would soften his anger and bring back the kind man she knew in Nebraska.

Outside, the birds began singing their spring songs. The recent snows melted, except in shaded areas and along the north side of buildings and trees. A steady stream of people, horses, wagons, and carriages stirred up mud in the streets.

Small boys played in puddles of melted snow, sometimes accompanied by dogs. A few chickens left behind by homesteaders roamed freely, spending their days dodging horses and wagons, while feral cats kept the mice and rats at bay.

Despite the mess, Sarah decided on a walk through town. Maybe some fresh air would make her feel better. *Maybe I'll even go for a ride . . . it's been months.* She knew Neal wouldn't approve, but right now she didn't care. There was a feeling of spring in the air, and, no matter the consequences, she wanted to ride. By the time she reached the stable, though, she realized riding horseback would be dangerous to her baby at going on six months along, so she asked Jacob Helms to hitch a buggy instead.

"Okay, let's go," said Sarah as the horse trotted from town. The cold air smelled of sage all around. It felt good in her lungs and against her face. She threw caution to the wind and urged the horse faster. Each stride gobbled up the road, and she was soon in the foothills of the Laramie Mountains southeast of the Meadows ranch.

After a while they slowed, and Sarah laughed out loud. "That was fun." The horse and buggy splashed through numerous small streams before reaching Sybille Creek. Snow still clung to the ground here, higher up and closer to the mountains.

Sarah recognized a spot along the creek where she had learned to swim. She shut her eyes and could almost relive that moment. Fish swam in the clear, cold waters of the creek, darting about in their own element.

Her first sight of the ranch up close drove the day's pleasure from her mind. She was shocked to see how badly the place needed upkeep, from the corral fence rails in disrepair to faded and peeling paint on the house and other buildings. Only the bunkhouse rebuilt after the fire remained in good shape.

Where was Trace Johnson, or José? She didn't see anyone as she urged the horse and buggy past the house, though she noticed a thin line of wood smoke coming from the chimney. Was Trace in there, or maybe in the barn? She drove the buggy toward the barn and pulled up, hearing voices from inside.

"I tell you, come summer there's going to be a bloodbath," said once voice. "When Neal unleashes all his gun hands on those sheep herders, it's going to be horrible. That whole sodbuster thing will seem mild in comparison."

A second voice spoke up in agreement.

Sarah felt alarmed at what she was hearing. *A bloodbath. A massacre of sheepmen.* If the men talking knew she was listening, it might get ugly. She gripped the reins, ready to turn and leave, when a familiar voice spoke from behind her.

"Don't go, Mrs. Neal. I think it's time you and I had a chance to visit. Your husband can't interrupt us out here."

A chill went up her spine, colder than the icy wind blowing down from the Laramie Mountains. Swagger stepped in front of her horse, a predatory smile on his face and his eyes gleaming like a wolf about to devour a newborn elk. His hungry stare frightened her.

Sarah tried to turn the horse and buggy away from Swagger, but he grabbed the animal's head and held tight. "No need to rush off. That's not very friendly."

"Let me go!" she shouted. "We have nothing to say."

"Why don't you just get down, and we'll see?"

"I need to get back to town. Jason is expecting me."

"Get down, or I'll pull you out of that buggy."

"No!"

He moved to her side. She kicked at him but missed. He grabbed her, yanked her roughly from the buggy, and pulled her close to him. "Now isn't this cozy? I've been waiting for this opportunity."

She fought to pull away. "Jason will kill you. You're an animal. I'm having a baby, for God's sake!"

"I know you feel like I do. I've seen the way you've been looking at me."

His unshaven, dirty face was pockmarked with red spots where pieces of skin were coming loose. She slapped him hard and lunged for freedom. He only held tighter. "Missy, you ain't going nowhere, so stop fighting me."

He leaned in and tried to kiss her. His foul breath and his unwashed stench made her gag. She managed to turn her head so his whiskered face brushed against her cheek. He pulled her closer, and she screamed, with little hope of anyone hearing her.

Swagger laughed and spun her around, then wrapped his arm around her from behind. "Behave, now, or I'll have to get rough." She felt the strength in his grip as he kissed the back of her neck and fought even harder to break his grip.

"Let her go!" It was Trace's voice, coming from the direction of the horse corrals.

"What the—" Swagger loosened his grip slightly as he turned to see who was talking.

"I said, let her go!"

Sarah tore free from Swagger's hold, then stepped clear and wiped her face. Trace Johnson stood just beyond Swagger, pointing a rifle at him.

Swagger glared. "Boy, you need to stay clear of this. This ain't none of your business."

"You need to leave her alone. Now back away!"

"I'm warning you, boy. Mind your own business. You're gonna get hurt," Swagger growled as he inched toward Trace, one hand just above his pistol.

"Sarah, get back in the buggy, and get out of here!" Trace shouted.

Sarah hesitated, unwilling to leave her friend confronting Swagger alone.

"Go, Sarah . . . now!"

She got in the buggy and picked up the reins. This was her chance to escape—maybe her only chance—and she had to think of her baby. Swagger shouted at her to stop. She wheeled the horse in a half circle and snapped the reins, urging the animal into a run. As she cleared the ranch house, she heard pistol fire followed by a rifle shot. A sob escaped her, but she didn't look back.

The buggy rattled over the ground toward Chugwater. Once, Sarah thought she heard a running horse behind her, but when she glanced over her shoulder, she saw nothing. *Unless he had a horse saddled and ready to ride, he hasn't had time to chase me yet.*

The distance to town was too far for her own horse to run all the way, and the bouncing buggy was taking a toll on her and the baby. She slowed to let the horse catch his breath and rest.

When they finally reached town, the horse was lathered in sweat. As they drove down Main Street, people scattered, along with a few free-range chickens and a mud-covered cur. At the stable, Jacob Helms grabbed the reins and gaped at Sarah. "What happened?"

"Never mind," she said. "I'm sorry I drove the horse so hard. I've got to get home."

Neal and Beatrice weren't at the house, thank God. Sarah went to her bedroom, found her pistol in a box, and held it tightly, trembling as she recalled the incident with Swagger. "Just let him come now. Let that animal come."

More than hour passed. Sarah sat in the kitchen with a wool shawl wrapped around her shoulders, shivering. There was no sign of Swagger, so she let herself relax a little. She guessed he wouldn't follow her into town and risk Neal seeing him.

Should she tell Jason what happened? No. Swagger would deny her accusations, making it her word against his. She decided to keep quiet and never again go anywhere unarmed. Heartsick, she wondered whether Trace was dead, or wounded without anyone to help him.

Her thoughts turned from Trace to what she'd overheard in the barn. Neal's gunmen, they'd said. She felt sick. *I should warn somebody. Who can I tell? Obviously not Jason. Sending a telegram to anyone would most certainly get back to him. Besides, where would I send it? I don't know what to do.*

Another hour later, Beatrice came home, followed shortly by Neal. Both were upset that Sarah didn't have a meal prepared, so they left to eat at the café. They didn't invite Sarah to join them.

Outside, the sun disappeared behind the mountains, and a cold wind drifted over the valley. The Chinook was gone . . . spring was still weeks away. Another snowstorm was building on the backside of the Laramie range, and up along Iron Mountain the snow was already falling.

Swagger sat on his horse behind Sarah's house and watched her through the kitchen window. The end of his cigarette glowed in the darkness. Light from inside streamed through the window glass and reflected off a nearby shed. The gunman finished his smoke, licked his cold lips, and backed his horse down the alley. The animal nearly stepped on a stray dog, which gave a ragged growl in response.

Sarah heard the dog and glanced outside but saw only darkness. She strained her ears, but all was quiet. She took a deep breath and touched the pistol hidden in her apron pocket.

CHAPTER 27

A cracking, ripping sound broke the silence of the night as a branch heavy-laden with snow and ice tore away from its mother tree and fell to earth. The ugly sound sliced through the dark morning air and woke Amos from a deep sleep. The silence that followed was deafening, leaving an eerie soundless void in which the imagination was free to roam.

With eyes wide open, alert, and searching, he saw only darkness in the small sheep wagon he called home. The night was quiet, and he found no answer to what had roused him. Yet something had stirred his sleep-bound senses, forcing him wide awake.

Maybe wolves in the flock.

When he got up and opened the wagon door, he saw only a peaceful, snow-covered landscape bathed in the moon's fading light. The sheep were silent, apparently undisturbed by whatever woke him. Although he couldn't see them in the ebbing moonlight, he assumed the flock was bedded down along the windbreak out of sight. Hank lay quietly inside near the wagon door, still recovering from his injuries.

Amos fixed a cup of thick, black coffee, rich and bold to the taste, put on his heavy coat, and stepped into the new day still deep in its black, pre-dawn womb. He put the dog outside in a comfortable spot under the wagon with food and water. The temperature was near zero. He felt its sting on his face, and his nostrils failed to warm the cold air before sending it into his lungs. He shivered and pulled his wool coat tight around him.

With his rifle in his gloved hand, he walked toward the windbreak and belatedly sensed something wrong. The flock was too quiet. His pace quickened, his strides across the snow-covered terrain toward the tree line driven with urgency.

The sheep were gone. He saw where they had bedded down for the night, but now the area was empty. The entire flock had disappeared.

Along the eastern horizon, the first shafts of sunrise explored the new day. Shades of purple and pink fringed the morning sky, and bright orange streaks pushed back the fading night. As the growing light of day chased the darkness westward, Amos found where the flock had trailed a few lead sheep into the nearby timber, like the masses that often blindly follow one person into an uncertain future. He saw no evidence the flock might have been driven from the area.

I hope you've chosen your leaders wisely, Amos thought.

With the sunrise, the trail was easy to follow, and Amos went in pursuit. The sheep had not drifted toward the main flock at the far end of the valley like he expected. Instead, they'd gone in the opposite direction. He found it strange they would move as one away from shelter and feed. The flock had wandered higher through a stand of ponderosa pine, then followed a cold, boulder-laden stream. The stream flowed down from a rugged nearby mountain range before dropping into a small canyon. Amos kept going and eventually found the flock under a massive outcropping, protected from the wind. Still, he saw no apparent reason for their behavior.

Do sheep really need a reason for acting strange?

He searched the area and discovered signs that a pack of ten to fifteen wolves had been trailing the flock. He tightened his grip on his rifle as he surveyed the area again and was surprised to find steps near the outcropping. Dug out of the rock wall, they went up about forty feet before disappearing on top of an overhang. He was curious where they led. He also suspected the wolves were close by and might attack the flock at any moment. He needed a better vantage point to see the surrounding area.

He slung his rifle over his left shoulder and began to climb. Every once in a while, his foot slipped on the narrow steps, and twice he nearly fell.

After about ten minutes, he reached the top of the ledge, where he found a large cave. Rocks laid carefully on top of one another created a stone wall blocking much of the cave's entrance but leaving a small opening.

Outside, long-cold ashes marked the remains of an old fire pit. He looked back over his shoulder, and, to his surprise, in the distance he could make out the valley where the Lincoln family made their home. Here, several miles away and higher up someone might be able to see everything that went on in the valley.

The landscape triggered a flash of memory. *There were three of us . . . no, four . . . following cattle rustlers. Am I a cattleman? We were looking out at a valley just like this one. There was a meadow, or was that someone's name? Meadows? And there were shots. A kid was there. Was he shot? Is that when I was shot?*

Much closer by, someone had created a small enclosed area for keeping livestock . . . sheep, goats, or even horses. The sheep in it now were the Lincoln flock, at the end of their morning adventure.

They looked well and safe enough, so Amos ducked into the cave. He found a pool of water near the entrance, and along one wall were smooth rock benches apparently used for sleeping. Near another fire pit inside lay pieces of shattered pottery. "Wonder who lived in this place?" he murmured. "It's not big enough for a tribe, more like home for a small family."

In his eagerness to explore this ancient dwelling, he failed to notice the sky had grown dark, and the wind was rising. It was already mid-afternoon, and the smell of snow hung on the thick, damp air.

The first big flakes came down as he emerged from the cave, then began falling heavy and thick as he stepped toward the edge and looked down at the flock. They huddled in the enclosure, out of the wind. Their heavy wool coats kept them warm even at this altitude, and, with the stream nearby, they had access to water. Feed was another matter.

It was snowing harder now, and Amos decided it was too late in the day to try driving the flock back to the Lincoln valley. Going home would have to wait until morning.

He decided to stay in the cave until the storm passed. His pockets contained only the dried remnants of a sourdough biscuit and a few pieces of venison jerky. However meager, it would have to sustain him. He built a small fire, and heat soon filled the gloomy chamber. He ate the biscuit pieces and made sure the fire had enough fuel to last a while, then went back outside.

The snow quickly accumulated on his hat and coat. As he checked again on the flock below, he noticed subtle motion along the rocky, man-made wall. The wolves were on the move, no longer able to see or smell Amos standing on the ledge above them.

An old alpha male with fiery black eyes was the first to advance from behind the rocks. Two young, nearly black females followed. One walked with a slight limp and had a white scar along her left shoulder. The second female trotted alongside, her tongue out as if trying to collect the falling snowflakes. The rest of the pack approached cautiously, following their leaders.

A young ewe, heavy with an unborn lamb, was their target. She stood slightly apart from the flock and stared in nervous disbelief at the approaching wolves. Despite the obvious threat to her life, she didn't move.

The heavy snowfall made it hard to see, but Amos took careful aim at one of the young females and fired. The shot rang out hard and loud in the mountain air, its echo rattling off nearby rocky ledges and canyon walls as it found its mark.

The second female flinched and turned away, escaping into the snowstorm. The others hesitated, unsure of what was happening, as Amos fired a second shot in their direction. The bullet missed and kicked up snow in the face of one of the males. The pack turned as one and ran, except for the leader.

The older alpha continued to advance, hunger overwhelming any fear. He hurried toward the ewe, then stopped in mid-stride as Amos's third well-placed shot found its mark in the wolf's head. The nervous ewe took an uneasy step back, as if not sure what had just happened.

Amos aimed a fourth, fifth, and sixth shot in the direction of the rocky wall from where the wolves had come, hoping to send a message. He thought he saw movement away from the rocks as the pack withdrew but in the heavy snowfall wasn't sure.

The young ewe inched toward the bodies of the two dead wolves. Red blood soiled the pristine white snow around their still-warm carcasses, and steam rose into the bitter cold air.

Satisfied that he'd turned aside any immediate threat to the flock, Amos retreated into the warm cave. Along one wall he found drawings of crudely painted animals and men with spears. In one drawing, a man held a long spear above his head while dog-like figures surrounded him. Amos shivered, recognizing the never-ending ritual of man and wolf laying claim to these mountains and isolated valleys. Later, even as he sought sleep in this ancient and abandoned, rock-walled home, he envisioned the glowing eyes of the wolves who surely waited outside in the cold night and darkness.

The flickering firelight gave motion to the drawings, bringing the paintings to life on the walls around him. The crackling embers sounded almost like voices of the men on the painted walls. The wind outside howled, rose, then fell back only to rise again. Amos shuddered and held tight to his rifle. Flickering firelight appeared as dancing shadows against the backside of his closed eyelids. Time passed slowly.

Before sleep finally caught up with him, he watched as, in his mind's eye, a spear-carrying petroglyph danced a warrior's fight, and outside the wind howled and wailed a warrior's death song.

During the night, the wolf pack returned and attacked the pregnant ewe along with three others. Only the blood-covered ground showed their coming and going, all traces of which would soon be covered with snow. The sheep huddled close together, blind to their role in life's never-ending struggle for survival, while snowflakes and death filled the night.

CHAPTER 28

Seven riders cleared the snow-filled mountain pass single file and dropped into a stand of pine and aspen trees, where more snow lay heavy on the ground hidden from the sun. Each man was well armed. Snow and ice clung to their unkempt facial hair and covered their shoulders. Each rider looked more like a long-neglected mountain man than a well-paid gunman from Chugwater, Wyoming.

None spoke. The seven riders had been told to put a scare into the Lincoln family, perhaps even convincing the sheep owner to move from his isolated valley home. If someone got hurt or killed, so much the better.

The child in Sarah's ever-expanding stomach had been restless through the night, keeping her awake. At three in the morning, she finally got up and fixed herself a cup of coffee. Neal had not come home the previous night, choosing to stay at the saloon instead. She sipped some coffee, then wrapped a shawl around her shoulders and stepped out onto the front porch in the cold morning air. Darkness still covered Chugwater, but she could see the outlines of several men riding down Main Street, heading out of town. She counted seven.

Why would anyone be up and riding out at this time of night? Abruptly, she remembered what she'd overheard at the Meadows ranch and shuddered. *A bloodbath,* they'd said . . . and her husband was involved.

Now that she knew about Neal's ruthless dealings, she suspected these men were riding out of town on his orders. There was nothing she could do. Her hands were tied. Without knowing against whom Neal's men might strike next, she felt helpless. She was seven months pregnant and couldn't even ride anywhere, much less provide any viable assistance to anyone.

Harassment against the sheep owners had started slowly, compared to the burnings and beatings of the sodbusters, but she knew now that Neal wanted them gone. He'd begun by targeting those who mainly raised sheep, but now and then his men took it upon themselves to assault other sheep owners, even those few cattlemen who were trying sheep.

Stories and rumors about beatings and harassment were rampant, and Sarah was afraid to ask if they were true, even though she knew they were. She had nobody . . . no knight in shining armor, no family or friends to help with any kind of resistance.

Former friends and neighbors shunned her, some blaming her because she'd married Neal, most afraid of retaliation.

There were also rumors about Cheyenne Mitchell, Neal's not-so-secret friend at the saloon. Word was, the young woman might be with child . . . Neal's child. He was seldom home anymore, choosing to stay in his office or at the saloon.

Sarah finished her coffee. She thought about returning to bed, but knew she wouldn't sleep, so she stayed up until the sun rose and then slowly set about making herself breakfast. Each day she did her chores and performed her responsibilities as a wife, trying to remain above the personal turmoil and anguish swirling within her. The same determination that had made her strong growing up now served her well.

She wanted to leave, maybe return to her uncle and aunt in Nebraska. But she worried about what Neal might do to her and the baby if she tried and failed.

Later in the morning, Sarah put on a wool coat, found a shawl, and draped it over her head. She needed supplies, and knew better than to ask her mother-in-law for assistance. Neal's mother ran the general store with an iron fist, charging outlandish prices for even the most basic daily necessities. Complaints about weevil-infested flour, rat-infested grain, and rancid meat were ignored, though she generally sold better foodstuffs to Sarah for Neal's consumption.

As she stepped outside, the cold wind of late March momentarily took her breath away. Her coat and shawl did little to stave off the biting chill. She gasped and hurried down the plank walkway toward the general store.

Mud and remnants of the most recent snowstorm, mixed with isolated piles of horse manure, created a strong smell on the morning air. Behind the café, two dogs fought over a bone. Their snarling voices carried loudly to Sarah's ears. The town smelled of decay and the moldy remnants of a long winter.

She reached the store and stepped inside, then halted as she realized Neal was there, arguing with his mother. They must be in the back. She heard the name Fernsmith, but little else. Apparently the town's only blacksmith had done or said something to make Neal angry. She thought of leaving but wasn't quick enough. Neal and Beatrice came out into the main room and spotted her.

"You listening to us?" Neal shouted.

"No! I just walked in."

Beatrice quickly busied herself arranging bolts of cloth on a store shelf.

Neal stepped closer to Sarah. "What do you want?"

"Supplies. We need supplies. Flour, sugar . . ."

"Mother can get your damned supplies. I told you to stay home. Stay off the streets. You never listen to me. I'm your husband, dammit."

Sarah nodded. An awkward silence fell as Neal stared at her. Finally, she said, "Can't I go ahead and get a few things since I'm here?"

"Get what you came for, and then get yourself home, out of my sight!"

He stayed and watched briefly as Beatrice took the short list from her and gathered the needed items, then abruptly left. *Probably going back to the saloon,* she thought. *That little tramp will be waiting for him.*

She moved closer to the counter next to a barrel of trash overflowing with rotten tomatoes, spoiled meat, and other discarded items. *How can anyone keep something that smells so bad inside? Take out your trash, Beatrice.*

Glancing again at the filthy pile, she noticed a garbage-stained envelope lying partially exposed under the remains of some moldy bacon. Then she saw it was addressed to *Sarah Neal, c/o General Store, Chugwater, Wyoming.*

Beatrice wasn't watching. Sarah pulled the envelope out of the trash barrel and looked at the return address. Her heart raced when she saw it was from Tom and Molly, and unopened. She quickly stuck it inside her bodice. There would be time to read it later on.

I wonder who threw it away, Jason or his mother? Regardless, I was never supposed to see it, she thought as Beatrice approached.

"Here's your stuff," the older woman said. "Now I've got real work to get done."

Sarah gathered up the items and left the store. She'd only taken a few steps into the street when she spotted Swagger and Lake standing in front of the blacksmith shop.

Robert Fernsmith was gesturing wildly, and she heard all three men arguing. She looked around for Neal but didn't see him. Fernsmith had dared to question Neal's motives and actions on several occasions over the past months, and her husband had tolerated the man's comments because the town needed the blacksmith. But Fernsmith had become more vocal lately, especially after the homesteader debacle and the harassment of local sheep owners.

Sarah knew it was only a matter of time before things boiled over. Where was Missy Fernsmith? Nowhere near, Sarah hoped.

Only a few people were on the street, all ignoring the confrontation at the blacksmith's. Arguments with Swagger and Lake usually didn't end well. Despite her own fear, Sarah crept closer.

"Listen, old man, you've got to pay the town business tax," Swagger shouted.

"I ain't paying nothing," Fernsmith said. "Now get out of my sight."

"You also owe for back taxes, and we aim to collect."

"I told you already. I ain't paying."

Lake moved toward Fernsmith. The blacksmith took two steps back. He was a big man with powerful muscles under his heavy coat. He never carried a gun . . . his size and strength were usually enough to help him avoid most fights. This was different. Both Swagger and Lake were heavily armed and had no qualms about using those weapons.

"Pay up, or we'll confiscate your property until you do," Lake snarled.

"Go to Hell!"

As Fernsmith turned to walk away, Swagger drew his pistol and swung at the back of the big man's head with it. Instead, he struck the blacksmith a glancing blow on the man's right shoulder.

Fernsmith staggered, then turned to face Swagger. He grabbed the surprised sheriff by his gun hand and spun him around. A bullet exploded from Swagger's pistol and hit the ground near a cur dog crossing the street a few yards away.

A big fist caught Swagger in the jaw and sent him sprawling backward into a mixture of mud and manure. Fernsmith turned his attention to Lake but was a split second too slow. The deputy yanked out his pistol and fired point-blank at the unarmed man.

The blacksmith clutched his chest and stepped backward, disbelief and shock written on his face. He stumbled sideways as Lake fired a second time. Fernsmith fell face down and lay still.

Bile rose in Sarah's throat. Then she heard Missy scream. Sarah hurried forward as Fernsmith's wife ran through a puddle of muddy water, narrowly missed by a team of horses pulling a freight wagon. Missy reached her dead husband just ahead of Sarah.

Swagger and Lake backed away.

"You saw it!" Lake shouted. "We was trying to arrest him, and he resisted. We was in our rights as duly appointed lawmen."

None of the few people on the street said anything. All that could be heard was Missy's sobbing.

Sarah knelt beside her friend. "Missy . . . I'm so sorry . . ."

Newly bereft, Missy Fernsmith looked at Sarah with burning hate. "Go home, Sarah Neal. Go home to your murdering husband."

Neal watched from the second-story balcony of the saloon, just outside Cheyenne Mitchell's bedroom. He smiled and turned to her. "All's well, sweetheart. Now, where were we?"

The seven riders Sarah had watched leave town before daybreak crossed Horse Creek and entered the Lincolns' valley. It was almost noon. They drew up near Jake's sheep wagon and waited while one of them checked and found it empty. There was no sign of life anywhere. The sheepdog cowered under the wagon, hidden by some tack. Even the sheep the men had seen days earlier were gone. The gunmen decided to ride on toward their intended target, the Lincoln homestead.

"Maybe they already got the message and left," said a man named Baxter.

"Not likely," another gunman said. "That old man is a tough old coot . . . harder than a woodpecker's beak. You gotta admire him for that. Take more than a few dead sheep to get his attention."

"That's why we're here," Baxter answered. "Time he got a personal invite to clear out."

The gunmen rode south toward the far end of the valley. It didn't take long before they heard bleating sheep. Dunwoody was the first to spot the Lincoln home a little distance away, with wood smoke curling out of the small chimney. "Looks like somebody's feeding hay to them woolies. See . . . off to the side near that lean-to. See them? Over there." Dunwoody pointed.

Baxter gave an ugly grin. "Let's go say hello. Pay 'em a friendly visit. I'm tired of riding, and my trigger finger is getting itchy."

Patrick Lincoln saw them first and looked for his rifle, but it was out of reach. He felt the hair on the back of his neck stand up as a cold shiver slid down his spine. Beside him, Willie looked scared.

"Patrick?" Willie whispered.

"Yeah, I see them."

"Wonder who they are?"

Patrick didn't answer. He tried inching closer to his rifle but stopped short when Baxter shouted, "Where's your old man?"

"Who wants to know?" Patrick answered with false bravado.

"Listen, kid. We're asking the questions here. Now, where is he? I won't ask again."

"He's at . . . at the house."

"We've got a message for him. You can tell him for us. Get out of this valley, and take these nasty-smelling woolies with him."

Again, Patrick eased toward his rifle. "Tell him yourself!"

Smoke from burning hay drifted over the lower valley and through the crevices in the cottonwood log walls of the Lincoln cabin. Little Ned, the youngest, was the first to smell the smoke and hear the gunshots. James Lincoln, who'd been standing near the fireplace talking to Martha, ran for the cabin's front door and flung it open. The hay shed was engulfed in flames, smoke rising thick and heavy before the wind snatched it up and carried it away.

Men on horseback were shooting the sheep. Their harsh laughter mixed with the frantic bleats of wounded and dying animals, and the crackling flames as the shed burned.

"The boys! Patrick and Willie!" shouted Martha.

"Stay with the girls. Barricade yourselves in the house, and don't come out unless I come get you. Make sure the rifles are loaded!" shouted James. He picked up his own rifle along with some extra cartridges and ran outside toward the melee, praying for Patrick and Willie. He couldn't see either of them.

He took cover behind a stack of wood near the cabin. As he returned fire, the men wheeled their horses toward the upper valley and Amos's sheep wagon. James ran through the thick smoke past the bleating sheep. Carcasses of several wethers and ewes lay on the ground. A few were still kicking. Blood covered the ground, turning large patches of snow crimson. "Patrick? Willie? Where are you?"

Moments later, he found Willie standing in a daze with a bloody gash across his forehead and dark bruises covering his arms. Willie led his father to a mud-filled ditch, lined with icy snow. Patrick lay there, his body limp and bloody. He moaned in pain as his father touched him.

It started to rain . . . an icy rain only found in high mountain valleys. The kind of rain that steals the heat of a man's soul and leaves him alone without hope.

CHAPTER 29

With sunrise Amos emerged from the cave, stretched, and looked off toward the valley the Lincolns called home. Nothing seemed out of place. He climbed down from his lofty perch on the ledge and prepared to drive the flock back toward the Lincoln valley and home . . . or, at least, the only home he knew. His task was simple . . . get the wayward flock home, and routine would be re-established. Normal would return.

He started the flock back toward the valley. The hungry animals moved quickly as if knowing feed waited at the end of their journey. Content to follow their course, Amos only now and then needed to redirect them. Snowdrifts created by the previous night's storm caused some delay, but by noon they had reached Horse Creek.

The sun shone brightly, and in places the snow had melted. Amos reminded himself spring was not far off, and such days were becoming more common, especially where the sun's warm rays penetrated the valley floor. He drifted into a quiet melancholy, wondering if his current situation bore any resemblance to his previous life. He knew come spring he would need answers. Perhaps someone in town might know him. But, for now, the Lincoln family needed him as much as he needed them.

Shouts of men up ahead jolted him back to reality. "Look over there! More sheep and lots of them, headed this way."

"Where did they come from?"

"Doesn't matter. They're sheep, ain't they? Start shooting!"

Amos could see riders now, on the pathway by the leading edge of the flock. Four . . . no, five, and there could be more. Each man pulled weapons and began firing into the sheep.

Amos swung his own rifle in their direction and fired back. Two lead ewes fell dead beside the stream. Another, badly wounded, lay kicking in the snow in her death throes. Two more shots rang out, and a wether fell dead. The second shot tore bark off a nearby pine tree. As the flock milled about, disoriented and nervous, Amos ducked for cover behind a pine log.

Two more riders were already on the far side of the stream. Amos fired wildly toward those still waiting to cross. He heard a shout: "Someone's shooting at us. Let's go!"

One of the remaining five gunmen urged his horse into the stream. This time, Amos took careful aim and fired. The man fell dead into the rushing water, and his body caught on the limbs of a partially submerged tree. The corpse's eyes stared blankly skyward as the stream pulled at the lifeless limbs.

Two more riders whipped their horses into the water, while their fellows on the opposite bank dismounted and tried to provide cover fire. Amos's next shot caught one of the men still in the water in the shoulder, but he managed to stay in the saddle, screaming in pain as he urged his horse toward the far bank.

Bullets came closer to the pine log as the remaining gunmen determined Amos's exact location. He tried changing positions, but the deep snow and deadfall prevented him from moving far. Still, it was enough to let him get off a couple more shots and hit one of the two men still needing to cross the stream. The gunslinger fell dead, his horse running off toward the valley and the sheep wagon. The remaining gunman had already turned downstream, looking for another place to cross.

Amos turned his attention to those on the far side of the

stream and watched as the men, including the wounded gun-man, escaped into the trees.

Once they were out of sight, he gathered the scattered sheep and again started them toward home, seriously worried now. These men had come from the valley and they were obviously on a mission. He kept looking back over his shoulder in case they returned.

He reached the sheep wagon and scooped up a new supply of rifle cartridges. He found Hank under the wagon, whimpering and trembling in fear from all of the shooting. He looked in the direction of the Lincoln cabin and saw smoke rising, dark and thick. Not the ordinary smoke of someone fixing a midday meal over a fireplace, but the deep ominous smoke of something tragic. He had to go find the Lincoln family, see if they were all right.

The deep snow made it difficult to walk. Amos tried follow-ing the tracks the gunmen had left behind in the snow, but even so the journey was hard and took valuable time. More than once he fell from fatigue and exhaustion. Finally, he reached the Lincoln cabin.

The area looked like a battlefield. Dead and dying sheep lay everywhere, their blood staining the snow. Amos feared the Lin-coln family might be dead as well. Then he saw James carrying Patrick's limp and wounded body toward the cabin.

Late in the day, Sarah remembered the letter from Molly and Tom. Hoping for solace, she pulled it from her pocket and opened it. Her friends wrote they were returning to Chugwater soon. She glanced at the date and saw it had been mailed three weeks earlier. That meant they could arrive any time.

Neal stepped into the early evening and watched five of the men he'd sent out before daybreak riding slowly down the main street. One man's clothing was bloody, and he was taken straight to the doctor's office.

There were seven men this morning.

Neal met the remaining four gunmen in front of his office and demanded to know what happened. "Everything went fine until we ran into some fella with a rifle, herding a sheep flock along Horse Creek," Baxter told him. "Sheep owners never fought back before, not with bullets."

Furious, Neal blamed the Lincoln family. "Somebody's going to pay dearly for this!" he shouted. "I want someone's hide."

"Boss, I ain't rightly sure it was Lincoln. Not the second fight. Pretty sure it wasn't old man Lincoln, in fact. We left him down by his cabin. He was shooting at us as we rode away."

"Who, then?"

"Maybe somebody who works for him. Maybe he's hired himself a herder. Or maybe another sheep man moved in up there. We did find a sheep wagon, and it was a different flock."

Neal stalked into his office and slammed the door behind him, leaving his men standing in the street. He snatched up a cigar but didn't light it. Instead he stood looking out the window, deep in thought. A woodstove burned hot in one corner, and its heat warmed the right side of his face. A lantern provided the room's only light.

Outside in the dusk, people moved about, some headed for Cheyenne, Deadwood, or Sheridan, still others merely going about their daily business before going home. Neal felt empty, misunderstood, and underappreciated.

How have I come to this? he thought. *Back in Nebraska I had a successful law practice, a nice home, and lots of friends. The women all loved me. Now I'm stuck out here with a bunch of uneducated morons and a wife who hates me.*

Don't they understand? I'm a good person. If everyone would just listen to me . . . follow my instructions. I know what's best. We could all be rich. Everyone is just jealous. Only Cheyenne understands me.

He sighed and turned toward the stove's warmth as Swagger, Lake, and Baxter entered the room. "If all these damn sheep owners would just leave peacefully," he said. "If they would just realize this is cattle country, I wouldn't need to use force. That's prime grazing land, and I need it for the Swan Land and Cattle Company. I don't want to hurt anyone, not really. It's their own fault for pushing me."

The other men said nothing. A large chunk of ice and snow fell loose from the roof of a nearby building and crashed to the ground. Neal heard the noise and glanced toward it.

"Lincoln is responsible for killing my men today. He's got to pay for that. Those people just keep pushing me. Now I've got to make them understand."

"We'll get 'em," said Swagger.

The lantern flickered as if in agreement while a dog barked outside. The last light faded, and darkness consumed the town, matching Neal's bitter mood as snow from another winter storm began to fall.

CHAPTER 30

Cold drizzle mixed with snow fell throughout the night, meandering back and forth between freezing and something slightly warmer. Patrick Lincoln hovered near death, often crying out in pain. The morning broke dark and grey, with no sign of improving weather. A sorrowful, fearful mood matched the outdoor landscape.

The boy needed a doctor's care, and soon. James Lincoln was afraid to leave his family alone in case the gunmen returned, so Amos volunteered to bring Patrick into Chugwater. He would take the sheep wagon and try to make the injured boy as comfortable as possible. The sheep he'd watched all winter would be moved back near the homestead and mixed with the remainder of the main flock.

Preparations were made, and by noon Amos was under way. Behind him, Martha Lincoln's sobs filled the air as she watched her oldest son being taken from home.

The going was slow and methodical. The wagon couldn't follow the same trail as someone on horseback, so it would take hours longer to reach town. They followed Horse Creek and crossed farther down. Near sunset they passed through the small town of Iron Mountain, which had no doctor, and camped along an unnamed creek. Patrick remained unconscious.

Best for him, Amos thought. *Shield him from the pain.*

Neal's wounded gunman died during the night. Leaving the

house just before dawn, Neal found Swagger and Lake in the café eating breakfast. Their presence kept other potential customers away, allowing Neal to talk freely.

"I want the Lincoln family wiped out, every single one of them—man, woman, and any children, along with anyone who's helping them. Burn that place to the ground, and kill all those stinking sheep. Leave nothing up there alive, and bring me the head of whoever killed my men.

"Take today, even a couple days; gather the men you need to get it done. Take men you can count on, good with a gun. Send a message once and for all. Let me know when you're ready, and see me before you leave. You understand my meaning?"

Swagger glanced at Lake and grinned.

"Boss, we got this. I hate them woolies, and them dead boys were friends of ours."

Amos was up and moving with Patrick before daybreak, hoping to make Chugwater by mid-morning. Patrick was still unconscious, but breathing. The terrain east of Iron Mountain was smoother and the hills more rolling, so they traveled easier and faster. Once in town, Amos stopped a freight wagon and asked the driver where to find the doctor.

"Doc Collins has his office near the stable," the driver said. "But mister, you'd better hide that wagon. It smells like sheep, and this ain't no place for a sheep man right now. The fellow who runs this town hates sheep men, and he will kill you with no questions asked."

The freight wagon moved off. Amos looked around, then turned his own wagon into a nearby alley. Following a series of back streets to keep out of sight, he reached the doctor's office.

Doc Collins, a youngish man with light-brown hair and beard, immediately took Patrick inside and began to examine him. Amos stepped out onto the plank walkway and looked up and down the quiet street. It felt familiar, in a way he couldn't quite explain.

Seems like I've been here before. Down there's the blacksmith shop and the hotel. Over there is the café and the saloon . . . and the bank. I know this place.

He spotted the general store and decided to go there, see if someone might recognize him.

Inside, an old woman with dark eyes and a sour face waited on two young men buying extra cartridges. The men were bragging about going to kill sheepherders. Amos stepped behind some fencing supplies and harness, just as one of the men mentioned the name Lincoln. A chill climbed up his back, and he fought down panic. The two men laughed about killing woolies and sheep lovers as they collected their purchases and went out the door.

The old woman spotted him and turned in his direction. "You there! Why are you hiding?"

"I'm not. Just checking out this equipment."

"What do you want? Come out of there."

Amos stepped out from behind the pile and started toward the counter. "I was wondering—"

"Oh, my goodness," the woman shouted. "You stink!"

He hesitated, realizing for the first time he hadn't shaved or taken a bath in weeks, if not months. His own mother wouldn't recognize him.

"When was the last time you washed? My God, you smell like rotten sheep."

"Listen, lady. There's no need to be rude. There's a reason—"

Again, she cut him off. "We don't allow sheepherders in here. No woolie lovers in my store. Now get out!"

"I have a right to be in here. I'm just looking for some information."

"Get out!" She pulled a small pistol from behind the counter and pointed it at his chest. "I said, get out!"

Startled, Amos held both hands up, well above the pistol on his hip that he'd borrowed from James Lincoln. "I'm going. I'm going," he said.

Once on the street again, he headed back toward the doctor's office. A young woman heavy with child was headed toward him, in a hurry. He stepped aside and into the doorway of the doctor's office as she passed. She turned her head away and seemed to flinch as she went by and smelled him.

He watched her retreating figure a moment longer. *She looks so familiar. I wonder—*

"Stranger?" said the doctor.

Amos turned. The doctor stood near the examining table where Patrick lay. Concern for the boy banished all thoughts about the woman.

"The boy is in really bad shape," the doctor said, his face grave. "I think he will survive, but he needs to stay here a few days so I can watch him."

Relief spread through him. "That'll work," Amos said. "I need to tell his family." He rubbed his bearded chin. "By the way, is there any chance you might know me? I was hurt last fall and can't remember much about my past."

Doc Collins looked closely at him. "No, I don't know you. Then again, I arrived in town myself just before Christmas. The old doctor retired and left town. I'm still meeting everyone."

Disappointment left him cold. "Just thought I'd ask."

"You say you don't remember much?"

"Just bits and pieces. Like this town. It looks familiar. And that woman who just went by out there . . . seems like I should know her."

"Sounds like your memory is gradually returning. Chances are it'll come back. Probably happen suddenly when it does."

"Thanks. Guess I'd better get out of here. I was told I stink like sheep."

"I've smelled worse. But then, they'd been dead for a few days. You *are* a little rank, but nothing a good bath and shave wouldn't cure." The doctor laughed. "That's my diagnosis."

Amos looked out the front door just as the stagecoach from Cheyenne rolled past and stopped in front of the general store. He watched as two elderly men stepped out of the coach, followed by a woman with bright-red hair and a tall man about his own age. The man draped an arm around the red-haired woman's shoulders.

Amos moved into the doorway. "Those people. Those people who just got off the stage. The young couple. I think I know them." He turned toward the doctor. "Do *you* know them?"

"No. But like I said, when your memory does come back, it could happen suddenly."

Amos resisted the urge to go ask the young couple if they knew him. So far, he hadn't been well received in town. Then the woman he'd passed on the street rushed up and gave each of the new arrivals a big hug.

"Tell me, Doctor . . . who's that woman?"

"Sarah Neal." Doc Collins stepped up alongside him. "She and her husband Jason Neal are expecting a baby in a few weeks."

Amos took a deep breath.

"Son . . . you want to stay away from her. She's a nice person, but her husband is the most hated and feared man in the territory. The only thing he hates more than homesteaders is sheepherders. I'd bet good money his men were the ones who hurt your young friend here. I'm almost sure of it."

The doctor clapped him gently on the shoulder. "You'd better go out the back and get your wagon out of here before someone sees it. Your life won't be worth a plugged nickel if the wrong person spots you, especially smelling like sheep."

"Yes . . . yes, of course. Thank you." Amos recalled the boastful men buying cartridges at the store and shivered. "I've got to go warn the Lincolns this man Neal is sending gunmen to kill them."

He left through the back door, climbed onto the wagon, and left, following the same back streets he'd traveled upon his arrival. The hurried trip back to the Lincolns' valley was uneventful, which gave him plenty of time to think. The town and people had triggered something, but he wasn't sure what. The memories felt just out of reach, and he was frustrated.

He stopped the wagon to rest the horse along a narrow stream near Iron Mountain. He built a small fire to fix some coffee, then rolled a cigarette and tried to relax. The day's events raced through his mind. The young couple from the stage, the pregnant woman greeting them like family . . . he knew them all, but how?

Suddenly, everything came clear.

"Jake!" he stammered. "I'm Jake Summers. That was Tom and Molly in town . . . they went away for a while. That's right, they got married. And the other woman . . ." he hesitated. "Sarah . . . Sarah Meadows. But the doctor said Sarah Neal."

His heart sank as he realized that, in his absence, Sarah had married Jason Kelly Neal. "And she's having his baby. Oh, my God . . . his baby."

Memory flooded through him like the water running over the rocks in the nearby stream. All of it came back clear, the reality cold. "She married Neal. She married that worthless no-account. It must've been his men who shot me and left me for dead. Now she's with him. How could she do that?"

Restless, he stood and paced. "And old man Meadows, I wonder what he thinks about them being married? And Tom, and Molly? Do they know? They must. So much has happened.

I don't belong there anymore."

In the distance, a coyote yipped for his mate, a cry of desperation and loneliness. Jake moved closer to the fire, sat down, and threw on another stick of wood. More memories rushed over him like the cold Wyoming wind. He shivered as his mind grew crowded with past and more recent events. Thoughts of his family in Texas . . . his trip north with Harry Haythornwaite's cattle drive north to Ogallala, Nebraska . . .

Made $30 a month. The boss paid us a dollar bonus for every new stray we could add to that herd. Met Tom Scott up in the Judith Basin Country of Montana. We came south together and ended up on William Thompson's Box T Ranch. I was foreman of that cattle outfit. Then I ended up helping Meadows near Chugwater . . . meeting Sarah.

"I've been involved with cattle since my young days, and now I'm helping sheep people. I owe them my life. They're good people. I need to help the Lincolns. The rest will take care of itself."

Having rested his horse, he moved out, pushing to reach the Lincoln cabin as fast as he could. Upon arrival, he relayed the good news about Patrick, and that his own memory had returned. The brief, happy mood quickly turned somber when he told them of Neal's plan to attack them, taking revenge for what happened a few days earlier. They had to get ready.

For the first time in weeks, Sarah found herself smiling. The return of Molly and Tom brought a sense of relief and hope. She invited them to dinner, knowing Neal probably wouldn't join them. Beatrice would be there, but she would be either interested in their brief stay in St. Louis and news of the "civilized" world, or not interested at all.

After a few pleasantries over dinner, Beatrice brought up "sodbusters and sheepherders" and her dislike for them.

"Why, just today, one of those sheep people came into my store. He smelled so bad . . . not just of sheep, but of gross uncleanliness. He needed a shave and a long bath. And he was so rude! I kept telling him to leave, but he wouldn't. Finally, I had to get my gun."

Sarah glanced at Molly and Tom, then turned a smile on Beatrice.

"You mean someone actually stood up to you? Why, how dare he? And a sheepherder with backbone. That's amazing."

Beatrice scowled. "Shut up, young lady. I'm your husband's mother. You'll treat me with respect."

Feeling good for the first time in weeks, Sarah wouldn't let up. "Maybe I'll get to meet your sheepherder friend one day," she said. "Sounds like a good man. In fact, I think I passed him on the street today."

Beatrice got up and stormed out of the room. The three friends finished their dinner and then talked long into the night, catching up. Neal never showed. Likely he'd found comfort with Cheyenne Mitchell at the saloon.

Later, finally settled in her bed, Sarah heard the call of a coyote on a distant hill near town and wept softly into her pillow. Seeing Tom and Molly had brought back memories, of their friendship and of Jake Summers.

"Oh, how I miss you," she whispered in the darkness.

The coyote's lonely yipping seemed to answer back but then was lost in the blackness of the Wyoming night and the ever-present wind.

CHAPTER 31

The cold winds of early dawn howled a mournful song. Cracks in the walls of the Lincoln cabin allowed the wind to penetrate, its wail like a warning on the fading edge of night. In place of the yips and cries of wolves and coyotes, there was silence. Even the sheep milled with nervous energy, as if hearing some unseen voice foretelling the fight to come.

Jake had warned them Neal's men would arrive soon. This time, they would come with numbers and intent to slaughter. They would not be turned back until the unsavory deed was done.

Sunlight pierced the mists throughout the valley as James Lincoln and his family prepared to defend their home. He and Martha had sent word to other sheep owners in neighboring areas, but nobody was expecting any help. They'd moved the flock into a narrow canyon downstream, near where the Lincoln boys had found Jake.

If Neal's gunmen find the sheep, it'll be like shooting rats in a barrel, Jake thought. *But we have no choice. If we can't defend the valley, the sheep will be killed anyway.*

He and James both knew they would be vastly outnumbered and outgunned, but running was not an option. As the sun began its climb toward midday, they declared themselves ready.

Jake figured Neal's men would follow much the same course as in the previous two raids. They wouldn't know they'd lost the element of surprise. In fact, it was Neal's men who were about to be caught off guard.

About noon, the sound of riders approaching carried to where Jake was. He guessed around twenty armed men had reached Horse Creek just above the place where Jake had spent the winter. Crossing the creek here was tenuous, made slightly worse by the early spring thaw higher in the mountains. Still, fording the stream anywhere easier meant going several miles in either direction.

The gunmen would need to cross in single file. Jake counted on as much. Martha Lincoln and the girls, along with little Ned, positioned themselves upstream behind the same deadfall Jake had used in his previous encounter with the marauders. Martha and the oldest girl, Catherine, were armed with rifles. Just downstream, Jake and James were equally armed and ready. They'd left the cabin and sheds unguarded, counting on the predictable nature of Neal's men. Jake had told everyone to hold their fire until at least five men had crossed the stream.

They all waited, tense with anticipation and fear. Once the initial five had crossed the stream, the rest would be either in the water or waiting on the far bank. The swift spring runoff would force each rider to concentrate on not being swept away by the current. Martha and Catherine were to shoot at those in the water. While Willie held their horses out of gun range, Jake and James would fire at those waiting on the far bank, forcing them back into the trees.

"Steady . . . don't shoot yet . . . steady," whispered Jake as Neal's men emerged from the trees along the stream. He counted twenty, led by so-called Sheriff Swagger. "Easy now."

Leaders of the group eased toward the water in single file, just as he'd figured. Swagger pulled up on his reins as his horse hesitated, then slid down the bank into the cold water. A second horse also balked along the snow-covered bank, and his rider spurred him forward hard.

Once the fifth man and his horse started up the near bank, Jake shouted, "Now! Start shooting!"

Rifle shots cracked through the air. Jake killed a rider about to enter the water. The dead man's horse bolted wildly back up the bank and into the next man in line. James shot a second man, creating bedlam on the far bank. The two attackers were down before the rest realized they were under attack.

Martha and Catherine fired at the riders in the stream. One man was struck in the shoulder and fell into the rushing water. His horse turned sideways, blocking the others from moving forward. A second shot hit another rider in the leg, and he screamed in pain. His horse lunged in panic, and he also fell into the water.

The element of surprise and the crossfire caught Neal's men unprepared. Swagger and Lake, in the first group of five to cross, didn't wait to learn the fate of their companions. The five men spurred their horses and rode. "Come on . . . follow me!" shouted Swagger. "We have a job to do. Forget those cowards that ran. We'll deal with them later."

Eight gunmen remained on the far bank, three in the stream. With a second round of shots, three more men died, two in the water and another on the far bank as he tried to get out of gun range. Martha's next shot struck a rider whose horse struggled to climb out of the stream. The man fell backwards into the churning, swift water.

The remaining seven men on the far bank scrambled for cover. Their taste for battle with sheepherders suddenly gone, they blended into the trees and disappeared.

Jake, James, and Willie finally withdrew toward the Lincoln cabin, following a little-used, narrow pathway along the stream.

Martha, the girls, and little Ned had pulled back once the shooting stopped and headed upstream out of harm's way. They would stay hidden until James Lincoln sent for them. Jake had told them about the cave he'd found days earlier, which would provide a good vantage point to defend themselves if someone followed.

"They ambushed us!" shouted one of the five men who'd crossed the stream. "They knew we were coming!"

"Never mind!" Swagger shouted back. "We still outnumber 'em. We'll deal with those who ran when we get back to town. Let's get this over with."

The remaining riders spread out and started down the valley.

"Kill anything you see," Swagger ordered. "We ain't supposed to leave anything up here alive."

As the group drew closer to the cabin, one rider spotted a little boy on horseback near the trees farther down. "There's one of them!" he shouted, pointing in the boy's direction.

Despite Swagger's warning that it could be a trap, the other four riders pulled their pistols and spurred their horses forward. The sting of being ambushed still fresh in their minds, they urged their horses into a run, eager for revenge on the closest target.

Willie waited, fighting the urge to turn and run. He'd been instructed to lure the attackers away from the cabin. At the last possible second, he turned his horse into the trees toward the stream and the open area where only a few months earlier he and Patrick had found Jake. He could hear the leader of the gunmen pleading with his men to slow down and watch out for a trap. They didn't listen.

Once Willie made the clearing, he slid down from his horse and ran to hide behind some boulders. As the gunmen reached the clearing, Jake and Willie's father opened fire.

One pursuer fell off his horse, dead. The three others realized their mistake and wheeled their horses around to escape the gunfire. They ran back toward their leader.

"Burn the damn cabin!" Swagger shouted as Lake and the other two men arrived from the trees. "Burn everything!"

They turned back toward the cabin and found themselves facing a small group of men . . . five on horseback, two on mules, and another in a well-worn carriage. All held rifles.

Baxter swore. "Sheepherders! Where the hell did they come from?"

Realizing the battle was lost, Swagger spun his horse away. "Every man for himself! I'm getting out of here." Lake and Baxter were right behind him. The remaining gunman fled in the opposite direction. Gunfire followed their escape.

Jake, James, and Willie emerged from the trees to cheers from their neighbors. The newcomers to the fight were sheepherders from neighboring valleys, all of whom had been harassed by Neal and his men. Now it was time to unite and defend themselves.

"I'm glad to see you guys. Not sure what we were going to do next," said James. "You saved our home and us. I can't ever thank you enough."

"We'll start gathering up the wounded and any horses we can find," said one of the other herders. "Then we'll take them to the authorities in Cheyenne. Not sure if we can get any justice down there, but we know we won't in Chugwater."

Jake mounted his horse and looked at the sheep owners, then longest at James Lincoln. "You know where to find Martha and the others. I've got to go finish something."

"Jake, be careful," James said. "From what you've told me, you've always been a cowpuncher. Seems strange, a cattleman helping us, but we're forever in your debt."

"You saved my life. Opened my eyes about a lot of things, but especially about how cattlemen and sheepherders can get along. Just now it's not about cattle and sheep . . . it's about right and wrong. Neal has got to be stopped."

Jake turned his horse into the late afternoon shadows and headed for Chugwater. He scarcely noticed the birds singing again, or the warm spring breeze against his face. His eyes and his focus were on what had to be done. Sarah had chosen this vicious man to be her husband, and to carry his baby. Maybe Jake didn't know her after all.

The time had come for justice, and maybe even vengeance.

CHAPTER 32

Noisy black flies darted from one brief landing spot to another, searching for whatever flies need to find. Otherwise, the saloon remained quiet, except for the occasional clink of beer glasses being washed. Neal sat at a table in one corner of the room along with Cheyenne Mitchell, awaiting news about the Lincoln raid. They seldom spoke.

Twenty men had gone out to clear the mountain valley of the Lincoln family and all their sheep. Neal expected little resistance and told his men as much. Until they returned triumphantly, he planned to sit in nervous silence nursing a small glass of whiskey. Not even Cheyenne dared disturb him while he waited.

"Lincoln doesn't seem to understand. I want him and his woolies gone. They will finally get the message today. Swagger is leading a small army up there."

One especially large fly found a temporary home on the rim of Neal's glass. Neal smashed it with the butt of his pistol. The action sent whiskey and broken glass in all directions, but the fly was dead. Cheyenne gasped. Neal smiled and said, "Collateral damage, my dear."

Two dust-covered young men, both wearing low-slung pistols, rushed into the saloon and demanded cold beers. A third man followed. Their horses stood outside with heads down, sweat drying on their shoulders and flanks, out of breath and exhausted from being ridden hard without rest.

One of the men spotted Neal and quickly looked away, as if

235

hoping beyond all hope not to be recognized as part of the group sent to eliminate the Lincolns earlier that day.

Neal stood and moved toward the bar. "What happened? Where are Swagger, Lake, and the others? Did you get the job done? Are those woolie lovers dead?"

"Don't know. We got separated," said another of the men and took a long draw of beer.

"Separated? Didn't you all ride together?"

The man set his beer on the bar. "They ambushed us. They knew we was coming."

"Ambushed? What do you mean, ambushed?"

"They caught us in a crossfire as we tried fording that stream up there. Swagger, Lake, and a few others got across. Some of the others were shot off their horses in the stream. Two others were shot on this side of the creek. We had no chance."

"What about you three?" Neal snapped. "You didn't stay and fight? Help the others?"

"Men got shot on both sides of me," said the first man. "I ain't being paid enough to die killing sheep. You said it would be easy. We had no choice but turn and run for the trees."

"You lousy cowards. Get the hell out of my sight and out of my town, you worthless tramps." Neal pulled his. 45 and held it at the ready. "I mean now, before I start shooting."

All three men hurriedly left the saloon. Neal followed them out onto the plank walkway, gun still drawn as the men mounted their tired horses and rode off. Farther down the street, Neal spotted Swagger, Lake, and Baxter headed his way.

"We gotta talk," he shouted at Swagger. "Get in here. And I don't want to hear that those damn sheepherders are still alive."

Swagger and the others reached the saloon, dismounted, and followed Neal inside. Neal waited, anger boiling inside him, as they went to the bar for something to drink. He felt ready to explode. "What the hell happened out there?"

Swagger looked beaten, for the first time since Neal hired him. "Boss, we took twenty men . . . should have been plenty. But only five of us got across that big stream up there. Everyone else was wounded, killed, or just plain ran."

"What the—"

"They surprised us. Caught us off guard. Somehow they knew we were coming."

Neal glanced at Lake and Baxter, who stared at the floor, their beers untouched. "Lake, that true?"

"Yes . . . yes," Lake stammered. "We was ambushed. Shooting from every direction. Blood everywhere. Horses squealing and lunging."

"You three among those that crossed?" Neal asked.

"Yes," answered Swagger.

"Sheepherders fighting back . . . with guns. I can't believe it. They got more guts than them damn sodbusters, for sure. What happened next? Surely five of you could still get the job done."

Swagger shrugged. "We rode for their cabin, but along the way a couple of the men spotted one of the Lincoln boys and rode after him. I warned them it could be a trap. But they wouldn't listen."

Baxter spoke up for the first time. "The boy was right in front of us. We chased him into some trees. Next thing we knew, we were in a clearing next to a stream."

"And—"

"And they opened fire on us from behind some rocks. It was a trap, like Swagger said. By the time we escaped back toward the Lincoln cabin, more men had been killed or wounded. Everything was happening all at once. Then the others showed up with guns."

"What others?"

"Sheepherders."

"What other sheepherders?"

"We didn't stop and ask for names, but I've seen some of them before over near Iron Mountain. They threw down on us, so we ran. We got away. Can't be sure about anyone else."

"How did they know you were coming?" Neal demanded.

"I don't know, but someone told them," said Swagger.

Neal slammed his fist on the bar. Beer glasses bounced from the impact, spilling much of their contents onto the floor. He uttered some obscenities and glared at the three gunmen in front of him.

"I've had enough of your incompetence. Somebody told them . . . a poor excuse!"

"Now wait," said Swagger. "You have no right blaming us. We've been loyal to you. Done everything you've told us to do."

Neal ignored him. "This is bad, real bad. Makes me look weak. Few sheepherders challenging me. Next thing, others will be doing the same. No, we've got to wipe them out for sure. Make people understand no one defies me."

Swagger glanced at Lake, then at Baxter. "Fine. Tell us what to do, boss."

"Hell, I *been* telling you. Seems you men can't get it right. Looks like I'll need to be more personally involved in the future if I want something done. Meet me in my office later. Now get out of here."

As the gunmen stepped into the street, Neal turned to Cheyenne. He said nothing, only stared blankly at her. Then he remembered his mother telling him about a foul-smelling sheep man in the store a few days earlier. Not expecting Cheyenne to respond, he said, "Maybe he overheard something, but who was he?"

Word of the debacle in Lincoln valley spread like a prairie fire through town. A crack in Neal's bluster and ruthless ways had emerged. Unlike the homesteaders, sheepherders had fought back and for the moment had won out. A thin thread of hope emerged that maybe one day Neal could be stopped, but nobody dared say it out loud.

CHAPTER 33

The winds of winter are often bitter, making no pretense of kindness or sympathy. Jake had felt their cold wrath. He'd learned to engage and endure, taking nothing for granted. Now he rode with a singular purpose. Life had dealt him a cruel hand of misfortune and lost opportunity. The young cowpuncher felt the need to stand up for justice, no matter the consequence.

Meeting Sarah had given him hope, the promise of a life he'd hardly dared grasp. Now that was gone. Fate and circumstance had done their deeds and done them well. Alone, his memory restored, he recognized an irony in his intentions. He wanted Sarah to be happy but couldn't leave her husband and his ruthless ways unchallenged. By confronting Neal, he would invariably cause her pain, if she loved the man.

After camping for the night in a small canyon along North Chugwater Creek, Jake was up before daybreak. A small fire provided little warmth but was enough to heat much needed coffee. He drank it and swung up in the saddle. He rode without a plan, no sense of real direction except his desire to teach Neal a lesson. Events would play out in some preordained manner, so he left fate to its own course.

Snow remained under shaded outcroppings and on the north side of boulders and trees, but a warm wind melted anything out in the open. Jake rode from the canyon onto a plateau covered with sage and small evergreen shrubs.

His first stop would be the Meadows ranch, where he hoped

to learn more details from the missing months of his life. When he left to follow the rustlers, the ranch had been viable, with Sarah and her father running the place. They were having financial problems, but he'd developed a plan to help them. Now he wondered what might have happened to force Sarah into marriage and off the ranch she loved.

In town, Tom had point-blank asked Neal for his old job back as foreman of the Meadows ranch. After discussing the matter with Sarah and Molly, they decided the direct approach was best. The move caught Neal off guard. He glanced at Sarah, then at Molly, both standing near Tom in Neal's office.

"Just think, Jason. Having Tom run the ranch would add value to the place," Sarah said. "He could rebuild the cattle operation. It's either that or they stay here in town with us, or at the hotel, until Tom finds work somewhere else."

Neal didn't like any of the options. The last thing he wanted was his wife having friends close by that might further turn her against him.

"Now's the time," said Tom. "It's calving season, and I'm sure you've got cows out there needing to be watched. You need someone with experience, not just a few gun hands."

"Tom already knows the ranch," Sarah added. Then her voice faltered. "And since Trace was killed, nobody's been taking care of things out there."

Neal turned toward the window and looked outside. He needed time to think. Getting Tom and Molly out of town and out of Sarah's way, at least temporarily, was probably his best option. He planned to sell the ranch to the Swan Land and Cattle Company by summer anyway, but maybe Sarah was right.

"Okay . . . okay. You go play foreman. I've got more important things to worry about right now. I'll send word to my men to come back into town and let you handle things. But remember,

241

you work for me. Watch out for my interests. Hire yourself a couple of hands, and get the place up and running again. Make it worth something."

"Thank you." Tom turned to leave, with Molly and Sarah right behind him.

"Sarah, stay here a minute," said Neal.

He waited until Tom took Molly outside, then glared at his wife. "Don't you ever . . . I mean ever . . . put me on the spot like that again," he told her in a low, threatening voice. "Now get out of here before I lose my temper."

Despite Neal's anger, Sarah was excited for Tom and Molly. They immediately made plans to move. Tom hired two young out-of-work cowhands, Jeff Phillips and Barry Smith, who'd remained in town through the winter doing odd jobs for local ranchers. With the approach of spring, they jumped at full-time work and a chance of their fortunes turning better.

A couple of days later, Sarah and Molly rode together in a one-horse buggy, followed by Barry Smith driving a wagon loaded with supplies. Neal had told his mother to give them whatever they needed, at a fair price. Jake's sorrel gelding, tied behind, was excited to be out of the stable and back in open country. Tom and Phillips rode alongside leading three additional horses.

After some time, they reached Sybille Creek and followed the trail toward the ranch. All around were traces of the prairie fire that had burned the valley. Here and there they could see small amounts of emerging spring growth. Soon the valley would be green with new grasses again.

Sarah moaned when she saw the ranch complex and its rundown condition. "Going to need plenty of work," said Tom as the group pulled up to survey the buildings and broken corral fences.

Once everything was unloaded, they cleaned the inside of the house where some of Neal's men had been living. Sarah agreed to help and spend the night, which would also give them a chance to celebrate Tom and Molly's return. Sarah would leave early the next morning for town.

Tom was anxious to be back in the saddle again, to inspect the ranch and inventory any cattle still on the place. But for the moment there was too much cleaning to be done. They went through the ranch house, the bunkhouse, the barn, and other buildings, gathering debris and unwanted items. Outside, they built a fire pit and disposed of it all in the hot flames.

Toward evening, with shadows covering the landscape and the sun nearly hidden behind the mountains, Jake stopped on a ridge above the ranch and saw the fire burning. There was activity in and around the house, and there were horses in the corrals. He couldn't see who was down there, so he elected to remain out of sight. *Too late to ride down there tonight. Can't afford any of Neal's men spotting me.*

He turned back toward a small cave he remembered seeing along Sybille Creek. Morning would come soon enough.

"Besides, might be wise to clean up a little," he told his horse. "Given my welcome in town and my apparent smell of sheep, meeting up with Neal's men could be deadly. Morning will be just fine."

Jake got up early and found a clearing near the creek, where he built a fire to heat plenty of water for a bath and shave. The hot water felt good on his body in the cold morning air. It had been weeks, maybe even months, since his last clean up. His bath water reflected as much, turning an ugly mix of brown and grey. He was forced to repeat the process twice before he felt any real sense of cleanliness. Most of the lye soap Martha Lincoln had sent with him quickly disappeared.

"No wonder everyone in town thought I stank."

He grabbed a handful of his ragged hair and used a knife to remove the excess. Without a mirror, he had to feel his way. The process took time, but he managed to get it cut to a respectable length, so at least his hat would fit properly.

Then, using the knife and the remaining soap, he shaved, leaving a mustache. The cold morning air on his chin and cheeks stung, and at one point he admonished himself for not leaving a few whiskers for protection.

The fire quickly consumed his clothing. Every garment smelled of sheep. He put on some clean clothing provided by Martha that once belonged to her husband. Jake glanced into the stream, where earlier he'd seen the reflection of a rough-looking mountain sheepherder called Amos. Now he saw Jake Summers.

Sarah was making her way toward town when she smelled smoke. She pulled up, trying to decide what to do. The smoke drifted in her direction, but she couldn't see its source. Not wanting to meet any strangers, especially Neal's men, she decided to turn the buggy away from the trail and try to go around. The thought of an encounter like the one at the ranch with Swagger left her cold and made the risk seem worth taking.

The seldom-used path she chose near the stream was steep and worn. As she started up it, the buggy slid sideways toward the cold, rushing water. The horse struggled to keep his footing on the snow-covered embankment. Too late, Sarah realized her mistake. She tried to get out, but the buggy tipped. She screamed as it toppled into the chilly creek.

Jake heard a woman's scream and quickly mounted his horse. The sound had come from upstream, though he wasn't sure where. He soon found buggy tracks where someone had turned off the trail and followed them.

After a few minutes, he saw the horse still hooked to the mangled buggy, struggling for footing in the rushing water. The animal was exhausted as the swift current pulled at it. There was no sign of anyone in the buggy.

Jake dismounted and stepped into the cold water to cut the horse out of its harness.

Wide-eyed and panicked, the horse lunged free, found the bank, and with some effort climbed from the creek. The animal stood out of breath, his sides shining with icy wetness.

Jake peered downstream, searching for whoever'd been driving the buggy. At first, he saw nothing. Then he spotted a piece of clothing, a hat caught in some debris, and finally a woman, caught against a dead tree trunk in the stream. Her head, just above water, bounced like a cork on a farm pond.

He got a rope from his saddle, tied one end to a small cottonwood along the creek and the other end around his waist, and stepped into the water. Its powerful surge against his legs tried pulling him deeper in and down. He stumbled, staying close to the bank.

Again and again the water tore at him, seeking to make him its victim. Now nearly up to his waist, the current carried him toward the woman, so fast he was afraid it might carry him past her. At the last possible moment, Jake grabbed a dead limb that stopped him close to her.

He recognized Sarah, and his determined effort turned to desperate panic. Twice he felt her nearly slip away as he freed her from the debris. Then, with considerable effort, he pulled on the taut rope and managed to reach the bank and safety.

Both of them were soaking wet. Sarah drifted in and out of consciousness. Her lips were blue and her body ice cold.

Jake realized she needed medical help, and quickly. The nearest doctor was in Chugwater, but that might take too long. Behind them lay the Meadows ranch, but he didn't know who he might find there and guessed it wouldn't be good. His only other choice was to carry her into the cave where he'd spent the night and try to get her warm.

The buggy was beyond use, but the two shafts or poles were intact. Using his saddle blanket and the buggy bench seat, Jake made a travois and managed to lay her on it. He led his horse slowly back to the cave. The buggy horse would have to wait.

He lifted Sarah off the travois and carried her inside the cave, where he built a large fire and removed her wet clothes. He wrapped blankets from his bedroll around her and worked to get her body temperature back up before changing into dry clothes himself.

Sarah moaned in discomfort but continued to drift in and out of consciousness. Once he had her quiet and resting comfortably, he went back for the buggy horse. As he approached the spot where he'd left the animal by the stream, he heard men's voices.

"She must be in the creek. Look, the buggy is smashed to pieces."

"Looks like it. Let's search along the creek bank for any signs."

He'd know that second voice anywhere. "Tom . . . Tom Scott." Eagerly, he moved toward the sound.

As Tom and the other man edged along the creek bank, Jake stepped from among some cottonwood trees. Tom gasped, as if seeing a ghost, and nearly lost his footing on the bank. Staring in disbelief, he searched for words.

Jake moved toward his friend. "Hello, Tom."

Still in shock, Tom said, "Jake? My God, is that really you?"

Jake smiled . . . a real smile, for the first time in months. "Yep, it's me."

Tom strode forward. "Man . . . you're dead. Everybody said you were dead."

The two friends embraced, then stood eyeing each other at arm's length.

"I can't believe this," said Tom. "Seriously, everybody thinks you're dead."

"I *was* dead, in a manner of speaking. Shot and thrown over a cliff. No time to explain now. I found Sarah. She fell in the stream with the buggy. I pulled her out, but she's unconscious. We've got to get her to a doctor, and soon."

"Wait until she finds out you're alive. She'll faint," said Tom.

"No . . . she can't know. Promise me you won't tell her."

"Why not?"

"She's married now. She's going to have Neal's baby. She's got a new life . . . her life. I'm not going to mess that up."

"But, Jake, she needs to know."

"No! Promise me!"

Tom hesitated. "Okay . . . for now."

"No . . . never! She must never know."

"Okay. Okay, I promise."

Jake glanced at Tom's companion. "And your friend here. Not a word."

The other cowhand looked mystified but nodded in agreement. He gave his name as Phillips as he shook Jake's hand in greeting.

Tom sent Phillips back to the Meadows ranch for the wagon and told him not to mention Jake's involvement, but to bring Molly back with him. Then Tom and Jake went to the cave. Afraid Sarah might have regained her senses, Jake didn't go back inside, sending Tom instead.

After several minutes, Tom came back outside, where he found Jake mounted and ready to leave. "You can't go. Not now."

"I'm not going far. After you get Sarah into town and she's okay, I'll come by the ranch, and we'll catch up. Bring Molly up to date. You won't believe where I've been all winter and what's happened." At the clatter of the approaching wagon, Jake wheeled his horse away and shouted, "Until later, my friend."

Once in town and with the doctor's assurance that Sarah and the baby were not harmed, Tom and Molly stepped onto the plank walkway in front of the doctor's office.

"What happened?" Molly asked. "How did she end up in the creek? How'd you get her out?"

Pausing at first to gather his thoughts, Tom explained how the buggy had slid into the stream, and Sarah was swept away. He kept Jake out of it as best he could, but it made for awkward telling.

As the sun began to descend behind the Laramie mountain range, they started back toward the ranch. Streaks of orange and blue filled the distant horizon, and the wind eased to a gentle evening breeze. Darkness had fallen by the time they reached the ranch house. Tom pulled the team to a stop and started to climb down. "Tom?" asked Molly, speaking for the first time since leaving Chugwater. "I've got a question."

Tom glanced sideways and lifted one eyebrow.

"Before we left Sarah, she mentioned something about seeing Jake's ghost, and being carried away on horses."

"She was just rambling, still confused."

"Makes sense, I guess." Molly climbed down from the wagon.

"Sure it does. I'm hungry. Let's fix some eggs and bacon."

"Tom?"

"Yes?"

"The cave. How did she get in there? After you and Jeff Phillips rescued her from the stream, you didn't have much time to find a cave, build a fire, get her warmed up, and still come get me."

"Well—" Tom avoided her stare.

"And how come neither you nor Jeff were wet? You both were completely dry. And those blankets she was wrapped in . . . you didn't have any blankets with you this morning. I took them off your horse so I could wash them."

Tom sighed and looked toward the mountains, hidden by darkness. "We need to talk."

CHAPTER 34

The strong smell of alcohol and other slightly less pungent chemicals filled Neal's nostrils as he entered the doctor's office looking for Sarah. He hadn't gone to see her the night before but thought he should make an effort now. The waiting room was empty, but he could hear voices coming from a back room.

He glanced around. A desk covered with papers and medical books lined one wall. A stethoscope lay over the back of the desk chair, and an old, dark-green sweater hung from a coatrack in one corner. Inside a storage case near the front door were various bottles and boxes. The shelves held bottles of laudanum, morphine tablets, carbolic acid, arsenic, ipecac, chloroform, and various herbal pills.

Neal drew breath to call out just as Doc Collins walked into the room. "Morning. I suppose you've come to see your wife?"

"Yes. Where is she?"

"I'm surprised you didn't drop by to check on her earlier. She had quite a scare. Lucky her friends found her when they did."

"Where is she?" Neal asked again, ignoring the doctor's sarcasm.

Collins gestured behind him. "In the back. But you shouldn't go back there. She's sleeping."

"Is she all right?"

"A little rough around the edges, but yes. And no harm to the baby that I can tell." The doctor sat at his desk and thumbed through some papers, ignoring Neal.

"I want to see her."

Collins didn't glance up. "Like I said, she's sleeping. Maybe later."

"When can she go home?"

"Day or two. I want to watch her to be sure she's really okay."

"Doc? Doc?" A young boy's voice came from the back room.

"Who else is in there?" Neal demanded as he stepped toward the rear doorway.

Collins called out, "Be there in a minute, Patrick. Hold your horses."

Neal scowled. "Who?"

"His name is Patrick Lincoln. I'd guess he's about thirteen, maybe fourteen. He was hurt by some men who attacked his family and home. I don't suppose you know anything about it? He's been here a few days now. With all your sources, I'm surprised you didn't know that already."

"Lincoln?" stammered Neal. "He's part of that damn family of sheepherders that's been killing my men. I thought I smelled sheep in here. I want to see the little animal."

The doctor quickly stood and stepped between Neal and the back-room doorway. "He's a boy, frail at that. Not likely he's been killing your men. And he was here when your men were up there."

"His pa killed my men. I want to see him." Neal tried to step around Collins, but the doctor moved sideways to block him.

"Nobody's going back there upsetting my patients. I suggest you leave. Come back later and see Sarah."

Neal hesitated, then turned toward the front door. "I suggest you get that little sheep lover out of here, and soon. If word gets around he's here, I can't be responsible for his continued health, or yours."

"Come back later, Mr. Neal. I'll worry about Patrick Lincoln. Maybe you should be more concerned about your wife."

Neal stepped outside and felt the cool morning air against his red, flushed cheeks. He adjusted his wool coat and looked up and down the street. Only a couple of freight wagons passed by while an old man walked slowly toward the bank. Otherwise, the street was empty.

Sarah lay quietly in her bed, having listened intently to the exchange between the doctor and Neal. Next to her, on the other side of a thick, off-white curtain hanging from the ceiling, was Patrick Lincoln. His wounds were healing, slowly.

"I suppose you heard all that?" asked the doctor as he stepped up to the end of Sarah's bed.

"Yes. Now I'm worried about the boy," she whispered.

"No need for that," came a voice from behind the curtain. "We Lincolns can take care of ourselves."

Sarah smiled. "Yes, Patrick, I'm sure you can."

Molly and Tom walked in to visit Sarah as the doctor packed his black bag, then put on his coat and hat. "She's in bed. I got a boy with a broken leg over at the Nettles place that needs setting. Be back shortly."

They found her sitting up, a look on her face like she was plotting something. She motioned for them to come closer and whispered, "Jason has been trying to run sheep owners out of the territory for weeks now. Only one family stood up and fought back . . . the Lincolns, up near Iron Mountain. The boy here—Patrick Lincoln—says a stranger named Amos helped them. They found him badly hurt, but Patrick doesn't know where he came from or what happened to him. Patrick was seriously hurt when some of Jason's men went up there and attacked them. He thinks Amos brought him here to Doc Collins."

Molly glanced at Tom. Before she could speak, he said, "That a fact?"

"You can stop whispering over there," Patrick said. "I can hear everything. Amos was good to us. We named him because he lost his memory."

Tom pulled back the curtain. "You might as well join in. We're talking about your folks."

Sarah looked Patrick in the eye. "I'm sorry, but I believe my husband, Jason Neal, sent those men to hurt you and your family. I am so sorry for that."

"Figured as much after hearing all the talk today."

"Now that he knows you're here, you may be in danger."

"I don't—"

"Listen, we have to get you out of here and to a safe place until we can get you home. Jason may try to harm you."

"What should we do?" asked the boy.

"I figure Tom and Molly can sneak you out of town in their wagon. You can hide out at the ranch for a few days until we can contact your folks."

"I don't know—"

"It sounds like a good plan," said Tom. "Can you travel, Patrick?"

The boy nodded.

"I'll pull the wagon around back, and we'll hide you in some blankets in the wagon bed. Nobody will be able to see you. Before you know it, we'll be on our way home."

"Tonight after the doctor goes to supper, I want you, Swagger, and Lake to go get that boy. Take Nelson with you," said Neal. "I saw a bottle of chloroform on the shelf in his office. Use it if the boy gives you any trouble. Put him to sleep, and keep him quiet. I'll make sure my wife is out of there before tonight."

Swagger and Lake grinned at each other. Then Baxter spoke up. "I should have finished that runt off when I had the chance out there. I want to go instead of Nelson. This time, I won't be so gentle."

"Don't hurt him. He's our bargaining chip," said Neal. "But go ahead."

When the doctor returned from the Nettles place, Patrick Lincoln was gone, and Sarah lay apparently sleeping. He smiled.

"You can wake up now. Your friends took him, didn't they? I know you were concerned Neal might harm him."

Sarah rolled over, smiling. "Let's just say he's in a safe place now."

A short while later, Neal walked into the back room. "I'm here for Sarah. She'll be better off at home. And—" Neal paused, looking at Patrick's empty bed. "Where's the boy?"

"He's gone," the doctor answered. "I don't know where. He wasn't here when I returned a few minutes ago."

Neal turned to Sarah. "Where is he?"

"How would I know? I was sleeping. Maybe he heard you talking this morning and snuck out."

Neal stormed out of the office, slamming the front door as he left. The doctor and Sarah smiled at each other. "Wait, didn't you forget someone, Mr. Neal?" the doctor called to the closed door.

A little later, after Collins left the room, Sarah slowly dressed and prepared to go home. She was feeling much better and decided she could learn more about Neal's plans at home than confined to the doctor's sickroom.

It didn't take Neal long to figure out there were only three possible explanations for the boy's disappearance. He might have gotten up and left on his own . . . but where would he go without a horse? An elderly couple had come to town in a small buggy shortly before noon, gone to the general store, and then left. Not much chance they'd taken him.

That left Sarah's good friends, Tom and Molly Scott. They'd been seen going into the doctor's office, then later leaving town with a pile of blankets in the back of their wagon.

Neal gathered his men at his office and outlined a change of plans. "Go to the Meadows ranch and burn them out. I want them all dead. Do what you must, but bring me that kid. The Lincolns are going to pay dearly for fighting me."

Patrick sat on the porch in a well-worn rocking chair while Tom sat nearby. Molly prepared fresh coffee, steak, and fried potatoes for everyone to eat, then joined them on the porch. In the growing darkness, the boy thought he saw the light of a lantern near the creek but decided it was only his imagination.

Jake watched from Sarah's old secret hiding place on the ridge as six men rode along Sybille Creek up to the ranch. One man, in the lead, fired at the house. The shot ricocheted off the stone steps at the base of the porch and sent everyone rushing inside.

"Send the boy out and nobody gets hurt!" the gunman shouted. "You've got five minutes, or we're burning you out."

A second shot shattered the kitchen window. Jake could hear Tom shouting at Molly and Patrick Lincoln to take cover.

Two of the men on horseback never heard the shots that killed them. Jake's well-aimed rifle shot got the first one. The second came from Phillips in the bunkhouse. Tom returned fire from the ranch house, wounding a third man who managed to stay in his saddle and ride into the darkness. The lead gunman wheeled his horse from the scene and headed back toward town, followed closely by his remaining two companions.

As Jake rode down from the ridge into the open area in front of the house, light from lanterns held by Phillips and another ranch hand illuminated the yard. Patrick stepped outside, caught sight of him, and gaped. "Amos, is that you?"

Jake smiled. "Yes, it's me."

Molly gasped as she stepped out on the front porch and saw Jake in the lantern light. "Oh, my God. We thought you were dead. I couldn't believe it when Tom said he'd seen you. He told me it was you who pulled Sarah from the stream. You saved her life."

Jake dismounted and gave her a hug. "Everyone keeps telling me I'm supposed to be dead," he said with a laugh. "In time, maybe, but I've got a score to settle first."

The next morning, Neal learned of his men's latest botched attempt to follow orders. Word of the failed attack on the Meadows ranch spread like a prairie fire through a mature wheat field. He sensed things were starting to crumble around him.

As Baxter finished his sorry account of the raid, Neal yanked out his own gun, put it against Baxter's chest, and pulled the trigger. As the man fell and blood splattered the floor, Swagger and Lake stepped back. Swagger reached for his gun.

"Relax." Neal waved a hand at them. "But someone please give me a reason why I shouldn't go myself and show each of you idiots how simple it is to find a little boy?"

No one said anything.

Neal glared at Swagger, Lake, and the two remaining gunmen. "Tonight we . . . yes, I said we . . . are going back out there. I'll show you how to get this done. I need a stiff drink. I'm going to the saloon."

Later, Sarah watched as Neal cleaned his guns and prepared to leave town. "What's going on?"

She hadn't expected him to answer, and it frightened her when he did. "Patrick Lincoln is at your precious ranch. I know your friends have him, and I know you helped them. I plan to go liberate the boy."

"What about Molly and Tom?" she asked, fearful for their lives . . . and her own. What would Neal do to her for defying him? Her hands curved around her bulging belly. *Surely he won't harm the baby . . .*

"They'll be fine unless they try to stop me," said Neal as he strapped on his gun belt and headed for the front door. "I'll be certain to take care of them—and you, my traitorous wife— later."

She stood in the hallway for a minute after he'd gone. *It will take him a few drinks to build up his courage,* she thought. *He never does things like this. He always sends someone else to do his dirty work.*

Sarah slipped out the rear door and followed back streets to the stable. Jacob Helms wasn't around, so she took a dapple-grey gelding from one of the stalls and hitched him to a buckboard. She led the rig around the building, out of sight. With considerable effort she climbed onto the seat, picked up the reins, and slapped them across the horse's back. Soon they were out of town, unseen by anyone who might question her leaving.

Near the ranch, a barn owl hooted Sarah's arrival in the darkness. As she pulled up in front of the house, a man stepped off the porch. The moonlight showed his face, and Sarah gasped. *Jake?* Light-headed with shock, she fell from the buggy into the arms of the man she'd thought was dead.

CHAPTER 35

The pungent aroma of smelling salts quickly pulled Sarah back from the abyss. Awake once more, she stared wide-eyed in disbelief at Jake.

"Welcome back," he said. "You had us worried."

"You're alive," Sarah murmured.

Not sure whether she was asking a question or making a statement, Jake took her hand. "Yes . . . I'm alive."

"But, I don't . . . where have you been? I don't understand."

"Take it easy. You've been through a lot the last few days. I'll explain everything in due time."

"They said you were dead."

"Your husband said I was dead. Obviously, he lied. I'm back now."

Sarah shook her head. "I'm so confused."

Jake eased his hand from hers. "Since you're here, I'm assuming your husband is up to something. Tell us everything you know about what he's planning."

Neal and several hand-selected men, along with Swagger and Lake, rode north along Chugwater Creek. On the opposite side of the stream, the rugged cliffs hung over them as if watching their departure. Soon, they turned west toward the mountains and the Meadows ranch.

Nearly a year earlier, Neal had ridden much this same trail alone as an inexperienced young attorney fresh from the courtrooms of Nebraska. He was on a mission then to marry Sarah Meadows. Today he rode with brutality on his mind. No longer the naïve young man from Nebraska, now he was the master of his own destiny, and pity those who tried to stop him.

Despite warnings of danger, Sarah managed with help to climb into her borrowed buckboard. "I'll be back," she said. "Don't worry. Unless Jason has totally lost his mind, I should be able to stop him." She wasn't as sure as she sounded, but she had to try. Anything was better than a bloodbath, and the baby should keep her safe. *Even if he hates me now, he won't want to hurt the child.*

"I don't like it," Jake said. "I should go along. How do we know you aren't going to warn your husband we're waiting for him?"

Molly glared at him. "How can you say that? She came all this way to warn us, while expecting a child to boot."

"Maybe so. All I know is, I was barely dead, and she went running to him. Now she's leaving us to go meet him."

Jake's words cut deep. "You don't know how it was," she told him with tears in her eyes. "Despite what you think, I have to try to stop him." She snapped the reins and started toward Sybille Creek and the valley that led to Chugwater.

In the wake of Sarah's departure, an angry Molly stared at Jake but said nothing. Jake turned to Smith, another young ranch hand hired by Tom, and told him to take Patrick Lincoln to his family. "Ride fast, get him home, and then hurry back. If we're still here and alive, we'll need your help. Otherwise, it won't matter much."

Within minutes Smith and Patrick were mounted and riding toward Lincoln valley several miles away deep in the mountains.

Sarah met Neal and his men about three miles from the ranch.

They'd been riding hard, and their horses were well lathered. She pulled up when she saw them coming and waited.

Neal looked furious at the sight of her. "What are you doing out here?"

"I came to talk some sense into you. You can't do this."

"I can, and I will. Now get out of my way."

"Jason! Please!"

"Somebody tie her hands together," he snapped at his men. "Lake, tie your horse on behind that buggy of hers and drive her into town. Take her to my house, and hold her there until I get back. I've had enough of her interference. Don't you dare hurt my baby either, my son. Stay in town and guard the house. Only my mother can come and go."

Sarah fought, but her efforts were futile. Once her hands were bound, Neal rode up beside her, grabbed her by the jaw, and looked into her terrified eyes. "You stay put. You understand me?" He glanced at Lake. "Now get her out of here."

Neal and his men tied their horses by the creek and approached the ranch from the south. The buildings glowed in the early sunlight. Neal's coat pocket felt heavy, weighed down by the kerosene can and box of matches he'd taken from his saddlebag.

"Surround the house," Neal said. Then he shouted at anyone he thought might be listening. "You, inside. You're surrounded. Send the boy out. He's all we want. Send him out, and we'll leave. No harm done."

No one answered. He shouted again. Still no response.

Neal motioned Swagger and three other men toward the house. They obeyed with reluctance. Still no sound or motion came from inside.

"Boss, I don't think anyone's in there!" Swagger shouted.

"Find out. Rush the place."

Swagger moved behind an old wagon, then ran across open

ground toward rain barrels at the corner of the house. The other men found similar cover and moved in closer. Swagger yelled, "Anyone in there? Come out, or we'll burn you out!"

Again, no response.

Neal moved closer to the house but kept to the trees nearby for protection.

Swagger ran to the back porch, then motioned for one of the other men to break down the door. Neal followed. They searched the house but found it empty.

"They've probably run off. I'm sure my darling wife warned them we were coming. Go search the barn and bunkhouse. Shoot anyone you find. After that, I intend to burn this place to the ground. Now get going."

One gunman stepped onto the front porch. A rifle shot caught him in the stomach and nearly cut him in half. A second man was hit in the shoulder as he stepped through the doorway. Badly wounded, he fell backwards and landed at Neal's feet, his blood splattering on the attorney's boots. Neal swore as he realized he and his men were trapped.

Jake and Phillips fired at two more gunmen trying to escape out the back door. One man died instantly. The second fell off the porch, crying out in pain.

"Throw out your weapons, and come out with your hands up!" shouted Jake as he moved to the front of the house. He'd left Phillips guarding the back. "We'll stop shooting."

"Go to hell!" Neal yelled back.

"That's where you're headed," Jake responded. "You're surrounded. You can't escape."

Silence fell. Then Neal spoke again. "Okay . . . okay. We're coming out."

Two pistols and a rifle sailed through the front door, followed by a pair of Neal's men walking out with their hands raised. One shouted, "Don't shoot! We surrender." Neal and another man stayed behind.

A rifle shot echoed from behind the house. Jake glimpsed a tall gunman—not Phillips—dashing off toward the creek. Sick at heart, Jake ran toward where he'd left Phillips. The young ranch hand lay dying, his assailant gone.

"Set the house on fire," Neal snarled at the lone gunman still with him. "Maybe we can get out of here under cover of the smoke."

"We're trapped in here," the gunman said, wild-eyed. "I'm giving up."

"Like hell. We'll never give up!"

The man ignored him and started for the front door. Neal shot him in the back. "Damn coward. I said we won't give up."

He still had the lethal supplies he'd brought. He splashed kerosene around Sarah's bedroom, then flicked a lit match into it from the doorway and watched the flames shoot up. Soon, they began to spread throughout the house. The smoke made it hard to breathe. Neal cowered near the front door, watching for an opportunity to make a break. As the fire gained strength, smoke from the burning house spread throughout the barnyard. Deciding the moment was right, he ran down the front steps and dashed for the barn.

A hail of bullets followed him. He was hit but managed to stay on his feet. Clutching his left shoulder, he stepped into the barn, hoping to find safety. Instead he found Molly Scott holding a rifle.

Molly fired, then fired again. Neal reeled backward out the doorway. Jake and Tom headed toward the barn. Both of them halted at the sight of Neal, raised their rifles, and pulled the triggers.

Which shot actually killed the attorney from Nebraska didn't really matter, at the time or later. He was dead.

"One got away," said Tom. "Swagger, I'm pretty sure it was.

He killed Phillips."

"And there's no sign of Sarah," said Jake. "This isn't over. Let's ride!"

Sarah sat in her bedroom, a hostage in the Neals' home. From the parlor she heard Lake and Beatrice talking. Then came angry shouts and a third voice . . . Swagger! She heard Beatrice scream, "No! It can't be true. My son . . . my boy!"

As the woman moaned and wailed, the door of Sarah's room burst open. Swagger's large frame filled the doorway. He grinned like a hungry wolf with its fangs bared.

"We gotta get outta here!" Lake shouted from behind him. "They're bound to be following."

Swagger didn't take his bloodshot eyes off Sarah. "You go if you want. I need to take care of something here first."

Lake's feet pounded away. The front door slammed.

Sarah backed away and cowered against her nightstand. In the adjoining room, she heard Beatrice throwing clothes into an old brown trunk, also preparing to flee. No help would come from her.

"Get out!" Sarah shouted at Swagger. "Jason will kill you if he finds you here."

"Your man is dead. Your friends shot him. I saw him go down by the barn as I rode away. Now it's just you and me, sweetheart."

Sarah felt weak at the news. Something heavy scraped across the hall floor, followed by the front door opening and closing. *Beatrice . . . gone.* Sarah was alone . . . alone with a madman.

His face was bright red as he reached for her. "Come here, darling! I've been waiting for this moment a long, long time."

Sarah shrank back against the nightstand and felt something hard against her leg . . . the pistol she'd stuck in her apron pocket after the last time Swagger confronted her. She lifted the apron like a shield.

Swagger laughed. "You think that old piece of cloth is going to stop me?" He moved closer step by step, like a hungry cat preparing to attack its prey.

Sarah groped for the pistol and pulled it free of the pocket. She aimed at Swagger's chest and pulled the trigger as he moved to grab her. The gunfire sounded like an explosion.

Swagger stumbled against her, then slid to the floor. Blood oozed from his chest. From his mouth flowed more blood, mixed with bubbles. He stared up at her in shock.

"You done killed me," he whispered.

Jake raced his lathered horse down Main Street past the Cheyenne to Deadwood stage as it pulled away from the general store. He barely noticed Beatrice Neal inside the coach.

He rode toward Sarah's house and saw Swagger's horse tied in front. Sarah's horse and buggy were nearby. Jake pulled his mount to a sliding stop as an ashen-faced Sarah stepped out the front door, a pistol in her hand. Blood was smeared across the front of her clothing. As Jake went toward her, she collapsed into his arms.

Cheyenne Mitchell watched intently from the window of her room over the saloon. Word had already reached her that Neal was dead. Tears stained her face, mixing with cheap makeup. She pressed her right hand to her expanding stomach and vowed vengeance.

"They killed your father, son. They killed the man I loved. They will pay . . . they will pay dearly. If it takes the rest of my life, those people will pay with *their* lives, and anyone associated with them. I swear it."

Her anguished whisper was carried away on the Wyoming wind, unheard and unnoticed. Within her, Neal's unborn child stirred with a painful kick, and she grimaced. Cheyenne wiped her face with the back of her hand and smiled . . . not one of happiness, but of resolution newly born.

CHAPTER 36

Morning clouds made swirling white patterns over the Laramie mountain range and spread over the vast prairie to the east. Meadowlarks darted among the sagebrush, singing happy spring songs. Wildflowers and fresh green grasses waved on warm southerly winds, as if trying to push winter north into Montana. Any snow left behind was melting.

Two weeks had passed since the confrontation with Neal and his death. There had been no celebration of his passing, only relief. Sarah had passed swiftly through her initial shock to acceptance.

Everyone assumed she'd married Neal for love. Few knew it was born of desperation and financial necessity. Only Tom and Molly knew the truth. Expressing any outward fondness for Jake so soon after Neal's passing would not be right and proper in her eyes, although her heart yearned to do just that.

Respectful of Sarah's complicated situation, Jake decided to go visit the Lincolns. He met with Sarah briefly before leaving, gave her a hug, then saddled up and rode off. His own emotions were a twisted muddle. The sudden return of his memory, and finding Sarah married and expecting a child, jolted him. He needed time to sort through everything.

One day spilled into another. Each morning, Sarah asked Tom and Molly if they'd seen Jake. Every time they said no, she prayed for his return.

Cleaning up Neal's mess proved difficult, but Sarah took on

the task with fortitude and diligence, intent on making things right among her neighbors. She sent word to area homesteaders and sheep owners that they would no longer be harassed, though most viewed the news with skepticism. The chasm between cattlemen and sheep owners remained.

Where Neal had legitimate land claims, Sarah met with Swan and Epperson to discuss their interest in obtaining them. Both men were already acquiring large tracts of land from local ranchers for the Swan Land and Cattle Company, though Sarah planned to keep the Meadows ranch. The railroad from Cheyenne was moving ever closer, and cattle pens were already being constructed in Chugwater in anticipation of its arrival.

Beatrice Neal had disappeared. Word was she had left Wyoming and returned to her home in Nebraska. Sarah wrote her Aunt Ruby and Uncle Lewis for verification, but they wrote back that nobody had seen her. Other rumors placed her in Cheyenne, even Denver. Someone suggested she'd gone to Deadwood. Nobody really knew. Missy Fernsmith took over the general store.

Neal's remaining gunmen had also disappeared. Lake was seen riding hard out of town on the same night as the Meadows ranch shootout. Chester Headwright and Ben Childers reportedly left for Texas. Charles Mann was said to have been killed after being caught cheating in a card game in Sheridan. The others simply drifted out of town, seeking unsavory work involving their guns somewhere else. There was always someone needing a gun hand's assistance. Range wars, especially those involving sheep owners, were just beginning.

Day by day, Molly's pregnancy drew closer to full term. She had moved into town with Sarah instead of remaining on the ranch without medical care close by. Sarah's own baby was also near full term, so both women helped each other and made plans.

Tom came and went as work on the ranch permitted. Sarah had asked him to remain in charge until things calmed down and she could make decisions about the future. Without Jake to advise her, Tom also provided guidance on other problems Neal left behind.

"Just think, our children will be able to play together, grow up together, perhaps even be best friends," said Molly one day. "How exciting!"

Sarah laughed. "If we both have girls, just think of the mischief we can expect."

Molly smiled. "What about two boys?"

"Oh, my goodness, what a thought."

Three days later, the doctor sent for Tom, who had gone with Sarah to meet with the Swan Land and Cattle Company representatives in Neal's old office. Sarah left with him, hurriedly promising to resume the meeting another time.

Entering the doctor's office at a run, they were greeted with a baby's cry. Abigail Sarah Scott was healthy and letting the world know it. Tom beamed at the sight of his new daughter, and Sarah felt her own baby squirm against his tight surroundings. His time would come soon. Molly was in great shape, though exhausted. She smiled at Tom as he held their child.

Spring came full bloom into the Chugwater Valley, and the creek was running high. Warm winds melted the snow, and, though the nights were still cool, plants were growing again. Wildflowers in every color covered nearby hillsides and valleys, waving in the ever-present wind. A month had passed since Jake left. No one had seen him since.

Sarah grew fearful he might never return. She knew he was upset she'd married Neal so quickly after his supposed death, even questioning whether her feelings for him had ever been genuine.

One morning, she decided to get out of town and clear her mind of everything. So much had happened, so fast. Tom and Molly advised against her leaving town, even for a short trip.

"You're having a baby for heaven's sake," said Tom.

"And you're due at any time now," Molly added, holding her own tightly wrapped infant close to her chest.

"I need to feel the wind against my face," Sarah told them. "I love this country, the wide-open spaces, the mountains, rivers, and valleys. I miss getting out and being a part of the land. I need to get out in the countryside. I'll be okay. I won't be gone long."

"Maybe I should ride along," Tom suggested.

"No . . . I need to be alone. But I do appreciate your concern."

"Take a buggy and go slow," Molly said. "No wild rides, and stay clear of creeks and streams. Remember your last experience with one."

"I can do that," Sarah said.

Her friends stood in the stable door as Sarah drove away. Tom shouted after her, "Stay close to town. Be back in an hour, or I'm coming after you."

Sarah waved her hand but otherwise didn't acknowledge hearing him.

She crossed Chugwater Creek over a recently built wooden bridge and headed toward the high plateaus east of town. The climb was gentle, though there were a few rough spots that made the buggy bounce. Her baby expressed his displeasure at being jostled.

On each side of her she could see the high cliffs and bluffs that lined Chugwater Creek. Once on top, she stopped and looked back at the town below her. Toward the east were the scattered homesteaders who'd remained despite Neal's attempts to run them off. Families were plowing the soil for spring planting.

Wild grasses all around were green with new growth, and in places wildflowers danced gracefully in the wind. The prairie was painted in color.

Sarah found an isolated tree near where the bluffs gave way to the valley. Again, she looked down toward the creek and town. Behind her, the prairie stretched toward Nebraska as far as she could see. The wind blew softly against her face as she inhaled great gulps of fresh, sage-scented spring air. Then she noticed a solitary rider coming toward her from the direction of Chugwater.

"My gosh, Tom wasn't joking. I just got up here," she said as her horse grazed on new grass nearby. She shielded her eyes from the morning sun as the rider approached. There was something familiar about him. Her heart jumped, and she took a deep breath as she recognized Jake. She waited quietly.

"Fancy finding you out here," she said when he got closer.

Jake grinned. "Mind if I climb down?"

"You'd better, mister. Where have you been?"

"I needed some time alone, time to find myself and consider my future."

"And what did you learn?" Sarah asked. She felt almost afraid of the answer, but she needed to hear it.

Jake hesitated, turned his back, and walked a short distance out on the prairie. Purple, pink, and yellow wildflowers danced around him in the wind. He didn't say anything at first. Birds sang nearby, and, in the momentary lull in conversation, Sarah felt the land come alive with spring's chance at new beginnings.

She walked up behind him and took his hand. And, with that quiet gesture, Jake turned and looked into her soft, brown eyes.

"Sarah Meadows . . . Neal . . . whatever your name is . . . I love you. So much has happened, and now you're having a baby. But I've thought it over. If you'll still have me, I will love you and your baby every bit as much as if it were my very own."

Sarah smiled and moved closer. She felt his warmth next to her. She leaned into him and kissed him, then stepped away. "If we have a boy, we'll name him Cody Jacob Summers."

Jake touched her cheek. "That would be great."

Then Sarah turned playfully away and started picking wildflowers. "He should be named after you. After all, he's yours."

"What? What do you mean, mine?"

"You remember that beautiful afternoon last fall, in the meadow near the aspens up on Wild Horse Creek? We made love and talked about getting married?"

"Yes . . . but—"

Sarah just smiled and picked a few more flowers . . . red, yellow, and white.

Jake said, "Are you serious?"

Sarah nodded. "I'm carrying your child, Jake. I couldn't be with child and no husband. What a scandal that would have been. You were gone. I had to get married quickly. Jason was my only option."

Jake reached for her, and they embraced long and hard. High on the bluffs and bison jumps towering over Chugwater Creek, a young couple with their unborn baby became a family. And a good Wyoming wind blew while the wildflowers danced.

ABOUT THE AUTHOR

Phil Mills, Jr., is a longtime member of the Western Writers of America (WWA), Montana Historical Society, and a lifetime member of the Custer Battlefield Historical and Museum Association. In 2010, he was a WWA Spur Award Finalist winner for Best Western Audiobook for his novel *Where a Good Wind Blows*. *Where the Wildflowers Dance* is the second in his Good Wind Western series. His illustrated children's books, *Scooter: The Cow Dog*, published in 2016, and *Mud Between My Toes*, published in 2019, have received critical acclaim. His experience includes being a small-town newspaper editor, farm magazine editor, and work with two major advertising/public relations agencies. Phil lives in Gainesville, Georgia. Find him on Facebook, Twitter, or on his website: philmillsjr.com.

The employees of Five Star Publishing hope you have enjoyed this book.

Our Five Star novels explore little-known chapters from America's history, stories told from unique perspectives that will entertain a broad range of readers.

Other Five Star books are available at your local library, bookstore, all major book distributors, and directly from Five Star/Gale.

Connect with Five Star Publishing

Visit us on Facebook:
https://www.facebook.com/FiveStarCengage

Email:
FiveStar@cengage.com

For information about titles and placing orders:
(800) 223-1244
gale.orders@cengage.com

To share your comments, write to us:
Five Star Publishing
Attn: Publisher
10 Water St., Suite 310
Waterville, ME 04901